The
MOTORING MILLERS

GLORIOSA

The MOTORING MILLERS

by Alberta Wilson Constant

ILLUSTRATED BY BETH AND JOE KRUSH

THOMAS Y. CROWELL COMPANY

New York

by the author:

MISS CHARITY COMES TO STAY

THE MOTORING MILLERS

THOSE MILLER GIRLS!

WILLIE AND THE WILDCAT WELL

Designed by Sallie Baldwin
Manufactured in the United States of America
L. C. Card 69-11081

1 2 3 4 5 6 7 8 9 10

A NOTE *from the* AUTHOR

To follow the trip taken by the Motoring Millers, get road maps of Kansas and Colorado. Gloriosa and Arvin are both made-up towns, not on any map, but the other towns are all there along the route as they were in 1910. The New Santa Fe Trail of 1910 has become U.S. Highway 50. Start a little west and south of Emporia at Peabody . . . Newton . . . Hutchinson . . . and keep going west on 50. Cross the Kansas line at Coolidge. At Pueblo, Colorado, turn north on what is now Interstate Highway 25 to Colorado Springs. The trip the girls and Miss Kate took into the mountains follows the present route of U.S. Highway 24. Greystokes-in-the-Pines is a made-up place, but there were many fine resort hotels in the area in 1910.

This book is for my son-in-law,
William Henszey Ewing.

HELLO, BILL!

The
MOTORING MILLERS

Chapter 1

The Great Smith chugged down the street, hiccupped over the culvert, and rolled into the side yard. In the shade of a tall elm tree Professor Cyrus Miller switched off the engine and hauled on the hand brake. The Millers had owned the Great Smith for a year, but he still felt uneasy at leaving the auto "unhitched." It was a handsome machine, gleaming red with polished brass trim. The black leather upholstery had diamond-shaped quilting, and the black Pantasote top was folded down in the warm summer weather.

Professor Miller swung his long legs over the running board and stepped down to the ground. He looked critically at the right head lamp. Fingerprints marred the surface of the brass. From a side pocket in the rear door he took out a bottle of brass polish and a cloth, and began to polish the head lamp. Then the left head lamp looked dull, so he started on it, whistling and smiling at himself, knowing that once he started polishing there was no stopping until the Great Smith was a credit to its advertising slogan, "The Handsomest and the Best Automobile in America."

In 1910 there were ten autos in Gloriosa, Kansas, but the Great Smith was the best known of them all. The town took extra pride in boasting that it had been manufactured in Topeka, the state capital. When Lou Emma and Maddy Miller were introduced, they often heard, "They're the ones with the big red auto."

Lou Emma wondered about it: *Does the Great Smith belong to us, or do we belong to it?*

Right now Lou Emma was on the other side of the house, standing on tiptoe by the rain barrel. Somewhere in the dark water was a tadpole she had put in last week. She reached down with her arm as far as it would go, trying to catch the tadpole and see what progress it had made toward turning into a frog.

Swoosh. A soft, jellyish touch slipped by her hand. She shuddered. Probably it was the tadpole, but it might have been anything. The water made a dim mirror for her face. Did she really look like that strange, wavering reflection? Blonde and blue-eyed, people always said she looked just like her father. Would that change now that she was thirteen?

So much had changed since the three Millers moved to Gloriosa a year ago that Lou Emma had fallen into a habit of wondering about things she had long taken for granted. The biggest change of all was that she and her younger sister, Maddy, had a stepmother. Professor Miller had a wife. Gloriosa had the best millinery shop of any town its size in Kansas. And all those changes were wrapped up in one person—Miss Kate.

From the distance of a year Lou Emma remembered the first time she and Maddy had seen Miss Kate. She was wearing a blue linen coat suit, and her white hat with three pink roses was tied on with white chiffon

veiling. For months Lou Emma had hoped, dreamed, schemed, that her widowed father would marry Miss Kate. And it had come true. Even now the wonder of having a dream come true made her feel warm inside.

Only . . . only . . .

Stop that, she told herself and reached deeper for the tadpole.

To have a mother—a stepmother was the same only called by a different name—was the one thing Lou Emma wanted. She and Maddy had been Professor Miller's "poor little motherless daughters" for most of their lives. They had been clucked over by faculty wives, sent home by irate neighbors, and alternately spoiled and neglected by a series of housekeepers. Now they had Miss Kate to belong to and she belonged to them. "And they lived happily ever after," the old fairy-story ending came to Lou Emma's memory. Why did the stories always end right there? Why didn't they tell how to live happily ever after?

SWISH-SWOOSH. The tadpole slid through her cupped fingers. Lou Emma grabbed and came up with a handful of rain water, cool and the color of weak tea. Miss Kate said rain water was the only kind that washed hair properly. She knew a lot of things about good looks. Vinegar to rinse Maddy's hair because it was brown; lemon juice to rinse Lou Emma's blonde braids. And when eggs were down to ten cents a dozen, an egg shampoo.

High above the roof there was a shaking in the branches of the elm tree. It must be Maddy, for Maddy was a tree climber. Probably one of the Wackers from next door was with her. Hackberry, most likely. Well, let em stay in the tree till she caught the tadpole. He wasn't big enough to share. A black blob surfaced and disappeared. She had missed him again.

"Drat!"

With a net she could catch him. Or a flour sifter. Or

a tea strainer. Or best of all one of those fancy veils from Miss Kate's Chapeaux, her stepmother's millinery shop.

Some of the ladies in Gloriosa were raising their eyebrows because Miss Kate had not closed the shop now she was married. Married ladies did not run businesses. If their husbands were dead or heavy drinkers or poor providers, they might take in sewing or keep boarders. But Professor Miller was alive, stone-cold sober, and teaching history and assorted subjects at Eastern Kansas Classical College. Shocking, the whispers went, really shocking. Woman's place is in the home, especially with daughters like those Miller girls. Lou Emma knew what they were saying, and so did Maddy, but if Miss Kate knew she gave no sign of changing her ways.

Lou Emma made waves in the rain barrel. "Come on, Tad," she begged. "Come on up. Pretty please with sugar on."

Maybe Tad suspected that once she caught him she was going to take him to her father and ask about why he had legs—or why he didn't. She was ashamed of herself for her plot, but it seemed that she never got to talk to her father now. For all the years she could remember he had always called when he got home, "Lou Emma . . . Maddy . . . Lou Emma. . . ." Now when he came home, he called, "Kate . . . Kate. . . ." And they talked in low murmurs and smiled at each other.

Why not? Feet-on-the-Ground Lou Emma asked

Face-in-the-Water Lou Emma. *Fathers and mothers—even stepmothers—talk to each other.*

But I miss Papa. I miss him. Face-in-the-Water Lou Emma thought it so hard that Tad swished by again.

"Gotcha!" She clapped her hands together, then peeked between her thumbs. She opened her empty hands in disgust. Tadpoles must be smarter than people.

"Oo-*oo*-gah! Oo-*oo*-gah!"

The deep-throated horn of the Great Smith made Lou Emma forget Tad. Stripping the water off her arms, she ran around the corner of the house. Maddy dropped from the elm tree, barely missing the front fender of the Great Smith. Then Hackberry Wacker dropped like an overripe apple, his face as red as his hair. Vinnie Wacker, who had been picking beans in the garden, ran over with beans spilling from her gathered-up apron.

They clamored to know what Professor Miller wanted. He put the brass polish and the cloth back into the side pocket before he answered.

"I want to put a flea in your ear," he said mysteriously. "Your collective ear. The Ides of July approaches."

They waited for more, but without another word he took a green bean from Vinnie's apron and chewed on it as he sauntered to the house. He nodded to Swish, the Miller girls' white goat tethered by the door, and called over his shoulder, "Don't forget . . . the Ides of July."

Hackberry looked at his sister and the Miller girls. "The Professor's crazy."

"He is not," Lou Emma said. "He's just—" She stopped, finding it easier to say what her father wasn't than what he was.

"What's the Idezof? What's he mean if he's not crazy?"

"That's in Shakespeare," Maddy said, swinging her dark braids. "Some old fortune-teller told old Caesar to beware the Ides of March. And he didn't. And he got killed. Dead."

"But what's the IDEZOF?" The less Hackberry understood the louder he yelled.

"Papa said that meant the fifteenth of March." Lou Emma tried to soothe Hackberry. "So this must mean the fifteenth of July."

"Then why'n't he say so? Why'd he say IDEZOF?"

"There's a fortune-teller over to Waycross," Vinnie said, ignoring her brother. "Maybe we oughta tell the Law she's out to kill somebody."

"The fortune-teller didn't kill Caesar," Maddy said. "His friends did."

"Don't sound very friendly to me," Vinnie chewed on a green bean. "Mama says raw green beans'll kill you, but they don't kill Professor Miller."

Lou Emma chewed on one and spit it out. "They taste so *green*."

Hackberry gave an ear-splitting whoop. "I know what that old Idezof is, I knew all the time only I didn't know I knew. Betcha it's coming through Gloriosa!"

The girls looked at him blankly. Still determined to be superior, Maddy made whirling motions at her forehead. "Talking through his hat."

"Am not." Hackberry glared at her. "Coming right smack-dab through town."

"*What's* coming through town?" Lou Emma could stand no more mystery.

"Mama'll swat you if you tell lies," Vinnie warned her younger brother.

He gave her a hard push, then turned his back on all the girls and spoke to the Great Smith. "Girls are so iggerant. I don't see how they stand theirselves."

Maddy started for him, but Vinnie held her off. "Leave 'im be. He's bustin' to tell us. Mama says let 'im stew in his own juice till he's ready."

"It can't be Chautauqua." Lou Emma counted on her fingers. "That's in August. The Revival's over. The Fourth of July's on the Fourth. Tommy Biddle said there was some kind of race—"

"Hush your big mouth!" Hackberry whirled to face her. "Don't mess it all up tryin' to tell it when you don't know nothin' about nothin' about nothin'."

"Then go on your ownself," she said.

Hackberry took a deep breath and said without stopping: "The - Midwest - AutoMobile - Club's - havin' - a - big - old - Three - State - Race - from - Kansas - City - back - again - to - Kansas - City - an' - the - race - driver - that - wins - gets - a - silver - cup - big - as - a - WASHTUB." He collapsed on the ground, his face flaming.

"Shoo, I don't believe it," Maddy said instantly.

"There is some kind of cup," Lou Emma said. "Tommy told me—"

"Quit talkin' about Tommy. You act like you own him."

"I do not. I just said he said—"

"Silver cup big as a rowboat," Hackberry crooned from the ground. "Big as a circus tent . . . big as a roundhouse . . ."

"Why's Papa steamed up about it?" Maddy demanded. "Gloriosa's got a speed limit of six miles per hour, an' he won't drive that fast because he's a professor an' he's got to be an example." She made a face.

"Mrs. Biddle said for Papa to be an example, not Dr. Biddle, and he's president of the college even if she is bigger'n he is. Dr. Biddle'd get an auto and drive it thirty miles an hour if she'd let 'im, Tommy says."

"Tommy-tommy-tommy-rot!" Maddy put her fingers in her ears.

Lou Emma's face burned.

"Maybe the Professor wants a race so's he can anyway *see* how fast autos go," Vinnie said wisely. "There comes Eppie from the store."

Up the street came Eppie, her red hair bright in the sunshine. All the Wackers had red hair like their mother. Even Joy who was hardly more than a baby. From the day the Millers had come to the small brown house, the Wackers, next door, had been their best friends. Miss Kate had roomed at the Wackers' house before she was married. The grass between the two houses was crisscrossed with small paths.

Eppie handed the groceries in at the kitchen door and hurried over to join them. "Mama says to come on home; it's near dinnertime."

"My stomach says it's past dinnertime," Hackberry said. "I'm hungry."

"You're always hungry," Vinnie said. "Mama says you're a bottomless pit."

"The Professor's hungry." Hackberry defended himself. "He et raw beans."

"Papa doesn't hardly ever get hungry," Maddy said. "He has to be called four times for dinner—six times if he's working on the Book." By now the textbook Professor Miller was writing, "A Look at Early Roman History," had become the Book to the household and the neighbors.

"It's the truth," Vinnie said. "I heard Lou Emma call an' I counted."

"Once I called nine times," Lou Emma said. "N-I-N-E."

"That was when you were doin' the cooking." Hackberry made throwing-up noises. "Bet he don't hafta be called nine times for Miss Kate's cooking."

It was easier to pretend to pay no attention. Hackberry was years younger than she was—nine years to her thirteen— What did he know about it? Lou Emma busied herself picking Spanish needles from the hem of her dress.

Papa used to say I was a good cook. Has he forgotten?

Maddy said, "Papa'd eat sawdust if we put sugar an'

cream on it. Food's not his cup o' tea. Books are what he really likes."

"Girrr-uls . . . Hackberry . . . ," Mrs. Wacker called.

"I'll walk you home," Maddy said as if the Wackers lived a mile away.

Lou Emma watched them go, still working at the pesky Spanish needles. In the sunshine, between the two red-headed Wacker girls, Maddy's hair was almost exactly the color of Miss Kate's. All her life Lou Emma had delighted in being told that she looked "just like" her father. For an instant she wavered. *If I looked like Miss Kate, would it make a difference?*

One Sunday at church a stranger had said how much Maddy looked like her mother, and Miss Kate hadn't said a word to set things straight. Funny that Maddy hadn't said anything either.

Lou Emma had been the one that wanted a stepmother. Not Maddy. At least one thousand separate times Maddy had said *No* to her sister's question, Wouldn't it be nice if Papa got married? Maddy had wanted only the three Millers—no nosy housekeepers, no stepmother. They had their three family rules, and that was all they needed.

Rule Number One: The Family Sticks Together, No Matter What.

Rule Number Two: Never Interrupt Papa When He's Studying.

Rule Number Three: Keep Clean, Keep Fed, Keep Happy; Anything Else is Fancywork.

They hadn't done so bad, Lou Emma thought. They had got the housekeeping done, with a lick and a promise. But Professor Miller said too much housekeeping was worse than too little. Before they moved to Kansas, he had promised, solemnly promised, that the girls could manage on their own.

He had been as good as his promise. Burned steak, oversalted potatoes, gummy rice pudding, "sad" cake, iron-hard pie crust, holey socks, dusty furniture, rough-dry wash, he had never complained. Evenings when everything went wrong and there was nothing ready for supper he would laugh and bring out cheese and crackers, apples and milk, and call it a Roman banquet and name the food: *caseus, panis, malum, lac.* They would sit on and on in the dish-stacked kitchen, munching and making jokes and getting cracker crumbs on the floor, while the little gray dust mice gathered in the corners and the goat at the back door fattened on Lou Emma's cooking failures.

But all of that was part of the past. It was BMK as the Miller girls said in their private language to mark the years before their father's marriage. Before Miss Kate. It seemed so long ago, and it was only from December to July.

Miss Kate had done wonders. Now the small brown house was spick-and-span. No dust mouse dared show its gray nose. Meals were on time. Pillow cases ironed—even *sheets.* And side by side with all of this work the millinery shop went right along and prospered, and Miss Kate hired a helper, and ladies came from as far away as Emporia to have a hat made at Miss Kate's

Chapeaux. Lou Emma wanted to help in all this, but it wasn't easy. At first she had tried to do the chores that had been hers since she was big enough to stand on a box and dry dishes. It hadn't worked. Miss Kate did them so much better.

"Go on with the others, Lou Emma," her stepmother had said with a loving little push toward the door. "I want you to have a good time now."

One thing sure, Maddy didn't have to hear Miss Kate say that to her but once. With a hop, skip, and jump, Maddy left housework behind. She joined a Croquet Club, started a neighborhood newspaper, and organized a Sewing Society that never sewed but always planned to.

Lou Emma put her face down on the sun-warmed hood of the Great Smith. *I wanted it this way. Why don't I like it better?*

The Great Smith could not answer, but down underneath the red hood in the mysterious engine there was a tiny tick-tick-crack noise that sounded as if it were trying to answer. Whatever the sound Lou Emma felt better for having heard it, and she spread-eagled her arms over the hood and let the sun push her down closer. Crack-tick-crack.

Do things we talk to try to talk to us and can't? If we listened hard enough, could we hear?

She listened so hard that she was half-cross when Maddy disturbed her, coming back from Wackers' with the news that Joy had German measles.

"She looks like red pepper on cottage cheese. Mrs.

Wacker says for us to stay away, unless Miss Kate wants us to have measles now and not miss school."

"I'd rather miss school," Lou Emma said, still trying to hear the Great Smith. "I don't care what Miss Kate wants."

"Why are you mad at Miss Kate? She doesn't even know about Joy."

"I'm not mad at her. I just don't want to have measles." Lou Emma started for the house. She dreaded the way that Maddy could almost read her mind. Give Maddy the glimpse of an idea, and she could drag it out into broad daylight. Besides, she was *not* mad at Miss Kate. Nor at anybody except maybe herself. "I'm going in and cook the dumplings for dinner."

Maddy said, "BMK you made dumplings, and we had to bury 'em."

Dumplings were nothing but wet biscuit, Lou Emma encouraged herself. She took the dough Miss Kate had mixed earlier and pinched its waxy surface. The feel made it easy to pretend she had done the mixing herself.

In the black pot on the back of the stove a hen had been simmering all morning. When she lifted the lid, the cloud of steam made Lou Emma's mouth water. Cooking along with the hen in the rich yellow pot liquor were the "little eggs" discovered when Miss Kate cleaned the hen. There were six of them—solid yolk—and the bay leaf, red pepper, and quartered onion for seasoning. Watching the hen roll lazily in the pot liquor, a sudden hunger overcame Lou Emma, and she spooned out the biggest "little egg," blew on it, and ate it, loving the hot, choking goodness. Chicken livers, round-steak marrow bones, and "little eggs" were always the cook's choice to eat. Feeling more like a cook than she had for a long time, Lou Emma took some dough, rounded it between her palms—*I should've washed my hands*—and dropped it into the pot. Soon the dough balls would puff up into white, fluffy dumplings. Miss Kate would be astonished and delighted. Lou Emma planned that she would say, "But I always made dumplings before."

If Maddy says a word about those BMK *dumplings, I will kick her. I will—*

"That you, Lou Emma?" her father called from the front room.

"Yes, Papa. I'm cooking hen and dumplings." She didn't say Miss Kate had made the dough for the dumplings ahead of time. To tell the truth, she no longer remembered it herself.

Maddy came in, sniffing, as Lou Emma lifted the pot lid to add more salt. "Love-licious." It was a word she had made up and was working to death.

"Come look." With an air of authority Lou Emma sprinkled in more salt. Maddy peered through the steam. The dumplings were rising exactly as they should.

"They do look good," Maddy admitted.

The added salt made the pot liquor boil up fast. Lou

Emma decided not to put the lid back on the pot. Let the good smell remind her father of dinner.

"Here's a letter from Aunt Jesse." Maddy fished it from her pocket.

Lou Emma backed away. Letters from her father's spinster sister, who lived in Cleveland, Ohio, were likely to be filled with unwanted advice. When they had lived in Auden, she would descend on them about four times a year with plans for "Cyrus' poor little motherless daughters," which sometimes included young ladies, who would be the perfect wife for her widower brother.

"Why didn't you open it?"

"I didn't feel like a lot of Aunt Jesse-ing. You do it."

"Uh-uh. You." Lou Emma tossed the letter across the table.

"Uh-uh, uh-uh. You."

Back and forth the letter went until Maddy missed a catch and it fell into the butter. As a penalty for missing, she licked off the butter and opened the letter, but she only read the first page before she thrust it back.

"Murder! I think she's coming to visit."

"Not again?" Lou Emma read hurriedly. After she turned the page, she sighed with relief. "No, she's not. She says, 'I had planned to visit you this summer, but since Cyrus' wife continues to work (I fear I am too old-fashioned to understand this) a guest would be an imposition.' "

"Hurray for Miss Kate's Chapeaux!"

Lou Emma read on, " 'My friends the Mayfields—Cyrus will recall them—*very* wealthy, *very* influential, have invited me to share their suite at Greystokes-in-the-Pines during July and August. I regret that this means I shall not see my dear little . . . nieces.' She's scratched out a word in front of 'nieces.' "

"Lemme see." Maddy saw and snorted. "It's 'motherless.' Papa told her if she called us that once more he wouldn't be responsible for what he did."

"She did scratch it out."

"Not much. There's enough left to read, and she knew it good 'n' well."

"Thank goodness, she's going to Greystokes-in-the-whatchamacallit."

Promptly at noon Miss Kate arrived. The walk home in the heat had curled the stray ends of her hair, so that it ruffled out into a brown halo when she took off her hat. Her cheeks were pink, her eyes bright. She was even prettier, Lou Emma thought, than the first time she saw her.

Pumping water at the little red pump to wash her hands, Miss Kate asked the girls about their morning, and told them about her own as she tied on her apron.

"Cora Stumpf is determined to have a red hat, and she looks like a boiled beet in it. I'm trying to get her into green."

"Why'd you care?" Lou Emma asked. "If she wants red."

"For one thing it's poor advertising for the shop.

And for another—" Miss Kate turned her head to one side like a robin. "Well, I don't like boiled beets."

"I'll go tell Papa you're here," Maddy volunteered.

"Dinner won't be ready for a few minutes. I have to cook the dumplings."

Lou Emma forgot her prepared speech. She said nervously as Maddy left, "I cooked the dumplings. I . . . I thought you might be late."

"You don't need to bother with the cooking, I can . . . do . . . it . . . when . . ." Miss Kate's words slowed as she looked at the black pot steaming away. "Did you leave off the lid, dear?"

"When I put in more salt . . ." Lou Emma rushed to look. The puffy white dumplings had collapsed into small soggy balls. "What happened?"

Miss Kate answered in a voice so gentle it was as if she were afraid of breaking egg shells. "Never take the lid off dumplings till you're ready to dish up."

"I didn't know. I didn't mean to . . ." Lou Emma stared at the dreadful things. She would never eat dumplings again as long as she lived.

"There's plenty for dinner without them. Don't worry about it." Miss Kate patted Lou Emma's shoulder.

She stiffened against the pat. *How can I help worrying? I ruined 'em, and now you won't even get mad.*

Quickly, competently, Miss Kate lifted the hen to the platter, cut it into serving pieces, dished up green beans, set out cole slaw from the icebox, and sliced the homemade bread bought from Mrs. Wacker.

Professor Miller and Maddy came in, laughing over Maddy's latest spoonerism. The famous tongue twisters of Dr. Spooner of Oxford were favorite stories of the Miller girls and had become part of their family talk. "May I sew you to a sheet?" "Will you occupew my pie?" "A blushing crow," and all the others that Professor Miller had recited BMK. Now Maddy announced that dinner was "dicken and chumplings."

" 'Tisn't chicken; it's hen, really," Maddy explained, "but I think it sounds better that way. Dicken an' chumplings . . . dicken an' chumplings . . ."

"Dumplings were a favorite dish of the ancients." Professor Miller struck a pose and declaimed, "Diogenes ate 'em in his tub."

"Oh, Papa, he didn't," Maddy scoffed. But her father was looking at Lou Emma and Miss Kate standing by their places at the table, not saying a word.

"What's wrong, you two?"

Miss Kate said, "The dumplings for dinner aren't . . . didn't . . ."

"I ruined 'em," Lou Emma said flatly.

"We'll try again next week," Miss Kate hurried to say.

"Nonsense. I demand dumplings today." Professor Miller looked into the black pot. "Exactly the way I like 'em. Juicy."

In spite of her misery Lou Emma giggled. Her father forked up a dripping wad of dough and ate it as pot liquor dribbled down his chin.

"Best dumplings ever," he announced. *"De gustibus*

LOUR

non est disputandum. And that means don't dispute my taste or I'll wash your mouth out with soap."

Peace was restored around the dinner table. Miss Kate praised Lou Emma for adding more salt to the hen, saying she never got enough. Maddy told about her victory over the entire Croquet Club and how she was a Red Rover before anybody else. Lou Emma gave the news of Aunt Jesse's summer trip, carefully leaving out the remarks about "Cyrus' wife."

"The Mayfields," Professor Miller grinned. "Jesse'll be in her glory."

"Where is Greystokes-in-the-Pines?" Miss Kate asked politely.

"Near Colorado Springs, but farther up in the mountains. A lot of Ohio people go there," Professor Miller said. "It combines the Effete East with the Wild West for twenty dollars a day, American plan."

"Wow!" Maddy said. "They must be rich."

"The Mayfields have been rich so long they've forgotten about it. I suggest we forget it, too. I have an announcement to make." Having their attention Professor Miller folded his napkin, rolled it neatly, and put it in his silver napkin ring.

Maddy bounced on her chair. "Is it about the Ides of July approaches?"

Lou Emma started to quote Tommy but thought better of it.

The clock struck. Miss Kate started gathering up dishes. "I ought to get back. Mrs. Stumpf's coming in for another try-on."

"Be logical girls," Professor Miller scolded them. "No matter what you think of Hardy, his father is . . ."

"We know. 'The richest man in the county,'" Maddy quoted resignedly.

"And he gave the land to build the college on," Lou Emma finished.

"That is not what I was going to say. Mr. Garrett is a very able man. He suggested that Hardy be chairman. That means the Garretts will back the race, and backing is needed. Q.E.D."

"I'm not going to ask what that means," Maddy said rossly. "It's some old Latin something, and I don't ant to know."

"You'll find out when you take Geometry," Prossor Miller said. "Kate, I'll drive you to town. Seeing e Great Smith will keep Mrs. Stumpf in her place."

Miss Kate hurried after him. "Don't wash the dishes, ls. Just stack 'em."

'I won't watch their old race," Maddy said angrily. or let 'em sleep in our bed. Not on my side, any-."

Nor my side," Lou Emma said. "An' I won't shine r old shoes. Not if they beg me on their bended —knees. Why won't she let us wash dishes?"

et us? Lou Emma, you're crazy as a pet coon."

MK we washed dishes. Years and years we washed s."

umkopf old dishes," Maddy scowled. "Catch me ng any I don't have to."

"Sit down, Kate." Professor Miller rapped his napkin ring.

"But . . ." Miss Kate sat down. "All right, Cyrus, I'm sitting."

"On the edge of your chair," he said in his class-room manner.

Miss Kate ought to backhand him with the skillet.

Professor Miller cleared his throat. "The Midwest Automobile Club is holding a Three-State Race, the winner to receive a . . ."

"Silver cup," Maddy cut in. "Big as a washtub, Hackberry said."

"From Kansas City back to Kansas City," Lou Emma said.

"Through Kansas, Nebraska, and Missouri, I heard," Miss Kate concluded.

"Sanguine Saturnini!" Professor Miller growled the Latin oath that meant he had been pushed too far. He slapped the table; his napkin ring jumped nervously. "Am I never to finish a sentence in this house?"

Before either girl had to answer, Miss Kate put her hand over his. "It must try the patience of a man to live with three females. Please tell us."

He smiled at his wife. "Well, it's not exactly world-stopping news, but I wanted to tell my family before it appeared in the *Silver Bugle* tonight. Gloriosa is on the route of the race, and after a lot of wirepulling, the town has been slated as the first overnight stop."

"Gollywoggles!" Maddy yipped. "Hackberry don't know that."

Lou Emma wondered if Tommy did.

"The Mayor thinks it's the biggest thing since the Dalton gang held up the bank," Professor Miller went on. "The Commercial Club wants a public dinner with Congressman Clary to speak. Every auto entered will have a driver, an observer to see that all rules are kept, and possibly extra passengers. So for all those people rooms will have to be provided, and a hundred other details. Dr. Biddle wants EKCC represented in all this."

"And he chose you, Cyrus." Miss Kate's eyes shone.

"As the sole member of the faculty to own an auto, I seemed to be the logical choice for the Arrangements Committee." Professor Miller beamed.

"Can I tell Wackers?" Maddy shot out the door.

"Dr. Biddle couldn't have chosen better," Miss Kate said.

"Ad Astra per Aspera," Lou Emma said, feeling that the state motto of Kansas fitted in here somehow. She was rewarded by her father's smile.

"It's no tribute to me, my dears. I'm only the owner of the Great Smith."

No longer could Lou Emma sit still. She had to *do* something. Rushing out into the yard, she hugged the Great Smith's brass radiator cap; then, transfixed by a new idea, she ran for the kitchen and reached the door just as Maddy came racing back from Wackers'.

"Papa, can we have one of the race drivers stay here? All night?"

Maddy grabbed the idea and took it over as she al-

ways did. "Lou Emma 'n' me can borro
an' sleep out. He can have our room."

"What do you think, Kate? I don'
doing."

"I think it would be fun. I'll mak
the girls' room."

"I'll make a banner that says W
the mirror," Maddy said.

"I'll shine his shoes," Lou Emm

"Stop!" Professor Miller held u
count your driver before he's ha
will have to ask the Committee."

The excitement in the kitche

"I s'posed they'd ask you," Lo

Maddy scowled. "I told Wac
of the whole shebang."

"Then you were mistaken,
minute . . . but then you n
member of the Committee.
man."

There was a shocked sile
Miss Kate's discarded beau
the county, to be put ahea
than the Miller girls could

"Hardy's a nitwit, a .
compoop!" Maddy thump

"And a . . . a . . . n
Lou Emma used her o
peated it till Miss Kate s

"Really, girls, Hardy'

"But BMK . . ." Lou Emma started and then fell silent.

"Are we really not going to watch the race because Papa's not Chairman?"

"You were the one that said we weren't." Lou Emma absentmindedly ate a sliver of chicken. "I think we ought to watch, and even give 'em our bed. And if Miss Kate wants to make curtains, that's all right, too. But I won't shine their shoes, no matter what."

Maddy nodded. "And I won't make the WELCOME banner."

"That Hardy!" Lou Emma ate more chicken. "Trying first to marry Miss Kate, and having the nerve now to be Chairman of the Arrangements Committee."

"Looky," Maddy said, "Tommy and his gang are coming past McKelvys'."

The childless McKelvys with their perfectly kept yard and garden were in a continual state of war with the boys and girls of Gloriosa. As the Miller girls watched, Tommy and four more boys, all carrying long sticks, came to the heavy wire fence Mr. McKelvy had built to protect his garden. They spread out single file, dragging their sticks along the fence. The wires rattled and sang.

Mrs. McKelvy darted out her back door, shouting. The boys scattered like quail. When she reached the fence, not one of them was in sight. Her shouting went on.

"Look at 'er, talking to herself," Maddy said with satisfaction.

"Here comes Vinnie 'n' Eppie. Let's all walk to town." Lou Emma knew that when Mrs. McKelvy went back in her house the boys would come out and follow the girls, either ahead or behind. Not really with them, but not far apart either.

"Miss Kate said for us to stack the dishes," Maddy said.

"You stack 'em." Lou Emma walked out, knowing that Maddy would not do it, knowing, too, that Miss Kate would not say a word of criticism.

Like the forgotten tadpole in the rain barrel the resentment she felt against her stepmother surfaced and as quickly disappeared. A small black blob.

Well, she shouldn't have told us to stack 'em, Lou Emma argued with her conscience. *Stacking dishes is for little kids that don't know how to wash and dry.*

Chapter 2

Gloriosa was wound up like a top—and spinning. The race was all anybody talked about. "Auto Intoxication Takes Town," the *Silver Bugle* headline read.

On Assembly Avenue men and boys argued the merits of the autos entered: Franklin, Overland, Great Western, Auto Bug, Velie, Reo, Cadillac, Locomobile, Buick, Maxwell, and many others. The Millers were delighted that a Great Smith was on the list and downcast when later it was scratched. Mrs. Biddle was relieved.

"I know Cyrus would not race an auto," she told Miss Kate, "but his owning a Great Smith and being on our faculty might create a wrong impression in the minds of some people if there had been one in the Three-State Race."

"Don't tell your father that," Miss Kate cautioned the girls. "It would be just like him to try to get into the race to show Mrs. Biddle."

Every night Professor Miller had to go to a meeting of the Arrangements Committee. Work on the Book came to a standstill. At the table he shook his head in disbelief. "I had no idea a simple test of the combustibility of gasoline in an engine could cause all these complications."

"It's great for business," Miss Kate reported. "I've had to stop taking orders for new hats. The Bon Ton is sold out of satin. At Gibble's goggles are going great guns."

"Goody, goody gumdrop!" Maddy strung it out a little more.

"Which church is going to get to serve the dinner?" Lou Emma asked.

"None of them. Mrs. Moss, wife of the president of the Commercial Club, has decreed the dinner is to be served by wives of the members, thus saving the club the money they would have to pay the church ladies."

"My stars and garters!" Miss Kate said. "She'll have half the town mad at the other half before she gets through that."

"Mrs. Wacker was going to bake hams and make lemon pie if the Methodists got the job," Maddy said. "Three-inch meringue on the pie."

"The Ladies' Aid was going to make the preacher's salary in one swell foop." Lou Emma tagged on her most recent spoonerism. "Where'll the dinner be if it's not done by a church, Papa?"

"At the Masonic Hall. I don't want you overdoing on this dinner, Kate," he said sternly. "You have plenty on your hands now."

"But Cyrus—"

"That's my last word. Girls, see to it that Kate minds me."

They promised, threatening all sorts of penalties, until Miss Kate laughed and agreed. "All right. But that kitchen at the Masonic Hall is so little there won't be room for many workers. I doubt if I'm asked."

"We could help," Lou Emma offered herself and Maddy. "We could—"

"Hey! Professor!" Tommy Biddle was at the door. Lou Emma hurried to open it. "Pa said for me to get you to a special meetin', *pronto.* Hardy's got the word on how many's coming to Gloriosa with the race. Wanta guess?"

"Fifty." "Seventy." "Forty." "Eighty." The Millers registered their guesses.

"Two hundred and fourteen," Tommy said with satisfaction; then as if he thought they might not have heard, he whooped it out: "TWO hundred and fourteen PEOPLE."

"Are you sure?" Professor Miller questioned him.

"Yessir. Sure's sure. Dave Jones's on the telegraph key at the station, an' he lemme see the wire 'fore Hardy got it. That's the whole shootin' match. Drivers, observers, passengers, newspaper folks, pilot car, baggage trucks—everybody."

"How many autos?" Lou Emma asked.

"Forty-nine autos, thirty-five different makes." Tommy swelled with importance. "An' the Smith Motor Co. up to Topeka's asked 'em all to lunch."

"But when they get to Gloriosa, where'll you sleep 'em?" Lou Emma asked.

"Or eat 'em?" Maddy worried. "I mean feed 'em."

"Or where will you put all those expensive autos, Cyrus?"

Professor Miller's eyes twinkled. "That's what I'm going to ask our Chairman. I understand that's what chairmen are for. Come along, Kate."

Tommy cranked the Great Smith, then stood back with the Miller girls as the big red auto sped away. "I wish the Professor'd drive in the race. That's a real daisy, that auto."

" 'Built as well as any car in the world,' " Lou Emma quoted the motto of the Topeka manufacturer. "But a college professor couldn't be in a race. The Board'd have a fit."

"Mr. Garrett's on the Board," Maddy said. "Bet he wouldn't have a fit if Hardy wanted to race that fancy-antsy Stanley Steamer he drives."

"That's different," Lou Emma said. "The Board doesn't tell its own family how to behave. Just the professors and their families. But preachers' kids have it worse. The Jones girls can't go buggy riding on Sunday afternoon except to the cemetery."

"Na-na-na," Swish bleated, recognizing Tommy. "NANANANA."

"Hey, old Swish." Tommy rubbed the dark polished horns. "He's sure big now."

"And he's a jumper from Jumpersville," Maddy said.

"He jumped the fence into Wackers' chicken yard," Lou Emma said. "Their big red rooster took after him, and he jumped right out again."

"Don't let 'im jump McKelvys' fence," Tommy said

soberly. "Yesterday Mrs. McKelvy phoned Ma and told her our gang had to stop rattling their fence or she'd have us jailed. Every single one of us."

"What'd your mother do?" Lou Emma's eyes were big. Mrs. Biddle had been a real friend to the Millers since their move to Gloriosa, but she still felt in awe of the tall, imposing wife of the president of the college.

"She gabbed 'bout an hour on how us boys oughta be nice, p'lite, kind, consid'rate. All that. Then she turned me over to Pa."

"What'd he do?"

"Marched me out to the woodshed, but when we got there, he just told me to chop some kindling, and as for Mrs. McKelvy, he said to 'consider the source.' "

"What does that mean?" Maddy asked.

"Aw, I figger it means he don't really care, but to watch out and not get her riled too often."

"Miss Kate said we ought to be sorry for McKelvys because they have no children," Lou Emma said.

"Huh! I'd be sorry for the children if they did have 'em," Maddy said.

"She told Ma they had acetylene lamps put in downstairs because the doctor said electric lights fry the eyeballs," Tommy put in. "Everybody knows they just won't pay for runnin' the electric line to their house."

"They've got that carbide pit that the acetylene drips into, or something." Maddy held her nose. "It smells terrible, and they act like it was wonderful and keep saying nobody's s'posed to go close to it. Who'd want to?"

"Let's walk by their place and act like we're about to rattle the fence, only not do it." Tommy's eyes danced.

"Let's get Wackers," Maddy said.

"Let's take Swish," Lou Emma said, lifting the chain from the stake. Tommy took it from her and began to run Swish around the yard as if he were a trotting horse on a racetrack.

"Hi-up, Swish. Up-up-up, giddup!"

The three Wackers ran over, Hackberry with his iron barrel hoop and long-handled paddle. He challenged Tommy and Swish to a race, and they galloped around the two yards, the goat and the iron hoop side by side.

"Hoop! Hoop!" Hackberry yelled. "We're faster'n you. Faster'n anybody."

The girls ran behind them, heading toward McKelvys'. Maddy yelled over the racket of the race, "Two hundred's coming to Gloriosa for the auto race."

"Two hundred fourteen," Lou Emma panted.

"Three hundred," Maddy screamed. "The town can't hold 'em. It'll BUST."

She kept screaming BUST, and the other girls joined in. Swish, excited by the shouts and the chase, veered and ran into the racing Hackberry. The iron hoop escaped and hit the McKelvy fence with a rattling clang.

Mrs. McKelvy was ready for them. She rushed out of her back door, kid-leather curlers all over her head shaking like small sharp horns.

"Tommy Biddle! I told you yesterday. I warned you. I told your mother that thinks she runs this town.

I warned her. I've got to have peace and quiet. Do you hear? PEACE AND QUIET."

The six of them stood as if they were frozen. Even Swish was quiet.

"We didn't mean to," Lou Emma said at last. "Swish got excited and—"

"That goat's another thing," Mrs. McKelvy raged. "That goat's against the law. I'm goin' to the town council and tell 'em. I'm somebody in this town, and no goat's gettin' ahead of me, and another thing . . ."

"Let's beat it," Tommy said to the others.

"I won't." Maddy stood her ground. "We didn't do a thing, and she knows it."

"Don't you talk back to me!" Mrs. McKelvy turned on Maddy. "I've got my opinion of you. AND your step-mother that ought to be stayin' home, flauncing around selling hats for fifteen dollars that aren't worth fifteen cents. AND your father with his fancy big red auto. What kind of professor is he, I'd certainly like to know!"

"Greek and Roman History," Lou Emma said, sure of this anyway.

"Who cares about those old heathens? Couldn't even talk English." At this moment Swish reared to his long hind legs to nibble at a June rose trailing over the McKelvy fence. "Get that goat out of here! Now!"

Tommy jerked the chain, and Swish thudded down on all fours. Then all of them started running at once as if they suddenly could no longer endure the screech-ing of Mrs. McKelvy. For a little while her voice followed them; they huddled behind the Millers' barn in safety, staring at each other.

"Whaddya think she'll do?" Hackberry asked in a low quaver.

"Nothin'," Tommy said, swaggering a little. "Not one thing."

Lou Emma looked doubtful. "All that talk, and not do anything?"

" 'Twasn't a patch on what she said to us boys, and all she did was phone Ma and say she was gonna have us jailed if we did it again. Well, we didn't. It was Swish. All of us saw it. Five against one."

"But . . . jailed?" Eppie worried. "Girls, too?"

"Girls can go to jail as good as boys," Maddy said. "Suffragettes go to jail all the time. I just wish she would put me in jail."

Vinnie said, "I just remembered. The town Law's Mama's cousin. He wouldn't put us in jail for rattling a fence."

"Mama'd fix 'im if he did," Hackberry crowed. "C'mon, let's *really* rattle it."

His sisters grabbed one arm, the Miller girls the other.

"Too many against you, chum," Tommy grinned. "S'long."

He left, and after a violent struggle Hackberry shook off the girls and ran after him. The four girls shouted, but he only ran faster.

"Tommy'll look after him," Vinnie said. "He's not scairt of McKelvys."

"Tommy saved our lives the first day we came to Gloriosa." Lou Emma launched into her favorite story. "He jumped onto the running board of the Great Smith and grabbed the brake when we were *that* close to a herd of cows. Papa said he was a hero."

"Papa never said any such thing," Maddy contradicted. "You said it. You said it till I'm worn slick hearin' it. You're sweet on Tommy Biddle."

"I am not." Lou Emma's face burned. "Am I, Vinnie?"

"We-ell," Vinnie started. Lou Emma wished she hadn't asked.

"Girls— Oh, girr-ulls," Mrs. Wacker called.

"We'd better hush about you-know-who being sweet on you-know-who," Eppie said. "Mama'll say we're too young for such talk. I sure get tired waiting till Mama thinks I'm old enough for *anything.*"

Mrs. Wacker had some lemonade pinked with beet juice. The girls sat on the porch railing, swinging their legs and drinking. Mrs. Wacker in a blue-checkered dress rocked comfortably in the squeaky porch rocker.

"Wish we had ice," Vinnie said. "This'd be real good with ice."

Mrs. Wacker wagged her head. "When I was your age, we didn't even have lemonade. Our fav'rite drink was well-water, sorghum, and vinegar. Switchel, my ma called it. Why, when I was your age . . ."

Why do they always want us to know what they did when they were our age? Wondering, Lou Emma waited for Mrs. Wacker to finish. *Do they think we can be like they were? Does Miss Kate think that? What was she like when she was thirteen?*

Mrs. Wacker broke off her rambling and went to the porch steps.

"Clara!" She shouted in a voice that could be heard a half mile. "C'mon in."

"Mama, don't yell," Vinnie whispered, agonized. "It's Mrs. Moss."

"Well, good land, don't you think I know who it is? I've known Clara since we were six years old, south o' town. COME IN CLARA AN' BRING ADELAIDE."

Mrs. Moss rustled toward the porch. Hot weather or no, she was hatted, veiled, gloved, and dressed in the latest style. Behind her came Adelaide, the Mosses' only child, and the Miller girls' "bosom enemy." Adelaide had a peculiar way of walking, toes first, that always enraged Maddy.

"Look at 'er, tiptoein' through the Dismal Swamp," she muttered.

The girls giggled, but Mrs. Wacker frowned. "You young 'uns remember Adelaide belongs to the Willing Workers, same as you."

"She may belong to the same Sunday School class, but she's not same as me." Maddy said it too low for Mrs. Wacker to hear. "Not same as any of us."

Mrs. Moss took out a long list and consulted it. "I've come to talk about the dinner at the Masonic Hall for the race drivers, Jane. I want to talk to you and Miss Turner—I *mean* Mrs. Miller."

"She's at the shop," Maddy said. "She can't work on the dinner."

"Papa doesn't want her to," Lou Emma added. "He says she's got enough on her hands. But you can see her after supper, if you want."

Mrs. Moss looked at Mrs. Wacker through her dotted veil. "Really," she said. And again, "Really! Women who work outside the home—"

"Come inside out of the heat, Clara." Mrs. Wacker propelled her through the door with a warning look back at the girls. It meant as plain as if she had said it aloud, *Be nice to Adelaide, or you'll be sorry.*

Eppie offered Adelaide a glass of lemonade.

"I don't want any of that, if there's no ice," Adelaide said. "Why don'tcha have ice? Our ice wagon goes right past your place every day."

Lou Emma wondered what to say. Certainly not that the Wackers couldn't afford to get ice regularly from the Mosses' ice wagon. Adelaide went on talking.

"I've been out with Mama all afternoon. She's asked half the town to decorate the tables for the race drivers' dinner and nobody'll do it. Now she's going after Miss Turner—I *mean* Mrs. Miller. Whaddya call her anyway?"

Maddy's eyes narrowed. "What we call her's none of your business, but you'd better call her 'Mrs. Miller,' or you'll wisht you had."

"Well, don't get sore." Adelaide rearranged her sausage curls. "Let's go over to your house, Lou Emma. Come on."

On the short walk between the two houses Lou Emma tried frantically to think of something to pass the time that would win Adelaide's approval. Mrs. Wacker's warning look was heavy in her mind. In the shade of the grape arbor she got an idea.

"Want to look at Miss Kate's fashion books?"

Adelaide didn't bother to answer. "Where are the boys?"

The Miller girls and the Wacker girls looked at her blankly.

"You mean Hackberry?" Eppie said. "He's off someplace."

"Not him, silly. You know who I mean. Mrs. McKelvy phoned Mama that Tommy and his gang hung around Millers' all the time and it oughta be stopped."

"There's no boys here," Lou Emma said. "Unless you count Swish."

Swish had not been put on the chain again. He came trotting to them, twitching his beard as he chewed on some clover blossoms. Adelaide backed away.

"Will he hurt me?" she demanded.

"Good gravy!" Maddy started a defense of Swish, but Lou Emma pinched her.

"I don't know," Lou Emma said. "He could stomp you with his hoofs. And his horns are sharp. Want to feel?"

"You're trying to scare me," Adelaide said uncertainly.

"Believe what you want to," Lou Emma said, "but

I'll tell you one thing for sure . . . Swish's against the law." Mrs. McKelvy's words came out, dark and threatening.

"I'm going home," Adelaide announced. No one tried to stop her, so she started walking away, looking over her shoulder every few steps. Maddy gave Swish a shove. He trotted after Adelaide. When she saw him, she began to run. Swish, who loved a chase, took after her, running much faster on his four long legs. Adelaide gave a wild scream and ran as fast as she could, disappearing around the corner with Swish right at her heels.

Maddy doubled up with laughter. "Look at 'er! She's not tiptoein' now."

"Mama'll be mad as a wet hen at us," Eppie said. "But it's worth it."

"Mrs. Moss's the one that'll really be mad," Vinnie said. "When she gets through talking to Mama we'll have to weed strawberries till the cows come home."

"I meant to be nice to her," Lou Emma mused. "I really-and-truly-honest-and-bluely meant to. But she was so hateful. I'll help weed strawberries."

"Uh-uh. Miss Kate'll have you doing something else," Eppie said.

"Maybe."

Lou Emma agreed with Eppie by nodding her head, but in her heart she knew it wouldn't be that way. Miss Kate wouldn't punish her; she never had.

Our own mother would give me the dickens; I just know she would.

Chapter 3

Mrs. Moss appeared at the Millers' house just as Miss Kate finished washing the last dish. She was alone. When Miss Kate asked about Adelaide, Mrs. Moss shook her head until the tips of the ostrich feathers on her hat quivered.

"She was attacked by your goat this afternoon and badly frightened."

Lou Emma heard Maddy make a noise between a snort and a giggle. She nudged her sister in the ribs as they sat on the sofa.

"But Swish is as gentle as a lamb," Miss Kate insisted.

"Ask Emma Lou," Mrs. Moss said. "I *mean* Lou Emma. Her names always sound backward to me. But I am here about the dinner for the race drivers . . ."

Lou Emma quivered in indignation as Maddy elbowed *her* ribs. Emma Lou, indeed!

"Every detail must be perfect," Mrs. Moss said.

"This whole thing is getting out of proportion," Professor Miller spoke up from the Morris chair. "The Greeks said, 'All things in moderation, even virtue.' "

Mrs. Moss's eyebrows signaled shock. "Moderation in *virtue?* I hope you don't teach that to our young people at the college, Professor."

"Don't worry. Youth is no time for moderation. But, Mrs. Moss, I must insist that Kate not work on this dinner. She has enough to do. The shop . . . the girls . . ."

"We wouldn't want to add to her burdens," Mrs. Moss said sweetly. "But there is one thing I hope she will undertake. With your permission, of course."

Miss Kate's hands twisted nervously, and Lou Emma, watching them, wondered if she and Maddy were the burdens, or the shop. *They* must be what Mrs. Moss meant.

"I'm sure I'll be glad to do whatever I can," Miss Kate said.

Mrs. Moss consulted her list. "Lavinia Biddle is taking over Program. She has composed a Welcome Song, and the Willing Workers are to sing it."

"Yippee!" Maddy broke out. "We'll be at the dinner."

"Unfortunately not, dear," Mrs. Moss addressed her in iced-lemonade tones. "Because of the crowd, the class will only march in, sing, and march *out.*"

"That's not fair," Maddy protested. Professor Miller flagged her down.

Between gritted teeth Lou Emma whispered, "It's not fair. It's mean."

Mrs. Moss's gloved fingertip traveled down the list. "Mrs. Jones, in charge of mayonnaise . . . Mrs. Edmunds, silverware . . . Ah, here it is . . . I want you to decorate the tables, Miss Turner. I *mean* Mrs. Miller."

"I'm sure I would enjoy doing that," Miss Kate smiled.

"So happy that you will undertake it," Mrs. Moss murmured. "Neither Mrs. Stumpf nor Mrs. Elkins could, and when I asked Lavinia, she suggested you."

For once Adelaide had told the truth. Miss Kate was fourth choice. Lou Emma looked at her father's face and braced herself for an explosion. Miss Kate forestalled it by saying hurriedly: "I'll be glad to do the decorations."

"There are a lot of roses this year," Mrs. Moss said. "I will ask the committee members to contribute them."

"Don't give the decorations another thought," Miss Kate said. "I'll—"

"Roses. And asparagus fronds for greenery. A large arrangement for the speaker's table, and small ones for the others. Congressman Clary is speaking."

"Does he get to eat?" Maddy asked. No answer came.

Mrs. Moss went on. "Don't use honeysuckle. It droops in the heat. And you may count on me for cut-glass bowls. I'm sure you will be very, very careful."

"We have a cut-glass bowl," Lou Emma interrupted bravely. "Dr. Barnes that spoke at Chautauqua last summer gave it to Miss Kate for a wedding present. He went to Yale with Papa."

"What's that?" Mrs. Moss looked as astonished as if the sofa had spoken.

Miss Kate suddenly took charge, and Lou Emma went limp with relief.

"Now, Mrs. Moss, the table decorations are my responsibility. You needn't worry a moment longer. You have more important things to do. I think I'll ask the Willing Workers to help me, too."

"With the table decorations? Those children?" Mrs. Moss's voice rose.

We are not children. Not, not, not!

"Would the Willing Workers help with the decorations?" Miss Kate asked Lou Emma and Maddy, ignoring Mrs. Moss's protest. The girls loudly chorused promises.

"Then that's settled. What else can I do?" Miss Kate asked.

"Nothing." Mrs. Moss stood up, started to speak, then marched to the door.

She was barely out of hearing before the Miller girls were doing a war dance around Miss Kate. Professor Miller applauded.

"Just the way the barbarians took Rome, Kate. Surprise and attack."

"Don't call Miss Kate a barbarian," Lou Emma said. "It's not polite."

"It only means 'foreigner,' " her father said. "To our recent guest that is anyone not born in Gloriosa. So we are all barbarians together."

"If Miss Kate's one, I'll be one," Maddy said.

"Me, too." Lou Emma hugged her stepmother. The sweet smell of rose cologne came to her. This scent was her one certain memory of her own mother, and that Miss Kate used it, too, made a bond between the past and the present. How many years she had longed for a mother—and now she had one. She hugged Miss Kate harder. "What'll we decorate with?"

"I don't know yet. Something appropriate and different. You girls go round up the Willing Workers. Lemonade and cookies tomorrow at three sharp. Etta Mahaffey will keep shop for me, and we'll all plan the decorations."

"Now Kate, don't overdo," Professor Miller worried.

"Cyrus, if you say that once more, I'll—" Miss Kate stopped to think.

" 'Drop a tadpole down your back,' " Lou Emma suggested. "I've got one ready out in the rain barrel."

Upstairs, under the low ceiling, the girls' room was still stifling. The bed was shoved against the windows. Lou Emma could see the stars through the lacy branches of the elm tree. Tomorrow smiled at her. The Willing Workers . . . cookies . . . lemonade . . . Miss Kate at home with them. Now Mrs. McKelvy couldn't say a single word about Tommy and his gang hanging around. The Three-State Auto Race had turned the summer from dull to shiny. What was it her father had said? "I owe it to the Great Smith." To have a big red auto for a fairy godmother was so crazy that Lou Emma giggled aloud.

"What're you laughin' like a loon about?" Maddy asked.

"That we're Cinderella, and the Great Smith's our fairy godmother, and if we don't get home before midnight, it'll turn into a pumpkin pie."

"Silly!" Maddy hit her with a pillow. "There's no pie in it. Just pumpkin. But it still makes me mad the Willing Workers don't get to eat."

"If you eat, you have to listen to speeches," Lou Emma said wisely. "When we march out after we sing, we can go to the vacant lot and play Run, Sheep, Run."

Tommy's sure to be captain, and he'll choose me first.

The star she was watching winked in agreement.

With the help of the Wackers, the Millers told every Willing Worker about the meeting. Even the ones that came to Sunday School only at Christmas, Easter, and for the Picnic. Most of them promised to be there, except Adelaide who had an elocution lesson and Edna Grover who had joined the Congregationals.

In the early afternoon Lou Emma and Maddy squeezed lemons, sifted sugar, and chipped ice Miss Kate said they would splurge this time and have store-bought cookies—Nabisco wafers. The thin, sugar-filled strips meant "party" to Gloriosa girls; the boys preferred doughnuts.

"What'll we have for decorations? Really?" Maddy sucked on a chip of ice.

"Our cut-glass bowl full of something. But not roses and asparagus fern." Lou Emma chewed on a rind of lemon, shuddering at the taste but liking it, too. "I love roses. I wish we could have roses."

"Me, too. But if Mrs. Moss is for roses, I'm for sunflowers."

"Here come the Wackers, looking lower'n a snake's tail."

Vinnie and Eppie plopped down at the kitchen table and sat, wordless.

"What's wrong?" Maddy demanded. Eppie's chin quivered, but Vinnie took a deep breath, and the story came out in a rush.

On her visit the afternoon before Mrs. Moss had asked Mrs. Wacker to help with the dinner. Once she had agreed, Mrs. Moss took out her list and said Mrs. Wacker was to be in charge of mashed potatoes. That was all.

"All?" Lou Emma could not believe it.

"A-double-ell ALL." Vinnie spelled it out. Eppie sniffled.

"Good Granny!" Maddy exploded.

"Mrs. Wacker's the best cook in our church, and Mrs. Moss knows it," Lou Emma said. "What'd she say to that old—old—"

"Mossback," Maddy supplied. "Moss front, too. Moss-all-the-way-through."

"Mama said she hoped there'd be some more strong arms and weak minds to mash for all that crowd. An' Mrs. Moss said she was s'prised at Mama's saying such a thing, but in view of their long friendship she'd overlook it."

"The worst thing is that Mrs. Stumpf's in charge of ham," Eppie said between sniffles. "Everybody in Gloriosa knows she can't boil water without burnin' it. But he's a Big Bug, and—"

She didn't have to finish the sentence. The Miller girls knew well enough that Mr. Stumpf was president of the Gloriosa Bank and Trust, and Mr. Wacker was an off-and-on worker for the Santa Fe Railroad. Their wives were ranked in the same order, good cook or not.

"Miss Kate said Mrs. Moss'd make half the town mad over this," Lou Emma recalled. "Do you know what she did to Miss Kate?"

Before the Wacker girls could ask, Maddy had blurted it out.

"Got Miss Kate to promise to do table decorations, then told her she was fourth choice."

"Shhhh." Eppie peeked out the door. "Here comes Miss Kate now."

Behind Miss Kate in rapid succession came the Willing Workers. Ten girls and five boys. Edna Grover turned up and said her mother said she could come "for the time being."

"I guess you mean 'for the time being in the fun,' " Gracie Elkins said.

Edna's feelings were hurt, so Miss Kate asked her to help with refreshments. She passed the Nabisco wafers to the boys first and the plate got back to the girls *clean*. Fortunately Miss Kate had an extra hidden box, so everybody got some. There were two glasses of lemonade all around, and then the Willing Workers sat, rattling ice and drinking the faintly flavored ice meltings.

"Shall we plan the table decorations?" Miss Kate said. "Any ideas?"

"I read in a magazine about freezing a bouquet of

American Beauty roses in a block of ice," Vinnie said. "Could we do that?"

"I'm afraid that's too expensive." Miss Kate ticked off on her fingers. "We need something inexpensive, easy to get, appropriate, and different."

The room was so quiet the buzz of a fly caught in the window sounded loud. The Willing Workers stared, blank as a blackboard the first day of school.

"I can't think of one solitary thing that's all of those," Lou Emma said at last. "Except . . . maybe sunflowers."

"Sunflowers?" Gracie said. "I thought they were weeds."

"They'd better be," Tommy said. "I've been pullin' 'em up all morning."

"Sunflowers always have bugs on 'em," Eppie shuddered.

"An' sticky juice an' hairy stems." Vinnie made a face.

"Tacky." Edna rolled her eyes back till only the whites showed. "Tacky."

"Sunflowers, UGH!" Maddy turned her thumbs down as the Romans did on an unsuccessful gladiator. Lou Emma wished she had kept her mouth shut.

"What's the state flower of Kansas?" Miss Kate asked.

"The sunflower, since nineteen-OH-three," all of them droned.

"They teach us that in school," Maddy said. "But nobody decorates for dinners with 'em."

"I think having the Kansas state flower as a decoration would be very appropriate," Miss Kate said, smiling at Lou Emma. "Besides, they're pretty."

Tommy wrinkled his freckled forehead. "They are, kind of."

I can always depend on Tommy; he is a hero, no matter what Maddy says.

"They'd be easy to get and free-for-nothing," Gracie conceded.

Lou Emma took heart. "And they'd be different."

"I'll say they would," Maddy sniffed.

J. T. suddenly joined Lou Emma. "I'm for sunflowers if you'll take 'em out of our back lot. Ma keeps jawin' me to cut 'em."

"Hooray for Kansas!" Harris Jones yelped. "Sunflowers all the way!"

"Could we freeze sunflowers in a block of ice?" Vinnie wondered. The others hooted her down.

"Can we use our cut-glass bowl for the speaker's table?" Lou Emma asked.

"Sunflowers and cut-glass don't go together very well," Miss Kate said. "But I have an idea. . . ." She hurried from the room and came back with a hank of the natural-colored raffia that was all the rage for embroidering hats. Twisting the raffia until it stiffened, she coiled it around a pint fruit jar, row on row. The Willing Workers watched it grow before their eyes.

"We'll cover the jar with glue to hold the raffia, and when it's covered and dry, we'll shellac it. That way we'll have matching flower holders, just right for sunflowers. And no worry about breaking borrowed cut-glass bowls."

"All in favor of sunflowers?" Tommy shouted.

Every hand went up except Maddy's. The Willing Workers groaned. Maddy sat stubbornly on her hands.

Lou Emma said, "Come on, Maddy. You're the one that made me think of sunflowers. You said your own self if Mrs. Moss was for roses, you were for sunflowers."

Maddy's hand shot up. "Count me in. She'll be mad enough to bite nails and eat snails."

The next afternoon the Willing Workers gathered to work. Each one brought two fruit jars. This time Adelaide came with Gracie who brought extra fruit jars for her.

"My mother doesn't have any jars to spare," she reported smugly. "They're all full of fruit and in our fruit cellar."

"That will do, Adelaide," Mrs. Biddle said. She had come to practice the Willing Workers in the Welcome Song. "All line up and read the words aloud."

"Welcome now to Gloriosa,
To our city fair.
Brave and speedy drivers welcome,
Our repast to share."

"What's repast?" J. T. interrupted.

Tommy snickered. "Whadda you care? You're not goin' to get any."

"Next verse," Mrs. Biddle said.

"You have braved the open road,
Dared the dangerous valleys,
Climbed the hills and forded rills,
To get the winning tallies."

Eddie Gammon who had just moved to Gloriosa raised his hand. Mrs. Biddle nodded.

"You don't say 'tallies' in an auto race. You say 'check sheets.' The check sheets've got the demerits on 'em. Drivers get demerits for even lifting the hood or tightening bolts or putting water in the radiator . . ."

"S'pose it's a Franklin? They don't have no radiator," Harris jeered.

"Awright, smart-Aleck," Eddie squared off. "My dad's seen check sheets and he told me about 'em. You wanta make something out of it?"

"Boys, boys," Mrs. Biddle said. "Next verse."

Eddie was not to be silenced. "But it ain't tallies! Dare you to ask my dad."

" 'Check sheets' won't rhyme with 'valleys,' " Lou Emma explained. "It's got to rhyme."

"Even if it's not true? A Sunday School class oughta tell the truth." Without looking Lou Emma knew this came from Adelaide.

"We will discuss truth later," Mrs. Biddle said. "Last verse with *expression*."

"Gloriosa, EKCC,
And Congressman Ed Clary,
Bid you welcome HEROES ALL,
And hope you long will tarry."

Up went Eddie's hand. "If they tarry all that long, they'll get demerits."

Mrs. Biddle ignored him. "Memorize the words. Practice tomorrow at the church with music. Now mind Mrs. Miller and work on your decorations."

Away Mrs. Biddle rustled, leaving the Willing Workers muffling their laughter as J. T. mimicked her: "Mind Miz Miller . . . mind Miz Miller . . ." Miss Kate pretended not to hear what was going on and passed out raffia, glue, scissors, and ranged the fruit jars on newspapered tables.

In a few short minutes Harris broke a fruit jar, Tommy upset the glue, Bob Handy pinched Maddy and blamed it on Eddie. The house was in an uproar. There was so much noise they didn't hear the Great Smith arrive and Professor Miller walk in. With one look at Miss Kate, he took charge.

"What's going on here?" He pointed at Eddie. "You there, answer me."

"Aw, we gotta sing a song that's a crazy lie. I'm goin' home."

"Good idea," Professor Miller agreed. "I'll take you in the Great Smith and the rest of you boys can come for the ride. We'll get a valve check at the blacksmith shop. Girls, get to work on those doodads, and we'll bring you some sunflowers to try out."

Open-mouthed, Miss Kate saw order restored and the boys leave quietly.

Then the girls settled down to work. Jar by jar the flower holders were set on the apron of the kitchen range to dry. There was a quiet buzz of talk. Miss Kate went around encouraging, tightening the coils of raffia, pushing and patting the finished products. Thirty jars and one big stone crock for the speaker's table were complete before the boys returned, Eddie with them.

They carried armloads of sunflowers and sacks of roasted peanuts still warm from the peanut roaster on Assembly Avenue. Each Willing Worker had one sack. Crackling and crunching, they watched Miss Kate select the best sunflowers and fill two jars and the big crock. The golden petals, the brown centers, the rough green leaves, fitted with the raffia-covered holders as if they had been grown for the purpose.

Lou Emma wondered if they were really as pretty as she thought, but she waited for somebody else to say so. Gracie Elkins spoke first.

"I'll never say sunflowers are weeds again."

"We've got a Miss Kate Original." Vinnie named the most expensive hat in the millinery shop. But Miss Kate wouldn't have it that way.

"No. It's a Lou Emma Original. I just showed you how to work it out."

Lou Emma stared at the floor, unable to accept the praise but loving it.

"How come I never noticed sunflowers before?" J. T. puzzled.

"Because you're a peanut brain." Tommy hit him on the shoulder. Eddie blew up and popped his peanut sack. Adelaide shrieked and put her hands over her ears. Bob tripped Vinnie and said it was Harris. Gracie dabbed glue on Eppie.

"Outside everybody," Professor Miller shouted over the rising racket.

As the Willing Workers rushed for the door, Lou Emma waited for a moment to carry out the discarded sunflowers left on the table.

"Cyrus! Thank heaven you got here! I didn't know what to do," Miss Kate said.

"Teaching gives you a few ideas," Professor Miller said. "Such as never try to mix boys and girls and work. Not in one small house. Takes an acre at least."

"I don't know anything about boys," Miss Kate said.

"You can learn," Professor Miller said softly. Lou Emma saw him touch her stepmother's soft brown hair as gently as if he touched a butterfly.

In the shady yard the Willing Workers spread out. Peace was restored. Tommy and Harris tossed a baseball. Professor Miller, J. T., and Eddie opened the hood of the Great Smith and talked about motors. Swish came prancing around, and Adelaide forgot she was afraid of him and made him a cap of grape leaves. Miss Kate brought out her fashion books, and the girls selected fabulous wardrobes. Lou Emma remembered last night, and how she had hoped things would be. *And now they are. They really are.* BMK *we couldn't have done it.*

She smiled in dreamy content. Then the smile congealed on her face. Driving her high-stepping bay horse at a fast trot, Mrs. Moss arrived at the front walk. Every move she made showed anger. The Willing Workers stood as if they had been playing statue.

Only Swish, unalarmed, trotted to meet her.

"Get away, you nasty beast!" Mrs. Moss stamped her foot.

Adelaide said, "He won't hurtcha, Mama."

Maddy collared Swish. "She might hurt him," she said pointedly.

"Lou Emma, bring a chair for Mrs. Moss," Miss Kate said.

"I prefer to stand," Mrs. Moss announced.

Lou Emma looked uncertainly at her stepmother, who gestured her toward one of the chairs that had been dragged out in the yard.

"Do let me give you some iced tea," Miss Kate said. "It's so warm—"

"This is not a social call," Mrs. Moss snapped. "When I first heard what you were planning, I refused to believe it. I said flatly that Miss Turner—I *mean* Mrs. Miller—would not do such a thing."

"But what have I done?" Miss Kate looked bewildered.

The Willing Workers edged closer. Lou Emma tried to hurry, but the chair was heavy.

"Dis-grace Gloriosa." Mrs. Moss said it so there was no mistaking.

Professor Miller's face blazed red. "Now see here—"

Mrs. Moss turned on him. "What do you care about our town? You—you foreigner."

By now Lou Emma had wrestled the chair to the grown-ups. Cautiously she touched Mrs. Moss's arm. "May I . . . may I sew you to a sheet?"

The old tongue twister was like a trigger that set off laughter in the Willing Workers. They whooped; they screeched; even Adelaide doubled up shouting the spoonerism over and over. Lou Emma realized Mrs. Moss would never believe she hadn't meant to say it, that it had only been a slip of the tongue. But there was no use apologizing now. Mrs. Moss stalked past her as if neither she nor the chair existed. Fascinated, the others followed. Mrs. Moss picked up a sunflower from the heap Lou Emma had tossed on the ground. She held it at arm's length.

"So it's true. You are using sunflowers for table decorations?"

"Not those," Maddy said. "The good ones are in the house."

"In the flower holders we made out of fruit jars." Lou Emma tried to make things better. Mrs. Moss closed her eyes as if she had just been stabbed.

"Gloriosa's big opportunity, and you decorate with fruit jars of sunflowers."

"The sunflower's the state flower of Kansas," Eddie piped up. Then he ducked behind the Great Smith.

"If you would come inside and look at our arrangements," Miss Kate said.

Mrs. Moss cut her off. "I am going immediately to talk to Hardy Garrett. We'll see what he thinks about this. Come Adelaide."

"Aw, Mama—"

"COME."

The Willing Workers watched silently as the Mosses' surrey departed in a whirl of dust. Then Tommy Biddle gave a loud groan.

"Humpin'-jumpin'-jackrabbits!"

Professor Miller nodded. "Exactly what I was about to say."

"I guess the sunflowers weren't a very good idea," Lou Emma said.

"Yes, they were." Miss Kate put her arm around Lou Emma. "But perhaps . . . under the circumstances . . . I mean, after all . . . roses . . ."

"Kate, I'm ashamed of you," Professor Miller boomed. "Where's your Kansas spunk?"

"Roses are ordinary," Maddy said. "Everybody has roses."

"Roses 'd looked terrible in our raffia jars. Tacky," Gracie said.

"Tacky," Edna echoed her. "Tacky as tacky."

"Roses smell too loud," Harris said.

"Roses 're too sissy for race drivers," Eddie said.

Lou Emma said nothing, but she twisted her head back so that she could see Miss Kate, and Miss Kate could see the *please, please* she was thinking.

"Well," Miss Kate smiled, first at Lou Emma and then at the others. "You've convinced me. Sunflowers it is."

The Willing Workers cheered.

Chapter 4

Banners fluttered on Assembly Avenue. Gold and purple, the colors of the Midwest Automobile Club, were everywhere. WELCOME screamed the banners. WELCOME drivers, observers, officials, sponsors, onlookers! Even a few welcomed Congressman Clary and urged his re-election. The official fuel of the race was White Rose gasoline, and signs proclaiming its excellence were strung out for miles on either side of Gloriosa.

Business was booming in the town. The stores were crowded, and there was a festive air among the customers. A rumor was going around that two autos—a Moon and a Marmon—had been sold, bringing the total number of cars in town to twelve. And now another rumor added that a Baker Electric had been put "on order." A delegation of farmers complained to the town council that too many autos were scaring their livestock and ruining their crops with poisonous fumes, but nothing came of their complaint. Gloriosa had accepted what the *Silver Bugle* called the Auto Age and was not going backward.

The stores put on special sales. Berkemeyer's Confectionery offered a Three-State Sundae: three scoops of vanilla ice cream drenched in grape jam and pineapple preserves. Dillar's music store had such a run on the sheet music of "In My Merry Oldsmobile" that J. T.'s father had to make a trip to Topeka to buy more. Miss Kate's Chapeaux featured a gold-colored straw sailor with purple ribbons and pompons.

"The Ides of July." Professor Miller mopped his forehead. "I'll be glad when this is over. Not a page done on the Book since it started."

"Poor Cyrus," Miss Kate handed him iced tea. "Only one more day."

The Millers' house had its own whirlpool of activity, which mirrored that of every house in Gloriosa where a driver was staying overnight. New curtains were hanging in the girls' room. Every inch had been cleaned, washed, waxed, or polished. Maddy changed her mind, concocted a Welcome Banner, and hung it over the mirror. Lou Emma made a book of shaving papers, laced together with gold and purple ribbons. Enough shaving papers, her father said, that a man could wipe lather from his straight razor for 365 days, let alone one morning. Maddy put a pipe stand on the dresser, and now she added a cigar, traded from Eppie who got it from Mr. Wacker's vest pocket.

"It is kind of bent," Maddy admitted. "But it's better than none."

"I'm not so sure." Professor Miller sniffed the cigar. Lou Emma saw Miss Kate shake her head.

"You girls go practice the Welcome Song," she said. "When I get through mopping the kitchen, we'll go after sunflowers. Better wait till dark."

They climbed to their favorite spot, the top of the grape arbor.

"Welcome now to Gloriosa,
To our city fair . . ."

"Do you think Gloriosa's a city fair? Really?" Maddy asked.

"N-no," Lou Emma said. "Just fairly fair. But Mrs. Biddle thinks so."

"That stuff about 'fording rills,' sounds crazy."

"It's in 'My Country 'tis of Thee.' Rocks and rills."

"Writers ought to talk like people."

"Well, Papa's a writer. Or almost. I wish he'd finish the Book."

"I heard him tell Miss Kate that he wrote one page and tore up two. If he keeps backin' up, he'll be writin' about the Garden of Eden instead of Rome."

"Is it fun to write a book?" Lou Emma wondered.

"It's bound to be," Maddy said. "Look at all the books Papa's got. And all the ones in the Library. Nobody'd write 'em unless it was fun. But it's more fun to be a race driver."

" 'Next verse,' " Lou Emma mimicked Mrs. Biddle.

They sang the Welcome Song three times and then fell silent. The sunlight was nearly gone. A few birds twittered sleepily. In the grass below Swish stood up, shook himself, and cropped a few bites of clover. The Wackers' ginger-colored cat, Mr. Murphy, stalked like a tiger among the nodding prince's-feather. The world was full of peace and quiet. Lou Emma breathed deep to bring it into herself.

Maddy said, "Are we waitin' for dark so Mrs. Moss won't see us?"

"Crazy. So the sunflowers won't be buggy. Bugs leave 'em after dark."

"How do you know so much?" Maddy demanded.

"Miss Kate said so. Did you ever see an ant after dark?"

"I never looked for one," Maddy countered. "Old Hardy told Mrs. Moss a jugful about our using sunflowers for the dinner, didn't he?"

"Just that Mrs. Miller would decorate in good style, he was sure."

"That's a jugful when you're talking to Mrs. Moss." Maddy looked at her sister thoughtfully. "You know . . . Hardy's not so bad."

"He tried to marry Miss Kate. Don't forget that."

"You were clear off Miss Kate for a while. What got you back on the track?"

"Mind your own business," Lou Emma said, but she was quaking inside. The truth was that she changed her feelings about her stepmother as often as the wind changed. Maddy must not know this, or there was no telling what she would jump to or what she would say. "There's Tommy. It's time to go."

By the time Professor Miller and Miss Kate came out, Tommy had the Great Smith's acetylene head lamps lighted and was standing ready, crank in hand. He gave a mighty spin, and the engine responded at once. In the back seat with the Miller girls he sighed.

"I wisht Pa'd buy an auto. Everybody's got one but us."

"There's only twelve in town, maybe thirteen," Maddy scoffed.

"Then I wanta be one of 'em. I can drive, patch tires, rig a block 'n' tackle, put on chains, strain gas. . . . Say, do you know how to keep your windshield clear in the rain? Rub a cut onion over it."

In his satisfaction at giving information, Tommy perked up and forgot his autoless state. Lou Emma gave the Great Smith an unseen pat. Maybe Tommy would have liked her as well without the big red auto, but she was glad she didn't have to find out.

By the time they came to Dillar's corner it was dark. J. T. flagged them down.

"I can't give you the sunflowers," he said unhappily.

"Whaddya mean?" Tommy squawked. "You begged us to take 'em."

"Yeah." J. T. stared at the dust. "My mother's got real thick with Miz Moss, an' she told me . . . Anyway, I'm not s'posed to."

Lou Emma heard the sharp intake of Miss Kate's breath, but her father appeared undisturbed.

"Get in the auto, J. T. We can find plenty of sunflowers."

"There's a zillion back of Old Main at the college," Maddy said.

In the glow of the Great Smith's head lamps a wide field of sunflowers showed, their heads turned toward the west. All the long hot day they had moved so slowly that no one could see them, turning with the sun; now they waited for the sunrise to turn them back again. Aunt Jesse used to sing a song about it:

As the sunflower turns on her god, when he sets,
The same look which she turn'd as he rose.

Sometimes it was nice to think about Aunt Jesse. If only their father wasn't forever telling them, "Jesse means well." Lou Emma wondered why it was so hard to like the people you were hard-and-fast supposed to like.

The others were out of the auto, and Maddy called back for Lou Emma to bring the old lantern. It was a relic of the horse-and-buggy days in Auden and used to swing under the buggy when they went out at night. She lighted it and held it high so that Maddy, Tommy, and J. T. could find the best sunflowers. At the edge of the circle of light stood her father and Miss Kate; she was almost sure they were holding hands. An unexpected pang of hurt feelings made Lou Emma catch her breath.

BMK *Papa 'd 've held the lantern. Now all he thinks about is Miss Kate.*

At home they pumped buckets of cool water and plunged the sunflowers into it. Examining one of the largest flowers, Lou Emma found not one single ant or other bug. For some reason this made her feel better. If Miss Kate was right about ants and bugs, maybe it was right for her to hold hands; maybe it was all right for their father to. The hurt feelings slipped away. Not even Maddy's discovery of a sleepy bumblebee in a sunflower leaf made them come back.

When it was time for the boys to go, Tommy went out to crank the Great Smith. It kicked him so hard he grabbed his arm and yelled with pain. Then he accused J. T. of not retarding the spark. J. T. claimed that he had, and it looked like trouble, but Professor Miller stepped in, examined the arm, said it was all right, and gave both boys a lecture.

"Who's right or wrong makes no difference. Retard the spark before you crank the auto. Always. No exceptions. No excuses. This auto carries forty horsepower and that's *dangerous*. If you don't respect the rules the Great Smith will remind you by breaking your arm."

"You make the Great Smith sound awful," Lou Emma protested.

"Not at all. It's a machine, and a machine does what the man in charge directs it to do. It has no choice. Mind over matter, young people."

"Yessir," the boys said soberly. Tommy rubbed his arm.

"Now, repeat after me, 'Hark, hark, retard the spark.' "

They repeated, at first earnestly; then as they all chimed in and said it over and over, it became funny. Tommy put an end to the lesson by adding his own tag line, "Hark, hark, retard the spark, and don't never stay out after dark."

J. T. said, "I'm gettin' for home or Ma'll retard my spark for good."

The alarm went off very early the next morning. Downstairs Lou Emma heard the quick, light steps of

Miss Kate and the slower steps of her father. Professor Miller slept hard, the way Maddy did. Miss Kate must have worked to get him out early. Then Lou Emma's heart jumped as she remembered: *It's the Day of the Race!*

Hurrying down she found them in the kitchen. Oatmeal in blue bowls on the table, bacon in the skillet, coffee boiling, French toast browning.

It'd take me two hours to fix a breakfast like this.

"Thank goodness, you're here," Miss Kate said, and Lou Emma's spirits lifted. "I need you to help me arrange the flowers. If we get them in now, they'll have a chance to get used to the containers."

"Get used to the containers?" Professor Miller questioned. "You sound as if you thought those sunflowers had minds and feelings."

"Maybe they do, Papa. The Greeks had all kinds of myths about flowers. Why not Kansas sunflowers?"

"Good for you, Lou Emma." Miss Kate said.

"Sounds pretty anthropomorphological to me," the Professor grumbled.

"An-thro-po-WHAT?" Miss Kate looked at Lou Emma.

"I don't know," she said. "But I know when Papa gets that look on his face he means 'Women are silly.' "

"Perish the thought and pass the syrup," her father said.

"Let's ignore him," Miss Kate said. "Please put the irons on to heat so I can do up your dress and Maddy's. I starched them last night."

"I can iron 'em," Lou Emma said. She liked to iron when she didn't have to.

"Let her iron," her father argued. "Kate, you're overdoing."

"Not this time, Cyrus." Miss Kate spoke firmly. "Every girl in the Willing Workers will wear a dress ironed by her mother. Our girls must, too."

Professor Miller looked upward. "Forgive me, O Minerva, Goddess of Wisdom, but women *are* silly."

Lou Emma, getting out the sad irons and setting up the ironing board knew what he meant, but she knew what Miss Kate meant, too. Some things were special.

The Great Smith looked like a flower wagon. Buckets of sunflowers filled the back seat. Among them sat Lou Emma trying to hold them upright and keep the boxes of raffia-covered jars from tipping over. As they drove from the yard they saw the dumpy silhouette of Mrs. Wacker at her kitchen table.

"They also serve who only sit and peel," Professor Miller parodied.

"It's a shame, a waste of talent, to put Jane to mashing potatoes."

"If I was Mrs. Wacker—" Lou Emma burst forth.

"If I were Mrs. Wacker," her father corrected.

"Was or were. I'd put a quart of salt in those mashed potatoes."

Miss Kate laughed. "Not if you were Mrs. Wacker. But if you were Miss Turner—I *mean* Mrs. Miller—you might."

When they reached Assembly Avenue, plenty of people were ahead of them. Early as it was Gloriosa was hustling to have everything in readiness for the race. The big sprinkler wagon was out trying to lay the dust before it was raised. Moss's ice wagon was cramming store refrigerators with all the ice they could hold. Boys on bicycles with gold and purple crepe paper twined in the spokes wheeled in and out like decorated mosquitoes. The vacant lot that had been graded, graveled, and provided with overhead lights where the racing autos were to be kept at night was swarming with special police. With the Great Smith at the curb in front of the Masonic Hall, Professor Miller took out his pocket watch to check the time.

"Six thirty, and two hundred and fourteen people heading for Gloriosa."

Lou Emma wiggled with excitement. "I wish I could see 'em start."

"Eddie Gammon told me how they start these races. The drivers are lined up in Kansas City according to the number they draw. The starter sends them out exactly one minute apart. Our driver"—he consulted a paper—"is L. T. Wintergreen, driving an EMF Studebaker 30."

"Papa! Why didn't you tell us his name before now?"

"I only knew it last night. Why do you care about his name?"

"I could've spelt his initials in colored pins on the pincushion."

"He'll have to struggle along with plain pins. How may I help, Kate?"

"With Lou Emma I won't need you, Cyrus."

Does she mean that, or is she just saying it?

"Well, I do have some things. . . . Now, Kate, don't—"

"I won't overdo." She gave him a little push, and he drove away.

"He's going to work on the Book," Lou Emma said. "I can tell because he looks happy and secret."

"Do you think a secret shows on a person's face, Lou Emma?"

"Sometimes. I know when Maddy's got a secret; she won't look at me. Why, Miss Kate, you're red as a beet!"

"Just the heat," her stepmother said quickly. "Must be eighty already."

Long tables had been set up in the Masonic Hall, draped with snowy damask from the best linen closets in Gloriosa. Borrowed silverware, tagged with colored thread on the handles, marked every place. Upside-down water glasses and napkins folded like teepees completed the setting. At one side of the Hall an upright piano with some ivory key tops missing had a gap-toothed smile. Gently Lou Emma touched middle C. *"Welcome now to Gloriosa, . . . To our city fair . . ."*

She sang it softly, never quite sure of herself and the music. Then she went back to Miss Kate. "Mrs. Biddle wants me to lead the march. S'pose I do it wrong?"

"S'pose you do it right?" Miss Kate arranged sunflowers. "How does that look?"

"Love-licious." Lou Emma borrowed Maddy's word. "Even Mrs. Moss—"

"Shhhh."

"Good morning." Mrs. Moss walked rapidly through the Hall into the kitchen.

Lou Emma's mouth fell open. "She never said a word about the—"

"Shhhh," Miss Kate said again and went on arranging sunflowers. Lou Emma stood beside her, handing the right flower at the right time. They worked in silence. At last Lou Emma could stand it no longer and tiptoed to the kitchen.

There was no one inside. She ventured to the back porch. On it was a long table stacked with washtubs of borrowed plates, cups, saucers. No one was in sight. Lou Emma went back to Miss Kate who had placed the decorations on the tables. Their radiant golden color transformed the room.

"I never knew they'd be this nice," Lou Emma said with something like awe.

"A lot of work, but it was worth it." Miss Kate sighed in satisfaction. "Kansas flowers on Kansas tables."

"Why wouldn't Mrs. Moss even stop and look? Why did she act that way?"

"Forget it as fast as you can," Miss Kate said. "It's not worth worrying about. Now I'm going to the shop. Three hats to finish by noon and be back here by three o'clock. I hope L. T. Wintergreen comes in early so he can have some rest before the dinner at five thirty."

Miss Kate hurried away. Lou Emma repeated the name dreamily as she picked up boxes and buckets and leftover sunflowers.

L. T. Wintergreen. He would be tall, dark, and never need to rest the way Miss Kate said. *L. T. Wintergreen.* He would sit in the Morris chair, smoking a pipe, and he would say, *Miss Miller . . . May I call you Lou Emma? . . . Permit me to take those shaving papers as a fond remembrance of . . . of . . .*

"Hey, wake up!"

It was Tommy. He and J. T. almost covered by boxes, pans, pitchers, potato mashers, and long-handled stirring spoons were being herded along by Mrs. Biddle. There was a clatter as she unloaded them in the kitchen, and they dashed back, eating slabs of cake and scattering crumbs.

"Go on—go on—" Mrs. Biddle came behind them with a broom. "Lou Emma get these boys out of here. And Tommy, don't forget—"

Her voice trailed after the three of them. clear onto the street. The bright sun made Lou Emma blink. L. T. Wintergreen was suddenly eclipsed by the excitement of the day ahead.

More and more people were congregating on Assembly Avenue. Farm wagons loaded with families rattled up. Every auto in the county had been washed, polished, and decorated with gold and purple streamers. Lou Emma thought with satisfaction of the crepe-paper rosettes Miss Kate had made for the Great Smith's head lamps, hubs, and the biggest one for the horn. They were joined by Eddie who had found a check sheet; the boys pored over it, counting possible demerits.

The four of them strolled around town, bumping into people, almost getting their eyes put out by the ribs of umbrellas raised against the sun. At Miss Kate's Chapeaux Lou Emma glimpsed her stepmother stitching on horsehair braid, head bent, sewing machine flying. They tapped on the window, but she didn't look up.

"Miss Kate works makin' hats like she was killin' snakes," Tommy said.

"Yeah, but my mother says—" J. T. glanced at Lou Emma and broke off.

"Anyway she don't say 'tally' when she means 'check sheet,' " Eddie said. "Like that other 'un. The big one with the fan that bosses the Willing Workers."

"That's my mother," Tommy said. "Want a bust in the jaw?"

"Naw." Eddie backed away. "I didn't mean . . ."

"Forget it, you guys," J. T. urged. "Fight some other time."

"Let's go back to the Hall," Lou Emma said. "The rest of 'em ought to be there."

She was right. The Masonic Hall was a beehive of female activity. Only Miss Kate was not there. The mothers of every girl and boy Lou Emma knew were buzzing around, wearing cover-up aprons, and talking, talking, talking.

Miss Kate ought to be here. Why do we always have to be different?

Mrs. Wacker came in and spoke admiringly of the table decorations.

"Pretty as a speckled pup, those sunflowers. I knew Kate'd fix it nice."

The praise warmed Lou Emma's heart. If only Mrs. Moss . . . But that lady was busy in the kitchen, giving orders at the top of her voice.

Maddy, Eppie, and Vinnie tagged after Mrs. Wacker. And Hackberry was all over the place, more like triplets than one nine-year-old boy. Gracie Elkins arrived with her mother, bringing pans of radish roses, celery curls, and bread-and-butter pickles. Mrs. Stumpf forgot the salt dishes and cried when Mrs. Moss snapped at her. Mrs. Biddle and Mrs. Dillar got into a row over butter chips. Were they or were they not proper at a formal dinner? And was this a formal dinner?

As Mrs. Biddle said, "If not, why not?"

There was a crash in the kitchen and out ran Hackberry like a scared rabbit. Mrs. Moss came after him, swinging a tea towel.

"Get out! All you children get out!"

"Just a minute, Clara," Mrs. Wacker said ominously. Hackberry dodged behind his mother's broad back. "What'd Hackberry do, an' whose children do you want out?"

"Dropped a grasshopper in the iced tea, and everybody's children."

"I never did it." Hackberry peered out from the

safety of his mother's back. "*She* opened the door, and *it* come in, and *I* was fishin' it out."

"A likely story," Mrs. Moss said.

"Sounds likely enough to me," Mrs. Wacker answered. "Clara, you're all in a swivet over this dinner. I'm for clearing out the children, but you let me clear out mine, and you clear out yours. Adelaide's swiped ten radish roses a'ready."

Mrs. Moss dropped the tea towel. "Adelaide?"

Calmly Adelaide held out her hand with six radish roses in it. "I took 'em because I was hungry. We didn't have any breakfast so's you could get here early ahead of—"

"THAT will do, young lady," Mrs. Moss said. "Go home and practice scales."

Mrs. Elkins said, "Gracie, there's sprinkled-down clothes to iron."

"J. T., mow that back lot. Today." Mrs. Dillar snapped like a rat trap.

"Thomas, finish your weeding." Mrs. Biddle pointed to the door.

"Eddie, go help him," Mrs. Gammon said.

"Vinnie, Eppie, Charles Egbert"—Mrs. Wacker used the name that Hackberry detested—"hoe the sweet corn and carry those potato peels to Parley's pig."

One by one the mothers of Gloriosa gave their commands. In minutes the Masonic Hall was cleared of all girls and boys except the Miller girls.

Lou Emma cleared her throat. "We'd better go. Miss Kate wants us to . . ."

"To mop the kitchen." Maddy came to her rescue.

In the street the crowd was even larger. The three blocks of pavement had been roped off, and special police were guarding the entrance to the lot where the racing cars were to check in. Somewhere in the distance the town band was practicing "The Motor March." The first auto fire engine in the state had been brought from Hutchinson to add glory to the day. But in all the excitement Lou Emma felt sad.

"Everybody at the Hall had somebody there but us."

"Somebody to jump on 'em," Maddy pointed out. "Why'd you say Miss Kate said for us to do stuff? She hardly ever does."

"I know it," Lou Emma admitted. "But why doesn't she?"

Our own mother'd have us doing scales, ironing clothes, hoeing the garden.

"Who cares 'why'? Where are you going?"

"Home to mop the kitchen."

"Great Granny Goosebumps! I made that up. Miss Kate mopped last night."

How could Lou Emma explain that if she really went home and really mopped, she would feel better about saying Miss Kate had given them house chores to do? She knew Maddy would make it sound silly. Maybe it *was* silly.

"Anyway I'm going home and find some colored pins to fix the pincushion with our driver's initials. L. T. W. His name's L. T. Wintergreen, Papa said."

"I'll go along. What do you think he'll be like?"

Tall, dark, slender, handsome, the image of L. T. Wintergreen came back to Lou Emma, but she didn't want to share it with Maddy. "I don't know."

"I'll bet he's homely as a wart hog," Maddy mused. "And fat. And he'll hate the WELCOME banner I made, and throw out your shaving papers."

"Do you really and truly think so?" Lou Emma recoiled.

"Nope. But I'm gettin' ready in advance *in case* he's like that." Maddy hopped on one foot for three squares of pavement; then she threw over her shoulder, "I hate being chased out of the Hall. In Auden, Ohio, they wouldn't have chased us out—'Professor Miller's poor little motherless girls.' "

"Auden's too slow-poke for an auto race," Lou Emma said. "And if we still lived there it'd be about time for Aunt Jesse to come to visit. Now she's going to Colorado, and I say, 'Hooray!' "

Already she had forgotten last night and her memories of Aunt Jesse's song. She threw a small rock into a stand of ragweed to show how glad she was that her aunt was not coming. Three startled grasshoppers jumped away.

Maddy shook her head. "I wish we could go to Colorado. It's not fair."

"Those rich folks, the Mayfields, they don't even know you 'n' me."

"Then I wish we were rich and they were poor as Job's turkey."

"Does Job have a turkey in the Bible? I thought

nobody did till the Pilgrims and the First Thanksgiving."

Maddy said, "Ask Papa."

"He'd just tell me to go look it up." Lou Emma spoke from experience.

"There's Hardy Garrett, all dressed up like a plush horse." Maddy waved at the dapper Hardy, driving by in his Stanley Steamer. "I like him."

Lou Emma was shocked beyond words. Hating Hardy had been a pastime of the Miller girls the whole year past. She wasn't going to give it up.

"Don't act so s'prised," Maddy said. "He treated our Croquet Club to cherry phosphates. Every one of us."

"Cherry phosphates!" Lou Emma flipped her fingers in disdain. "Don't forget he tried to marry Miss Kate, and he kept Papa from being Chairman."

"They were large-sized cherry phosphates," Maddy said. "And Papa didn't want to be Chairman. He only got on the committee because of the Great Smith and Dr. Biddle. And Hardy *didn't* marry Miss Kate; Papa *did.*"

There was no answering Maddy, for every single thing she said was true. Still, Lou Emma was not ready to give up Hardy as an enemy. She decided to change the subject and picked on Mrs. Moss as a safe way to divert Maddy.

"What do you think Adelaide meant, that Mrs. Moss wanted to get to the Hall early, ahead of somebody?"

Maddy took the bait. "Who was there when you and Miss Kate got there?"

"Nobody. Just us. And she came right past us and never said one word about the sunflowers. Not one single-syllable word."

"Not even that they looked terrible?"

"She couldn't 've said that. They looked pretty. Everybody said so."

"Everybody who?"

"Oh . . . Mrs. Wacker, Mrs. Biddle, Mrs. Jones, and . . . "Lou Emma faltered.

Maddy's eyes narrowed. "Mrs. Wacker 'n' Mrs. Biddle are our friends. Mrs. Jones is our preacher's wife and not s'posed to say anything but nice stuff."

"But—"

"The rest of 'em are too scared of Mrs. Moss to say they like 'em, even if they do. Eppie says she's a ring-tailed tooter when she gets mad."

"Hardy likes 'em." Lou Emma came back in triumph. "He came in to see about the speaker's table, and he said they looked great."

"I thought you hated the ground Hardy Garrett walked on."

Lou Emma was trapped, and she knew it. Looking down she gave a quick dive into the thick grass and came up with not one but *two* four-leaf clovers.

"Looky!"

"Put 'em in your shoe," Maddy advised her sister. "That's the best way."

"No. I'm going to put 'em under L. T. Wintergreen's pillow. That way he's sure to win the race."

Chapter 5

By three o'clock not one more person could squeeze onto the sidewalks of Assembly Avenue. Ropes had been strung to keep the crowd off the street. Hundreds of people strained against the ropes and struggled to catch the first glimpse of the first of the autos to appear. Upstairs windows were jammed. Boys climbed onto metal awning tops; they teetered dangerously along roofs. Men wearing the gold and purple badges of the Arrangements Committee were easy to spot in the crowd. Mrs. Moss had tried to get badges for the ladies working on the dinner, but Mr. Moss had refused.

"There's been enough bad feeling already," he was reported to have told the Mayor. "Black an' blue 's their color; not gold an' purple."

On one side of the entrance to the lot where the drivers were to check in was the Great Smith, wheels twined with gold and purple crepe paper, rosettes decorating every possible space. Mrs. Biddle and Miss Kate sat in front; Tommy and the Miller girls in the back. At the other side of the entrance was Hardy Garrett's Stanley Steamer. Hardy sat in it alone, his white linen duster ornamented with an extra-large badge, Arrangements Committee, CHAIRMAN. The sight of it set Lou Emma's teeth on edge.

"Wonder who Hardy's bringing to the dinner?" Maddy speculated.

"Vinnie said Goldie Harriman, but Eppie heard it was the Cates girl."

"He's not bringin' nobody," Tommy said with authority. "He told Jim Eccles, and Jim told Erma Bilson, and Erma is Hilda-that-works-for us's best chum, and Hilda told Ma that he didn't have time to treat a girl right, and he'd be dang-swang-hanged if he ever got roped into being Chairman of anything in this durned town again."

"Thomas, don't repeat idle gossip or bad language," Mrs. Biddle said without turning her head. Tommy rolled his eyes back till only the whites showed.

"Lissen," Lou Emma whispered, jerking her head toward a knot of people.

"Six bits the Cadillac gets to Gloriosa first," a farmer said.

"Dollar says it's the Franklin," countered a man from Moss's ice wagon.

"Two bucks on the Overland. I know the driver. He's a mean skunk, but he's shifty and *fast.*"

"Putcha money where your mouth is."

"I'll take the Reo and give you odds."

"Shocking!" Mrs. Biddle's cartwheel hat shook. "Open gambling in Gloriosa. The Committee should be informed. They should put a stop to it."

Tommy winked at Lou Emma. "I bet Eddie ten cents on the Auto Bug."

"Gambling's wrong," Lou Emma said, "but if you're

going to gamble you ought to bet on the EMF Studebaker because it's *our* driver."

Tommy groaned. "I bet to win, not to please a silly girl."

Lou Emma turned away. He let her stay that way so long she got a crick in her neck, so she decided to forgive him.

Professor Miller came plowing through the crowd. "Kate, this is as close as I'll ever get to a Roman chariot race. I'm taking notes for the Book."

"Wait," Mrs. Biddle called to him. "I'm sure there's gambling going on in the crowd. You should not ignore that."

"Great idea!" Professor Miller took out his notebook. "The Romans were gamblers, too. Perhaps I should put down a small bet . . ."

"Wait!" Mrs. Biddle called as he started away. "I do not condone . . . I meant, I think as a member of the Committee you should protest. . . . The law . . ."

But Professor Miller had gone.

"Don't worry," Maddy said. "Papa's only got a quarter."

"We are a little short of cash," Miss Kate explained. "Have you any idea when the college will pay last month's salaries?"

"I am sure Amos is doing his best," Mrs. Biddle said a little coldly. "He always pays himself last, in any event. We have been short of cash, too."

"Of course," Miss Kate murmured. "We'll get along . . . somehow."

So that's why we keep having macaroni and cheese, Lou Emma thought.

"Teachers should be the best-paid people in the community, and they are often the worst-paid," Mrs. Biddle sighed. "Amos says—"

But Dr. Biddle's remarks were lost in a roar from the crowd. Far down the street the first auto had appeared. It was coming so fast it was only a green blur. Lou Emma jumped to the seat to see better. Tommy and Maddy climbed to the folded-back top. The shouting and screaming stormed around them.

"Which one? Which auto?" Lou Emma pounded on Tommy.

"Whichizit?" Maddy howled. "Whichizit?"

"Looks like the EMF Studebaker," Tommy yelled back.

"Glory be!" Maddy shouted. "It's us . . . ours . . . our driver!"

L. T. Wintergreen! Lou Emma realized in a flash of astonishment that the four-leaf clovers had worked. L. T. Wintergreen was first to get to Gloriosa.

"You've done it; you've done it; you've done it!" She heard herself screaming. She would find hundreds more four-leaf clovers; she would make him a chain of four-leaf clovers. She shut her eyes to get the full glory of the moment and saw L. T. Wintergreen winning the Three-State Race, accepting the silver cup, and heard him say: *"Miss Lou Emma Miller's four-leaf clovers won for me. Give the cup to her, she deserves it."*

At a new shout from the crowd her eyes snapped open.

"The Packard! The Packard!"

A dark gray Packard forged ahead of the Studebaker. Lou Emma blinked.

"Look OUT!" As one the crowd shouted its warning. A maroon Overland coming in fast slewed to the right and hit a telegraph pole. The Packard took a left and struck the dip where the pavement began with a spring-breaking THUNK. Out of nowhere an Apperson Jack Rabbit tore around the Packard. Then out of the cloud of dust a tan Great Western was suddenly at the finish line. Far behind was the green Studebaker.

Lou Emma sighed. *I don't care really. L. T. Wintergreen was first first.*

Tommy, still standing on the top, gave a tremendous whoop.

"Looky what's drivin' the EMF Studebaker!"

"My word!" Mrs. Biddle fanned herself with her program.

"I can't believe it." Miss Kate peered through the dust.

Lou Emma pushed them apart so that she could see; then she, too, fell back. "Shaving papers!" She looked at open-mouthed Maddy. "I put out shaving papers."

The driver of the green EMF Studebaker 30 was a young woman. L. T. Wintergreen, tall, dark, slender, handsome, wearing four-leaf clover chains around his neck, disappeared forever.

The crowd broke through the ropes and swarmed

around the young woman. The special police tried to hold them back, but it was useless. Over by the Great Western that had reached Gloriosa first, Hardy Garrett thumbed through the check sheets. The Apperson Jack Rabbit and the Packard waited for him. Lou Emma almost laughed out loud. He had wanted to be Chairman, hadn't he? He'd never figured a pretty girl would turn up as a driver, and he'd be too busy to meet her!

The driver of the Studebaker was barely five feet

tall. Her outfit was of khaki-colored covert cloth with a divided skirt. She wore a long-visored cap with goggles, and when she pulled it off, it released golden hair arranged with frivolous curls. Under the goggles her blue eyes were enormous, white-rimmed; the rest of her face was covered with dust. Whipping a small mirror from her skirt pocket, she looked at herself and burst out laughing.

"Look! I'm Kansas-colored."

The crowd that had been only curious before was

completely won over. A cheer began, and as if on cue, the town band began to play "I'd Rather Have a Girlie than an Automobile."

"L. T. Wintergreen," Tommy said. "I call that pretty sneaky."

"Calling it sneaky don't make it sneaky," Lou Emma answered hotly.

"She's got a perfect right to her initials," Maddy said. "I'm gonna call myself M. M. Miller."

"Mean an' messy," Tommy jibed. "Look at Hardy sweat."

More autos were thundering, roaring, coughing up to the check-in spot. A sharp report meant an overheated tire had blown out. Hardy was nearly hidden by drivers demanding attention, shaking check sheets at him, arguing points. The driver of the first-in Great Western said the driver of the Apperson Jack Rabbit had strapped down his springs and ought to be disqualified. The baggage truck had missed the turn and gone on to Waycross. The route men who had the job of spreading confetti to mark the turn complained that the wind had blown it away. The Overland had to be pried from the telegraph pole and the driver taken to a doctor to get his broken ribs attended to.

In the midst of the hubbub, Professor Miller herded together the occupants of the Great Smith and led them through the crowd around the EMF Studebaker.

He bowed to the driver. "*Miss* Wintergreen, I presume?"

She laughed, pushing back blonde curls and leaving

another streak of black grease on her forehead. "Laura Thayer Wintergreen. Isn't that a mouthful? I hope you won't mind my using initials. Mother was so upset when I entered."

"We're delighted." Professor Miller introduced the Biddles and the Millers. "You are to be our guest. Our daughters have shaving papers and cigars all ready for you."

"OH, PAPA!"

"Thank you both." The blue eyes danced. "I'll give them to my brother, Jack. Mother wouldn't let me come without him. He's over there with my observer, Mr. Jenkins."

She pointed to a tall young man conferring with Hardy.

"That's Hardy Garrett," Lou Emma said. "He's Chairman."

"His father's the—" Maddy started, but Mrs. Biddle neatly smothered the rest of the usual "richest man in the county."

"Miss Wintergreen, I want you to know that I am highly in favor of your driving in this race. Women should advance their cause in every field."

Miss Wintergreen looked startled. "I didn't think about that. I just love to drive. Taught myself on our one-cylinder Trumbull when I was ten."

"What's that thing?" Tommy pointed to a seated china doll with pointed head and slanty eyes strapped to the dashboard of the EMF Studebaker.

"That's a Billikin, my lucky doll. Pat him for luck."

Tommy only grinned and backed away. Lou Emma patted the Billikin.

"Do you believe in luck? In four-leaf clovers, and all that?"

"I've got two four-leaf clovers in my shoe right now." An incredibly small black-leather pump was wriggled on a slender ankle.

Maddy said before Lou Emma could open her mouth, "And there's two more four-leaf clovers under your pillow. We put 'em there."

Someday Lou Emma knew she was going to hit Maddy for taking over her four-leaf clovers. But not today.

"Miss Wintergreen . . ." she started.

"Please call me Laura. I won't be twenty till May."

"Laura . . . Laura . . ." Lou Emma repeated the name for pure pleasure in using it. "We've got your room all ready. New curtains, and the best bedspread."

"And we'd better take Laura home now so she can get some rest," Miss Kate said. "The dinner's at five thirty, and we don't want her too tired to enjoy it."

"Oh, driving doesn't tire me, but I'd like to wash my face," Laura said.

"We made the decorations for the dinner," Maddy said. "The Willing Workers."

"Don't tell what they are," Lou Emma cautioned. "Let it be a surprise."

Tommy pulled on her arm. "Old Hardy's about to pop a gusset."

Looking back, Lou Emma saw Hardy, his white

linen duster crumpled, his straw hat barely hanging on his head, and his CHAIRMAN badge upside down. He gave her a despairing look as he tried to satisfy a driver who had lost his way.

"We can't help the wind, mister. It always blows in Kansas. Hey—Professor—Kate— We're sorry the confetti blew away, but we can't—Lou Emma— Hey—"

Serves him right!

She was the only one who heard him call, and turning back, she smiled sweetly and waved. "Good-bye, Hardy."

He beckoned wildly, but she waved again and hurried to the Great Smith.

Laura at the Miller's small brown house was even more enchanting than Laura at the wheel of the EMF Studebaker. She loved the Welcome Banner and the new curtains. She put the four-leaf clovers in her shoes, and the shaving papers, she declared, would make a perfect notebook for the trip. She gave the Miller girls a box a woman in Wellsville had thrown into the auto as it sped through the town. It was filled with fried chicken and apples. They ate happily, sitting on the floor of their room, which had suddenly become Laura's Room. She unpacked an oil-cloth wrapped suitcase, and out came a green silk dress, cut daringly low.

"For the dinner. But it does need pressing." She shook at the wrinkles.

"I'll press it." Maddy jumped up, scattering chicken bones.

"I'll press it." Lou Emma pushed her sister's hand away.

"I'll press it." Miss Kate took the fragile garment. "You girls get into your own dresses. They're laid out in the kitchen."

The organdy dresses had been exquisitely ironed; every ruffle, every bit of lace, every ribbon, smoothed with loving care. When had Miss Kate done it? At noon, or early this morning, stealing time when she might have been resting? *Every girl in the Willing Workers will be there in a dress ironed by her mother. . . .* In the middle of her bedazzled admiration of Laura, Lou Emma felt a moment's gratitude toward Miss Kate. She'd like to thank her for ironing the organdy dress, but Miss Kate was carrying ice water up to Laura. Before she came down, Maddy had taken Lou Emma's attention.

"Laura gave me a violet sachet." Maddy showed a square of padded satin, sweet with the scent of violets, handpainted with delicate purple flowers.

"She gave me a stick of orris root." Lou Emma held out a small woody stick that ladies chewed on to sweeten their breath. The sachet was prettier, but the orris root was far more to be prized because it had the mark of Laura's teeth on one end. "She's not a bit like I thought a race driver'd be."

"A million times better," Maddy said. "I'm going to be a race driver."

The Willing Workers—girls in white organdy, boys

in blue serge coats and knickers—were gathering at the Masonic Hall. Maddy won fame with her sachet.

"Laura gave it to me. She asked us to call her 'Laura.' She's coming back to visit and teach me to drive." Maddy looked at Lou Emma, daring her to contradict it.

Lou Emma kept the orris root hidden in her handkerchief. It was her very own, and she would never show it or share it with anyone in the world.

"Wisht we had somebody like her at our house," Adelaide said in honest envy. "We've got some old man 'bout thirty years old."

Mrs. Biddle appeared wearing a gold-colored surrah silk. Her hair was bound up with an aigrette that made her look a foot taller than Dr. Biddle.

"Are you ready, Lou Emma? Right foot starts going in, left foot coming out!"

"Yes, ma'am." Lou Emma had a moment of doubt as to which foot was right and which left. There was a mole on her right hand; she mentally worked her way toward her foot.

"March in. Sing with expression. Then stand there till the Reverend Tompkins asks the blessing. Then march out. Do you understand? Are you sure?"

Lou Emma was still struggling with "right foot in, left foot out." Then she realized that the Reverend Tompkins was the preacher famous in Gloriosa for the length of his prayers and his blessings. Her eyes widened. "*Him!*"

Mrs. Biddle nodded. "I know. But he's high up in

the Masons, and they're letting us have the Hall at no charge. Just stand still and listen. Then march out."

"Yes, ma'am."

Mrs. Biddle went on. "I want you to take this copy of the music for the Welcome Song to the back door of the Hall, come in through the kitchen, and put the music on the music rack of the piano. I'd do it myself, but I don't want to leave these boys and girls. Put it *right* on the music rack."

Where's she think I'll put it? On the floor? "Yes, ma'am."

Lou Emma pushed her way through the crowd, fearful of crushing her organdy skirt. As she neared the entrance, she saw the Great Smith drive up and Laura looking absolutely beautiful in the green silk.

More and more people arriving blocked her way. One of the special police turned her around and pointed her back where she had come from.

"You're goin' the wrong way, kiddo."

She tried to explain, but he didn't listen.

"Willing Workers this way—this way—" He gave her a shove.

Frantic at the delay, she dodged under his arm and ran into the street. The crowd was out there, too, talking, laughing, blocking her way. There was nothing to do but run a half block to the opening of the alley. She ran, feeling the sweat starting to trickle down her back. Her dress would be a mess!

A Pierce-Arrow arriving late, filled with drivers and their hosts, honked impatiently. Scurrying out of its way, Lou Emma almost ran into the side of a Winton Roadster. It was like one of those terrible dreams when you run and run and never get where you're going. The music for the Welcome Song was crumpled and damp from the sweat in the palm of her hand.

She *had* to get the music on the music rack. She *had* to get back to start the march. She had told Laura she would lead the others in. Pounding down the alley, she found the back door to the Masonic Hall. It was locked.

Lou Emma hammered with both fists.

"Let me in. LET-ME-IN!"

The racket inside was deafening. Women's voices, clanging kettles, clattering spoons. The steady thump-thump-thump of a potato masher. Through the small smudged window she saw Mrs. Wacker's broad back, but she could not get her attention. Again she hammered on the door.

"Please . . . somebody . . . let me in!"

With unnerving suddenness the door was jerked open. Mrs. Moss in a red taffeta dress, protected by a long white apron, glared at her.

"What do you want? Go away. We're too busy to—"

"Mrs. Biddle sent me to put the music on the piano. Mrs. Biddle—"

"Absolutely not. Tell Lavinia—"

"I've got to," Lou Emma babbled. "We can't sing . . . the lady can't play . . ."

"Clara!" A wail rose from Mrs. Stumpf, in charge of ham. "Clara, you've got to come here this minute—"

Mrs. Moss jerked the music from Lou Emma and slammed the door.

Her knees watery, Lou Emma leaned against the door. *I hope it gets to the music rack. I hope Mrs. Biddle believes me. I—I—*

She stopped thinking, stopped breathing. All she could do was stare.

Under the long table on the back porch were thirty jars of sunflowers in their raffia-covered containers. The big crock for the speaker's table was there, too. Bright and lively in the dreariness of the alley, the sunflowers nodded in the little breeze between the buildings. But what were they doing here? And what was decorating the tables for the dinner due to start in ten minutes? Five minutes!

Lou Emma began to run. Miss Kate, she had to find Miss Kate.

The crowd was inside now. The Willing Workers were lined up at the door. Mrs. Biddle grabbed Lou Emma.

"What took you so long? Never mind. Don't tell me. There's been a change in the Program. Listen closely. The blessing is to be first, *then* the Welcome Song."

"I've got to see Miss Kate." She shook off Mrs. Biddle.

"You can't." Mrs. Biddle caught her again by the arm and pushed Lou Emma to the head of the line. "You cannot dash in there now. They're all seated. Congressman Clary is beside Kate. Do you want to ruin the Program?"

The question stopped Lou Emma cold. "No, ma'am, but— Anyway, it's too late."

"What's too late?" Maddy asked over Adelaide's shoulder in the line.

Adelaide knows about the sunflowers. I know she knows.

"Nothing," she told Maddy. "Ready? Left foot first."

"It's s'posed to be right foot first," Adelaide said.

"When I say left foot, Adelaide Moss, I mean left foot, and you'd better believe it. Start."

The pianist was playing "Auto Race." It was a great tune to march by, but Lou Emma could not hear a note. All she could do was to keep walking, left foot, right foot, and strain to hold back the tears of rage that threatened to pour down her cheeks and disgrace Gloriosa, Kansas, before two hundred and fourteen strangers. No, two hundred and thirteen! Laura was a friend.

Now they were inside the Hall, and she was leading the marchers around the long tables. Before she saw them, Lou Emma smelled roses. Roses everywhere. Roses and asparagus fern jammed into cut-glass bowls, even into water glasses, overpoweringly sweet in the hot, crowded room. Behind her she heard the gasps of the Willing Workers. They buzzed like angry bumble-bees.

"What?" "Where?" "Who did it?" "Where are our sunflowers?"

Adelaide was strangely quiet.

They lined up to wait for the blessing. Lou Emma

saw Miss Kate looking a little pale but smiling politely at Congressman Clary beside her. *If Miss Kate can keep from crying, I can.*

On the other side of the Congressman was Hardy Garrett and then Laura, lovely, shining Laura, looking as if she wouldn't know a carburetor from a catfish.

That place card was for Mrs. Moss! Lou Emma had peeked at it early in the morning. Hardy must have changed it. Mrs. Moss was seated at the far end, her face the same shade as her dress.

Her eyes came back to Miss Kate who was smiling fixedly at Congressman Clary. She saw him pull a big white handkerchief out, hold it to his face, put it down, and take it up again. His face was as red as Mrs. Moss's. What was wrong?

Hardy announced the blessing would be by the Reverend Tompkins. There was the sound of shuffling feet and chairs as the crowd rose. The Willing Workers bowed their heads. Only Lou Emma did not bow. There was no prayer in her rebellious heart. The sunflowers . . . the raffia-covered containers . . . the hours of work . . . Miss Kate's afternoons away from the shop. . . . Head erect, she may have been the only one in the Hall to see Congressman Clary's shoulders heave, his chest jerk—once—twice—

"Bow your head," Adelaide hissed.

"Leave me alone," Lou Emma hissed back. "You—you snake-in-the-sunflowers."

The Reverend Tompkins, in full swing, asked divine blessing on the drivers, the autos, the Midwest

Automobile Club, the manufacturers of the cars, the roads, the Commercial Club of Gloriosa, their wives who prepared the food. . . .

A strangled snort came from Congressman Clary. Some curious people looked up. The Reverend Tompkins went on to the farmers who had grown the food, the good soil of Kansas, the rain, the sunshine, President William Howard Taft, . . .

"A-A-Ah-CHOOOOO!" Congressman Clary exploded. "A-A-Ah-CHOOOOOO!"

The long-suppressed sneeze had built up to a mighty volume. The Masonic Hall vibrated. The Reverend Tompkins hesitated, then went on with his blessing. But the Congressman once started seemed unable to stop. Sneeze after sneeze after sneeze. By now the Reverend Tompkins was the only one with a bowed head. Lou Emma could hear the boys in the Willing Workers snickering. Congressman Clary's face had turned from red to purple. He made a superhuman effort to control his sneezing, but he failed. The loudest sneeze on record shattered the Reverend Tompkins' "Amen."

Once more the diners shuffled and scraped their chairs, but now they were all craning necks to see the unfortunate Congressman. He continued to sneeze, but between gasps Lou Emma saw him point to the big bowl of roses directly in front of him, and say something to Miss Kate. Miss Kate leaned back and spoke to Professor Miller. He leaned forward until he got Hardy's attention away from Laura. It was like the boys' game of pass-it-on. Hardy stood and rapped for attention.

"Uh . . . ladies and gentlemen . . . I have just been . . . uh . . . informed that our distinguished speaker suffers from . . . uh . . . rose fever. I . . . uh . . . suggest that for his comfort we . . . get rid of . . . that is, we dispense with these beautiful decorations."

He looked around helplessly. Miss Kate whispered to him.

"Uh . . . Will the Willing Workers Sunday School Class kindly remove the roses, before they sing their Welcome Song, composed for this occasion by our distinguished fellow citizen . . . uh . . . citizenESS, Mrs. Amos T. Biddle?"

There was a spatter of applause, a murmur of sympathy for the Congressman who continued to sneeze. Mrs. Biddle motioned to Lou Emma.

"Do what Hardy says. Take the roses out back."

Once again the pianist played the "Auto Race." This time Lou Emma heard every note. There was a lilt to her step as she led forth the Willing Workers.

"Take two bowls each," she directed, and chose to remove the large bouquet from the speaker's table. Miss Kate gave her the tiniest nod, while trying not to smile. Congressman Clary did not see her, for he sat with his eyes closed, handkerchief held to his nose and mouth. Hardy winked; Laura giggled; and down the table Mrs. Moss's face could have stopped a clock.

Into the kitchen Lou Emma marched her followers,

their hands rose-laden. Mrs. Stumpf, in charge of ham, watched them, popeyed.

"Open the back door, please," Lou Emma asked. Mrs. Stumpf obeyed.

Lou Emma marched to the back porch. The music of the "Auto Race" was fainter, but it still urged them on. The Willing Workers followed like well-trained troops.

Lou Emma rapped out an order. "Put down the roses and *pick up the sunflowers.*"

"Sunflowers?" "Our sunflowers?" "What?" "Where?" "Who put 'em out here?"

Questions bubbled around her, but Lou Emma answered none of them. She was in charge, and she liked it. "Take the sunflowers back in the Hall and put 'em where you took off the roses."

In the hubbub Maddy squeezed Lou Emma hard. "You're a hero!"

Once again Lou Emma lined up the Willing Workers. At their head she marched back into the Hall, all of them carrying the golden flower of Kansas.

Applause began such as had seldom been heard in Gloriosa. The pianist changed over to the popular "Home on the Range." The crowd went wild. They cheered; they stamped; they whistled. It took Hardy five minutes to quiet them so that the Willing Workers—lined up by the piano and grinning like possums—could sing the Welcome Song.

They sang it better than they ever had before. Tonight Gloriosa really was a city fair. On the last

verse they bore down heavily on "HEROES ALL." Mrs. Biddle gave the pianist the signal to play the "Auto Race" and march them out.

Back of the big crock of sunflowers, Miss Kate looked directly at Lou Emma as she applauded, her face one big smile. Congressman Clary lumbered to his feet. The pianist stopped in midnote. He spoke hoarsely but without sneezing.

"For the first time in my life I am glad to have rose fever. Without it I might never have seen the floral tribute these young people prepared for the great state of Kansas. I say hurrah for the Willing Workers!"

They marched out to the intoxicating sound of cheering. The boys rushed into the street and began to play leapfrog, tossing off their coats as they ran. The girls clustered in the doorway of the Bon Ton, talking indignantly of the disappearance of the sunflowers. Between the march outside and the Bon Ton, Adelaide had evaporated. No one had seen her go.

"It was her doing," Gracie said. "Hers or her mother's."

"Mrs. Stumpf knew," Eppie said. "You shoulda seen her face when Lou Emma said, 'Open that door or I'll knock your head off.' "

"I never!" Lou Emma said, but her protest was lost.

"Mrs. Moss cheated my mother out of the prize when they played cards," Edna said. "It was last year, but a cheater's a cheater."

"We oughta vote Adelaide out of the Willing Workers," Gracie said.

"She deserves it," Vinnie said. "We oughta tell Congressman Clary what she did."

"Let's take a vote this minute," Gracie insisted.

"It's Lou Emma's say-so," Eppie said. "If it hadn't been for her, our sunflowers'd never have got to the dinner."

For one juicy moment Lou Emma thought about how she would enjoy voting Adelaide out, out, out. How she would march up to Congressman Clary and tell him exactly how the swap of flowers had come about. Slowly she shook her head.

"Let's forget it as fast as we can. It's not worth worrying about." They were Miss Kate's words. She felt safe using them.

Tommy ran over from the leapfrog game.

"C'mon you crazy girls. Stop gabbin'. We're goin'

over to Meyers' vacant lot and play Run Sheep Run. I'm captain, and I choose Lou Emma first."

There was a half moon and a lot of stars in the sky. The night smelled sweet with clover and honeysuckle. On the borrowed cot, set up in the side yard, Lou Emma dozed and waked and dozed again, hugging to herself the long day of the Three-State Auto Race, the Ides of July.

It had been a day of high spots and low spots. What was the best thing of all? Meeting Laura? Outwitting Mrs. Moss? Miss Kate's extra hug as she fixed the cots? Or was it playing Run Sheep Run when Tommy caught her hand as they raced through the dusk and then forgot to let it go again? She snuggled her cheek into her hand, remembering.

Faraway the Santa Fe night train from Topeka blew a long, lonesome whistle. In a minute it would go highballing through Gloriosa. She waited, but to her astonishment she heard the train slo-o-ow down, grind to a stop, and then quickly pull out. It gathered speed rapidly, and the dark sky blotted up the sounds it made. But why had it stopped at all? The Santa Fe night train never stopped in Gloriosa. Lou Emma puzzled until sleep crept upon her.

All at once she was wide awake again. Along the silent, deserted street came an automobile. It passed under the street light at the corner, and she saw it was the Stanley Steamer with Hardy driving. He stopped in front of the Millers' house.

She reached toward the other cot to wake Maddy, but drew her hand back. At this time of night, getting Maddy awake would take fifteen minutes and a wash-rag dipped in ice water.

"Sst!" Hardy signaled. "Anybody awake? Lou Emma?"

Why'd he call me? I de-test Hardy Garrett.

"It's me," she answered, knowing her father would correct "me" to "I." She slipped from her cot and put on her dressing gown. The grass tickled her bare feet. Hardy came toward her, and she could see he was carrying a long white box.

"I need some help, Lou Emma. A big favor. Will you help me out?"

He asked it as if he were just *anybody,* as if he had forgotten that his father was the richest man in the county. She had called him a *dumkopf* only a few short days ago and said she hated him for a whole year. How could she do him a favor?

"I don't know if I can or not," she said, her toes curling in the grass.

"You can. Kate said you were a girl to depend on. She said you had a lot more gumption than most people—young or old."

The stars whirled. When Miss Kate said gumption, she meant all the things Lou Emma had doubted in herself since her stepmother had come to live with them. If Miss Kate thought . . .

"Gumption?" she asked him slowly. He thought she didn't know the word.

"Good sense. Smartness. If Kate says you've got it, you've got it. She's got more than her share herself."

For the first time since she had known him Hardy Garrett seemed different to Lou Emma. He must have felt awful when Miss Kate turned him down, but here he was saying nice things about her. And asking favors of Lou Emma.

"Well . . . I'll try. What'd you want me to do?"

He held out the long white box. "Roses. For Laura."

"Laura's in bed," Lou Emma said, shocked. "Her brother brought her home and said Laura was to go to bed 'toot sweet.' I don't know what that means, but Papa said it was French for 'right now' and Laura'd better go or he'd tell her in Greek and Latin. Her brother's kind of . . . bossy."

"Kind of?" Hardy echoed bitterly. "You'd think he was driving that Studebaker. I was going to take Laura for a spin in the Stanley when he came around and practically shanghaied her. Acted as if I was trying to get her to lose the race."

"I guess he meant well." Lou Emma used her father's favorite excuse for Aunt Jesse. Then she blurted out, "Did you know he can't even drive?"

"I'm not surprised," Hardy said. "But this is what I want you to do . . ." He lifted the lid from the box. In the moonlight Lou Emma saw long-stemmed American Beauty roses nestled in lacy fern. She smelled the heavenly scent. These were no ordinary roses from Gloriosa gardens.

"Where in the world did they come from?"

"I telegraphed Topeka and got a florist I know to put the roses on the night train. Then I got hold of Hack Wacker and got him to flag the train and take 'em off. It wasn't anything."

"It was, too," Lou Emma said. "It took . . . gumption."

"You're a good kid," Hardy said awkwardly. "I'm glad you were the one awake."

"Maddy sleeps like a log," Lou Emma explained. "Laura'll love these."

"I hope so," Hardy said. "When I saw her that first minute, shoving back her goggles, her face dirty, and all—I was a goner."

"You changed the place cards at the dinner, didn't you?"

"Sure. Would you rather sit by Laura or Clara Moss?"

Lou Emma only giggled. By now she not only didn't hate Hardy, she actually liked him.

"We hit it off fine at the dinner, but it's kind of hard to talk to a girl with three hundred people watching. So I was going to take her home when her brother— But you give her these roses. In the morning. Early."

"No," Lou Emma said. "Tonight. Right now."

"But what about the Professor? Or Kate?" Hardy asked. "What'll they think?"

"They won't know a thing about it."

She went to the elm tree beside the house. Then she took off the belt to her dressing gown, tied it securely around the long white box of roses, and slipped her arm under the belt. Then Lou Emma, who feared high places and climbed trees only when Maddy called her "cowardly calf," went up into the dark mystery of the elm branches.

Up she went, slowly, uncertainly. Frightened by the creaking branches, hampered by her dressing gown and her nightgown around her ankles and by the long white box, still she kept climbing. The scent of the roses was so strong she thought she could smell it through the box, and once she put her nose against it and breathed in deep and then went back to climbing.

At the level of the upstairs window she leaned far out from the tree.

"Laura . . . Laura . . ."

Bedsprings squeaked, and there was Laura at the window. The moonlight touched the soft blonde hair that tumbled around her shoulders.

Rapunzel, Rapunzel, let down your golden hair. . . .

"Lou Emma? Be careful! What're you doing out in the tree?"

"It's for you, from Hardy." She pushed the long white box forward, slipping her arm from the belt and straining toward the window. Laura reached toward it, took it, and Lou Emma heard the rustle of tissue paper.

"They're gorgeous! Oh, how wonderful! Thank him for me . . . Tell him . . ."

"You tell him," Lou Emma said. "He's right here down on the ground."

Laura leaned from the window and talked to Hardy, who stood under the tree while Lou Emma backed slowly down. Coming down was even harder than going up, but she made it as scraps of whispers and laughter from Laura and Hardy drifted through the dark leaves. At last when she reached the lowest limb, Hardy jumped her down. It was good to have the solid ground under her feet and hear Laura's whispered praises fluttering down from the window above. But in a minute she felt a little like three's-a-crowd and hurried back to her cot. It wasn't long until Hardy came over to her.

"You're a good kid," he said again. "Laura dropped this one down for you."

It was one of the American Beauty roses. The velvety petals caressed her nose; the fragrance made her close her eyes in pure pleasure.

"Laura's a peacherino," Hardy was saying, "a real peacherino. When this race is over—" He broke off, whistled a tune, and did a fancy buck-and-wing step. "Good night, kiddo. If I can ever do you a favor, you name it. Just name it."

She watched him walk out to the Stanley Steamer. He was whistling again and the tune came back on the warm night breeze.

Lou Emma punched the pillow and made a place for her head and for the rose.

That's funny . . . it's as easy to like Hardy as it was to hate him. Must remember to tell Maddy, I like him now.

Chapter 6

The Midwest Automobile Club Three-State Race roared out of Gloriosa the next morning. Many of the townspeople followed the race to the next town and beyond. Interest was high, and each home that had put up a driver overnight wanted him to win, but at the same time *everybody* cheered for Laura. For the next few days reports came back by wire, and the *Silver Bugle* devoted columns to the race. It all ended in front of the Kansas City *Star* office at 11th and Grand at 12:45 P.M. The winner was an eighteen-year-old driving a Cadillac. He had made the 760-mile run at an average speed of twenty miles per hour, with a top speed of thirty-five miles per hour. His check sheet was nearly perfect.

Lou Emma and Maddy read every word, looking for Laura's name. All they found was a scant report that she had finished the course, "pretty as ever with her hands calloused from holding the wheel."

Lou Emma sighed. "All's well that ends well."

"You call that 'well'? I wanted her to win. Four-leaf clovers, phooey."

"Did you know Hardy went along to Omaha?" Lou Emma asked.

"No wonder she didn't win with him tagging along."

"Don't say that. I like Hardy. I meant to tell you, I like him now."

Maddy decided to be contrary. "He sure made a punk Chairman. Papa could've done a lot better."

"No, he couldn't," Lou Emma surprised herself by saying. "He'd 've run it like a Roman chariot race. Did you know Hardy swapped place cards at the dinner so he could sit by Laura and not by Mrs. Moss?"

"Well, he may have more sense than I gave him credit for. I'm tired talking about something that's over 'n' done with. Let's go see your tadpole."

They were astonished to find he was no more a tadpole, but a small perfect frog with no sign of the frisky black tail he had had before.

"I forgot about him, and he changed all by himself." Lou Emma peered into the dark water. "Where do you think his tail went to?"

"Bottom of the barrel, maybe."

"Whoops! There he goes—Catch him."

But he was even harder to catch with legs than without. Well splashed with rain water, the girls gave up and decided to walk to town. By the time they got to Assembly Avenue, their dresses were dried. The town was quiet. After the excitement of the race there was nothing to do and nothing to look forward to. The hot weather, which before they had hardly noticed, bore down.

In the window of Miss Kate's Chapeaux they admired the line of ladies' auto accessories she had added. Crepe de Chine scarves, chiffon veils, motoring bonnets, goggles, and a handsome ankle-length, summer-weight duster.

"Le's go in," Maddy said.

"Uh-uh. She's got a customer."

They wandered on. There was no use going home. Their father was spending every spare minute working on the Book, and Rule Number Two was in force all day. In the evening he went to the college and worked in the Library. They walked slower and slower, and at the bridge stopped moving altogether.

"SNAKE!"

The Miller girls screamed and ran. They ran for half a block before they looked back and saw Tommy Biddle, laughing his head off at them. Then they turned and chased him, but he was faster than they were, and when they got home, he was sitting coolly in the shade of the grape arbor, grinning.

"Where was any snake at?" Maddy demanded.

"Right behind the 'at.' " He grinned wider. "C'mon, sit down. Don't get sore. If you want a snake, I'll rustle one up for you."

"Don't you dare," Lou Emma said.

But they sat down. After all, there was nothing else to do. Swish walked over, and Lou Emma took off his chain. Tommy fed him clover blooms.

He said, "You know that Baker Electric that was 'on order' before the race? I hear old man Moss bought it for *her*."

The Miller girls screeched and collapsed on the grass.

When Maddy recovered, she sat up. "She can't drive, can she?"

"Aw, drivin' an electric's not hard. No gas, no crank. The big thing is you've gotta keep the batt'ry charged every twenty miles." He rubbed Swish's silky nose. "I hear she's braggin' she'll be the first lady driver in town."

The Miller girls sighed. Maddy said, "Anyway, we were the first girls in town to own a goat."

"We don't own Swish," Lou Emma said. "Tommy does. We're just goatkeepers till Mrs. Biddle says he can take Swish back."

"You can say you own him. Ma's never goin' to change her mind. She's got the hardest mind to change in eastern Kansas." Tommy dug a stick in the dirt. "She's absotively posolutely against us getting an auto."

"That's crazy," Maddy said. "Why?"

"Right now her big reason is that the driver in the Overland broke three ribs, so she says no auto's safe."

"Even the Great Smith?" Lou Emma looked at the big red auto.

"She'll ride in it, but only because she likes Professor Miller."

"Laura said the time would come when as many women would drive as men," Lou Emma said. "Papa laughed, but she didn't change. She said cranking was what held women back, but the Winton in the race had a self-starter and pretty soon they'd all have 'em."

"Miss Kate said cranking an auto's not a bit harder

than wringing wet overalls over a washtub," Maddy said. "Bet I could crank one."

Lou Emma asked if the Baker Electric was already in town.

"Nope. It's got to come from Detroit. It'll take a while."

"Then . . . why can't Miss Kate be the first lady driver in Gloriosa?"

"Who's goin' to teach her?" Maddy asked gloomily. "Not Papa. He said no man in his right mind tried to teach his wife. He wouldn't teach her Latin."

"I forgot that." Lou Emma frowned. Slowly her head swiveled toward Tommy. Maddy followed her sister's motion. Tommy jumped up in alarm.

"What's going on?" he demanded.

"You can teach Miss Kate to drive," Lou Emma said.

"Not me!" He started to run, but Lou Emma grabbed one ankle, Maddy the other, and brought him crashing to the ground. "Lemme up . . . lemme up. . . ."

"Not till you say you'll do it," Lou Emma bargained. "You drove the Great Smith the first day we came to Gloriosa, through all those cows."

"You've bragged you drove cars," Maddy pointed out. "A Franklin, a Studebaker, a Loco . . . Locomotivemobile."

"Locomobile," Tommy shouted and kicked loose. But he didn't run. He said, "Ma'd froth at the mouth. She'd put me through all that about the son of the President of EKCC's got to be an example."

"She told Laura women ought to learn to drive," Lou Emma said.

"But teach a grown-up? That'd be murder."

"Miss Kate's not as grown-up as lots of grown-ups," Maddy said.

Tommy spoke so low they could scarcely hear him. "Maybe I don't know how to drive good enough to teach anybody."

"Then you and Miss Kate can learn together," Lou Emma offered cheerfully.

Tommy found a ray of hope. "How about the Professor? He'll be sore."

"We won't tell him. It'll be a surprise," Lou Emma said.

"For his birthday," Maddy said. "Miss Kate can learn to drive for Papa's birthday present."

To the Miller girls' delight, Miss Kate fell in with their plan. They didn't mention Mrs. Moss but talked long and hard about their father's birthday.

Fortunately Professor Miller was so absorbed in the Book that Maddy said if Chicken Little told him the sky was falling, he'd have asked "Greek or Roman?" After supper when he walked back to the college, Tommy appeared in the doorway of the barn. This began to seem the best part of the scheme to Lou Emma, and she almost forgot that the idea had been to get ahead of Mrs. Moss.

Miss Kate insisted on paying for her driving lessons.

"Goodnightshirt!" Tommy said. "I can't take money for this. It's fun."

"The workman is worthy of his hire," Miss Kate said. At last it was agreed that Tommy should take twenty-five cents a lesson. This was half of what Mrs. Hamilton charged for piano lessons, plus guaranteed appearance in her Summer Recital.

"Our Summer Recital will be on Cyrus' birthday," Miss Kate said.

"I'm hemstitching handkerchiefs for Papa," Lou Emma said.

"Me, too," Maddy said. "I mean I'm going to. I'm not started yet."

"Let us go along when you have driving lessons," Lou Emma begged.

"Pretty please," Maddy added.

"It's up to the teacher." Miss Kate looked at Tommy.

Tommy closed his freckled eyelids as if in horror. Then he agreed. "All right. But don't gab. And you've got to crank the Great Smith. And learn to change tires. And put on a cold patch. And . . ."

They went by back streets to the Fair Grounds.

"Can't get hurt here," Tommy said. "Keep in the ruts and go 'round the racetrack. But first off you've got to learn the right names of things."

"Exhaust pipe, intake valve, pistons," Lou Emma chanted.

"Connecting rods, crankshaft, camshaft," Miss Kate went on.

"Flywheel, cylinders, spark-control lever," Maddy said. "That last's the most important. 'Hark, hark, retard the spark.' "

"Don't forget the crank," Lou Emma reminded her. "Tommy says—"

"You can't move unless you crank, so there's no use putting it in. And because Tommy Biddle says so don't make it so."

"Tommy's the teacher," Miss Kate said. "Let's go over it again."

The lessons went on every evening until the time Miss Kate went around the racetrack four times without stalling and backed the Great Smith into a complete turn. The girls changed a back tire, using one of the two spares, and got grudging praise from their teacher. "Not so bad. Not so bad. Considering."

Back at the small brown house Tommy said, "You know as much as I know, Mrs. Miller. For a lady you're pretty good. You learnt quicker 'n I thought."

There were grown-ups, Lou Emma knew, who wouldn't like that. Miss Kate only smiled.

"Remember, I've operated a sewing machine for years. Driving is fun."

"Most fun in the world, Laura said," Lou Emma remembered.

"I wish she'd won the race," Maddy sighed. "If Laura'd won, her picture 'd 've been in the Kansas City *Star.*"

"Laura may have won something else," Miss Kate said. "I hear Hardy 's gone to see her and meet her parents."

Lou Emma thought of the night Hardy had come with the roses; the sound of their voices in the moonlight: *Rapunzel . . . Rapunzel . . . let down your golden hair.* Would anyone ever call to her at her window? She looked over at Tommy. He made a horrible face.

"Hardy's no prize," he said. "That mushy stuff gives me the hully-gullies."

"You may change your mind later," Miss Kate said.

"Not me!" Tommy bristled.

"Not me!" Maddy echoed.

They looked expectantly at Lou Emma, but she refused to join in. She went over to Swish staked in the front yard. Tommy followed her.

"Mrs. Miller's asked me to the Professor's birthday party. Cake, ice cream, then her driving up, sis-boom-bah, like Barney Oldfield himself."

"It'll show Mrs. Moss," Lou Emma said. "To be second to Miss Kate'll kill her soul."

"Yeah." Tommy tossed his quarter into the air and caught it. "Only I got a feelin' Miss Kate wouldn't do it to spite anybody. Not even Mrs. Moss."

Lou Emma wasn't listening. "The day after Papa's birthday we'll get Miss Kate to drive us past Mosses', and I'll see Adelaide and yell 'Yah-yah-yah.' "

"You won't, either," Tommy said.

"I will, too."

"Well, it's your funeral." Tommy spun the quarter once more and left.

The next morning the Miller girls walked uptown. Gloriosa drowsed in the blanketing heat. Assembly Avenue looked deserted. The wooden blades of the electric fan over the entrance to Berkemyer's Confectionery droned around and around. A forgotten banner welcomed Congressman Clary and the race drivers.

Maddy looked around in disgust. "This town's a dump."

"A dead dump at that," Lou Emma agreed. "Let's walk by the peanut machine."

"Have you got some money?"

"You know EKCC hasn't paid salaries yet. But we can smell free."

They crossed the street, scuffing the toes of their slippers. The peanut machine was in front of the Big Dollar, where the Millers bought groceries. The dry, rich smell of the roasting nuts made Lou Emma's stomach growl.

"In the Bible Esau sold his birthright for a mess of porridge. I bet he'd have sold it quicker for hot roasted peanuts."

"Silly. Anyway, it's not porridge. It's pottage. It's like stew."

"Stew, phew," Lou Emma rhymed. "Anyway, I wish I had some peanuts." They looked at the window of the Big Dollar, dusty and smeared. "If we don't have money to buy peanuts, how do we still buy groceries?"

"Credit, maybe," Maddy said, then shook her head. "Nope, they've got a sign that says 'In God We Trust, All Others Pay Cash.' Maybe Miss Kate pays for 'em."

"You mean she's . . . supportin' us?" Lou Emma

felt as if she had had a blow in the pit of her stomach.

"I don't know for sure," Maddy said, "but she's got a checkbook, and she puts money from Miss Kate's Chapeaux in the bank."

"But . . . groceries . . ." Lou Emma could hardly stand the thought. "Aunt Jesse'd drop dead. She thinks Miss Kate ought to close the shop and stay home."

And I do, too!

"Aunt Jesse's off in Colorado eatin' five meals a day at Grey-Pines-in-the-Stokes." Maddy looked curiously at Lou Emma. "I don't see what's so bad about Miss Kate buying groceries."

"But . . . but . . ." Lou Emma stammered, and then burst out, "I wish there wasn't any such thing as money!"

"I'm going to make a lot of money when I grow up." Maddy always spoke as if she could read the future. "I'm going to be a—"

But Lou Emma never heard her sister's choice. "Look! Look there!"

Up Assembly Avenue at a stately, noiseless glide came a small, enclosed automobile. It was part shiny black metal and part heavy glass panels. Through the glass the gray plush upholstery was visible. Two cut-glass vases, each filled with an artificial rose, decorated the interior. In the driver's seat, grasping the guiding tiller with a firm kid-gloved grip, was Mrs. Moss. Beside her sat Adelaide.

"Great Snakes!" The man that worked the peanut machine stared. "What's that?"

Lou Emma was speechless. Maddy groaned. "It's the Baker Electric."

"Looks like a fishbowl that run away from home," the man grinned.

At that moment the electric slithered past the Miller girls. Mrs. Moss gave them a regal nod. Adelaide put her nose against the glass panel, thumbs in her ears, and wigwagged a greeting.

Maddy turned her back. Lou Emma looked intently at a peanut shell.

Assembly Avenue that had been deserted suddenly swarmed with people. All of them were staring, gawking, pointing at the elegant Baker Electric. Mrs. Moss halted the vehicle with a slight jolt. The roses bobbed in unison. Mrs. Moss and Adelaide stepped out, and went into Miss Kate's Chapeaux.

Once in Ohio Lou Emma had gone on a roller-coaster ride. She felt again the long, sickening drop that seemed never to end. *No, no, no!*

With the Mosses out of sight behind the pink curtains of the millinery shop, the Baker Electric was surrounded by curious people. Lou Emma and Maddy found themselves there without quite knowing how they got there or why.

"That's class. Real class." A female voice spoke enviously.

"Tim Moss really set his missus up in style."

"Yep. First woman driver in Gloriosa."

Lou Emma whirled. "She's not either!"

ROCERY
BECKEMYERS
G DOLLAR
PEANUTS

Maddy's hand clamped hard on Lou Emma's arm. "*Shhhh!*"

The unknown voice, cross at being contradicted, asked, "Who is first?"

Lou Emma thought fast. "Laura Thayer Wintergreen. That's who."

There was an indulgent little laugh. "Her? Better wait till Hardy hooks her, kiddo. We may never see her again."

Lou Emma knew she had reached the bottom of the roller coaster, the very, very bottom. A gray-haired farmer gave her a good-natured shove.

"Move over, you're hoggin' the view. Never thought to see one o' these critters live an' breathin'."

It was their chance to leave. The Miller girls wormed their way through the crowd and started for home. They got as far as the river bridge before either of them spoke a word.

Dinner was cold meat loaf. It was a dish Lou Emma detested. With her suspicion that she owed it to Miss Kate's Chapeaux, swallowing seemed next to impossible. Professor Miller was grumpy because a chapter wouldn't go right. Maddy wanted to hurry and get to a meeting of the Croquet Club. It was a dreary meal and no dessert. Miss Kate apologized.

"I meant to get home in time to make some apple snow, but Mrs. Moss and Adelaide came in to buy some of the automobile accessories. Did you know they have a Baker Electric, Cyrus?"

"I heard a rumor," he said. "I can't picture Tim Moss in an Electric."

"Not him. Her." Miss Kate spoke lightly. "She drove down Assembly Avenue and stopped right in front of the millinery shop. A big crowd gathered. It was better than an advertisement in the *Silver Bugle.* Money in our pockets."

Lou Emma jumped up from the table. "Money's all you care about. No matter what Mrs. Moss did to us, you'd sell her hats or whatever she wanted. She made us eat dirt, and you—you—"

"Stop it!" Professor Miller towered over her. "You don't know what you're saying."

"I do so. I know you ought to quit piddling with that silly book and make some money to buy groceries. So we wouldn't have to— And I hate cold meat loaf. And —"

Suddenly her anger ran out, leaving only dismay at what she had said, what she had done.

"Go to your room," her father said, his face like stone.

"Please, Cyrus . . ." Miss Kate whispered hoarsely.

"Lou Emma. Go . . . to . . . your . . . room."

She flopped face down on the bed and pulled the pillow over her head. Would nothing in the world ever go right? She tried; she knew she tried; but things never worked. Nobody liked her. Nobody knew what she meant. A smothering of self-pity came over Lou Emma, and tears began to wet her cheeks.

Much later she heard the Great Smith chug away, its engine sound fading in the distance. *Camshaft, cylinder head, carburetor . . .* She ran over the list. All of them worked together to move the big red automobile. If one of them was out of whack, all of them failed. She pushed the pillow away and tried to understand what she was thinking. The Great Smith was only a machine, her father said, that did what the driver made it do. But all the parts had to work altogether. *Spark plug, universal joint, king post.* Every one doing its part. Like Rule Number One.

The small brown house was very quiet. Maddy must have gone to the Croquet Club, Professor Miller back to EKCC— *Why did I say it was a silly book?*—and Miss Kate to the millinery shop. Lou Emma squirmed in misery as she remembered what she had said to Miss Kate. It was too bad to think out in words—just a big, black, slimy feeling.

I was awful. Worse 'n Adelaide and Mrs. Moss rolled together. I wish Papa'd whip me or Miss Kate slap me. But they won't. What am I goin' to do?

"I could make dessert for supper," she said aloud. "It's not much, but it's something."

Her misery eased a little as she got up from the bed and hurried downstairs. Peach tapioca? The new Chocolate Jell-o? No, it was too easy. Did she dare try cherry cobbler?

"Lou Emma?"

The sound of a voice in what she thought was an empty house startled her. It came from what she still thought of as Papa's Room. Face down on the bed, crumpled pillow close, was Miss Kate.

She must feel bad the way I feel bad. Why? She didn't do anything.

Lou Emma tiptoed in and took hold of a hand that groped for hers.

"I'm sorry, Miss Kate," she whispered.

"It's all right." Miss Kate's face was still down and her voice muffled. "I've been wrong about things. I should have explained. The house money . . . Cyrus' book . . . selling things to Mrs. Moss . . ." A little sob choked her.

"Please don't!" More than anything Lou Emma dreaded talking, explaining. *If grown-ups would just let you be and not make you say . . .*

"I'm glad I can keep on at the millinery shop. Getting the Book written means so much to Cyrus. And it will be a fine book."

"I know. I'm sorry I said—"

"It will be lots more important than who buys groceries. And who buys hats . . . That's water off a duck's back. Mrs. Moss, I mean. Someday I'll stop working and stay home, but till then if you . . . if Maddy . . ."

"I will. She will. We promise." Lou Emma didn't know what Miss Kate was going to ask, but she would have promised to climb the tower of Old Main one-handed to keep Miss Kate from crying. "Rule Number One," she added, thinking of the Great Smith and the auto parts that worked together.

"That's right. I forgot about the Rules." Miss Kate stood up and went over to the mirror. "I look a fright."

It was the same mirror Lou Emma's mother had looked into. Had she ever stood there with reddened eyes and dark smudges under them?

"I look a fright, too."

They poured cold water into the big china bowl; then Miss Kate and Lou Emma washed their faces and came up dripping. Eyes tight shut, they each found a towel and rubbed their faces.

"Wash together; friends forever.
Dry together; fight forever."

Lou Emma singsonged the old rhyme. "Maddy 'n' me say that. We learned it back in Ohio."

"My sisters and I used to say it, too, 'way out here in Kansas." Miss Kate began to take the pins from her hair. "Would you like to go back to Ohio?"

Lou Emma thought about it. "For a visit, but not to stay. We live here."

"Thank goodness for you, Lou Emma!" Miss Kate gave her a quick hug. "Now I can go back and fix Mrs. Moss's motoring bonnet."

"I wish you didn't have to. Fix things for people like her."

"In the hat business you don't think about whether you like a customer or not. Only how to get her to buy a becoming hat." Miss Kate began brushing her hair.

"Maddy told me about why you wanted me to learn to drive."

"It was wrong, I guess. Tommy said so, only I wouldn't listen to him. He said it was my funeral, and I s'pose it was."

"It wasn't wrong to get me to learn to drive." Miss Kate brushed hard and her hair crackled with electricity. "Only the part about Mrs. Moss was . . . Well, a mistake."

"Whatever I do 's wrong." Lou Emma slumped into the slough of self-pity again.

"That's foolish, and please don't say it again." Miss Kate spoke sharply. "We all do the right things for the wrong reasons sometimes. But think about this—we have a wonderful surprise ready for Cyrus's birthday."

"Na-na-na-Na . . ."

Hairbrush upraised, Miss Kate stood listening. Lou Emma looked toward the back door. It came again then, a high-pitched bleat. Of pain? Fear? Anger?

"Swish!" They both started for the door.

"Na-na-na-na." Now it sounded choked and faint.

"McKelvys'," Lou Emma shouted and started to run.

Miss Kate ran beside her, hair streaming down her back, hairbrush swinging.

There was one loud, one-note cry. Then a dreadful silence.

Chapter 7

They reached McKelvys' fence together and stared through the wire.

"Oh, no!" Miss Kate groaned.

"Not the carbide pit," Lou Emma moaned.

But groans or moans didn't change things. Swish was right in the middle of the carbide pit against which every girl and boy in the neighborhood had been warned. The sticky mass of white carbide drippings from the McKelvys' acetylene-light system held him as if he were in a big pot of glue.

"Swish!" Lou Emma wailed.

Miss Kate hushed her quickly. "Don't call him. He may thrash around and break his leg."

No more had to be said. A broken leg meant an animal must be shot. The thought of Swish's long, thin, high-jumping legs scared Lou Emma into silence.

"Is it poison?" she whispered. "Hackberry said it was mad-dog poison."

"N-no. People use it to whitewash fences. But it can't be good for a goat."

Swish turned his head and saw them. As if asking for help, he quavered out, "Na-ah-na-ah-na-AH?" Lou Emma's throat tightened.

"We're coming, Swish," Miss Kate said. Then she turned to Lou Emma. "I'm going to ask Mrs. McKelvy to let us into the garden."

"She'll have us put in jail. She said Swish was against the law."

"I know, but Swish is part of our family. Rule Number One."

Remembering the Rules stiffened Lou Emma's backbone. "I'll come, too."

"Good girl. Now, forward, march."

But their knock at the front door brought no answer. The windows were closed and the long lace curtains motionless. If Mrs. McKelvy was inside, she was not coming out. They went to the garden gate. It was wired shut from the inside.

"We could get the pliers and cut the wire," Lou Emma whispered.

Miss Kate looked at Swish. He seemed to be sinking lower. "It would take too long. We'd better climb the fence."

"Climb McKelvys' fence?" To Lou Emma there was less danger in climbing the Matterhorn.

"I'll go first." Miss Kate gathered her long skirts and climbed. At the top she teetered a moment but got down safely. "Hurry, Lou Emma."

Her heart thumping, Lou Emma got to the top of the fence; then she jumped and landed, SPLAT, in a patch of prize tomatoes.

Seeing them near, Swish began to struggle. The carbide held him tight. His fine whiskers were plastered to his chin; his curious golden eyes begged for help.

When Lou Emma and Miss Kate tried to get to him from the edge of the carbide pit, he was barely out of reach. But if they almost got hold of a horn or an ear, he jerked backward. Time after time he pulled away. He seemed weaker.

"We're not getting anywhere," Miss Kate panted. "We've got to coax him forward. What does he like best?"

"Tobacco," Lou Emma said. "And we don't have a bit."

"And Hack Wacker's off in the country. If we had one of his awful cigars . . ."

"If Laura hadn't taken the one Maddy gave her," Lou Emma said. "Wait a minute! Swish, hold on a minute longer!"

Darting down the garden path, Lou Emma ran to a small toolshed, nearly hidden by a smother of trumpet vine. Clay pots were stacked in the tangle of vines. Under one she found what she was looking for.

"Mr. McKelvy's." She held out a cloth sack of Bull Durham tobacco. "She won't let him smoke, but Maddy 'n' me saw him smoking out in the garden when she was gone. We watched where he hid his pipe and tobacco. Is it all right to take it to help Swish?"

"It's as all right as the rest of what we've done," Miss Kate said.

She tried to coax Swish forward with the sack, but he seemed too far gone to notice. His eyes were closed. Lou Emma took the sack and hurled tobacco onto the white carbide. A grain touched Swish's nose. He blinked, licked out his long tongue, then churned the carbide as he moved forward. The tobacco disappeared as he moved; he strained to reach it.

"More," Miss Kate commanded. "Like salt on a bird's tail."

Swish inched forward. They were so absorbed in his feeble motions that neither of them heard McKelvys' back door open.

"Now," Miss Kate said. "Grab his right horn! I'll take the left."

With one big heave they brought the goat scrambling from the carbide pit. Lou Emma tumbled backward into a row of onions, Miss Kate into some late lettuce. Swish, uncaring, snuffled at the tobacco sack. One gulp, and it disappeared, leaving the string and the tag hanging from his mouth. He chewed, unconcerned.

"You terrible awful GOAT!" Lou Emma scolded. But she and Miss Kate were laughing, plucking vegetables from themselves.

"Wilted lettuce." Miss Kate flipped a lettuce leaf from her streaming hair.

"Onion pie." Lou Emma responded with an onion flower. "Phew!"

Swish stopped chewing, the Bull Durham tag hung motionless. His ears pointed toward the house. On the back porch stood Mr. McKelvy.

"Jerusalem my happy home!" Lou Emma gasped.

Miss Kate made a desperate effort to twist up her

hair. She took hold of Lou Emma's hand, and they got unsteadily to their feet.

Mr. McKelvy watched them without a word. He was a small weather-beaten man with bright blue eyes. Lou Emma realized she had never heard him speak.

Never got a chance with her around.

"Our goat got into your garden," Miss Kate said in a brave voice. "He fell into your carbide pit. We came to get him out."

Mr. McKelvy glanced at the wired-shut gate, still without a word.

"We . . . uh . . . climbed the fence," Miss Kate admitted.

Mr. McKelvy scratched his head. "Breakin' an' enterin'. M'licious mischief. Trespassin'."

"Oh, dear," Miss Kate said. "But I'm afraid it's true."

"We had to get Swish out," Lou Emma said. "He might've *died.*"

"Ain't likely." Mr. McKelvy strolled past them to the broken tomato plants, the bruised lettuce and onions. As he went by, Lou Emma's heart jumped hopefully. She thought she glimpsed a twinkle deep in his blue eyes. Was he only having fun scaring them?

"Seems like you two did more damage than your goat."

"We'll pay for the damage," Miss Kate said. "We tried to get someone to let us in, but there was no answer, and Swish was getting in deeper."

"How 'd he get in, in th' first place?"

As if he understood the question, Swish trotted up to Mr. McKelvy. The Bull Durham tag was still swinging from his mouth. Mr. McKelvy grabbed for it, but Swish, startled by his movement, took off in a flying run. He sailed over the garden fence in one swift leap.

"I guess that answers your question," Miss Kate said.

Mr. McKelvy didn't appear to be listening. He looked after the galloping goat and frowned. "What's he got in his mouth?"

It was time for her to speak up, Lou Emma realized. "It's . . . it's your tobacco sack. Swish loves tobacco, so I took it to get him out. I'm sorry, but . . ."

Mr. McKelvy shifted uneasily. "Where'd you get it?"

"Oh Maddy 'n' me've known you hid it in back of the tool shed for a long time. We see you get it out when Mrs. McKelvy goes to town, an' your pipe, too."

"She's against tobaccy," Mr. McKelvy said. "Don't know where I keep it."

"We won't tell," Lou Emma said. "Will we, Miss Kate?"

"No, we won't tell." Miss Kate smiled. "Now if you'll let us out . . ."

Mr. McKelvy marched to the garden gate and untwisted the wire. As they walked through, he said, "She's *terrible* against tobaccy."

"Maybe she's right," Miss Kate said, "but that's between you two. Will you let me know about the damages?"

"Aw, it don't amount to much. We've got too much garden sass to eat, an' the stores don't give enough trade to be worth carryin' it uptown."

"Then let me make Mrs. McKelvy a hat," Miss Kate said.

"Say, she'd like that." The little man smiled. Lou Emma was sure of the twinkle now. "She's been wantin' one, but she never thought we could afford it."

"Tell her to come in. Anytime. We'd better wash Swish, now."

"Good-bye," Lou Emma said. "And thank you."

Mr. McKelvy winked. "Mum's the word," he said. "Mum's the word."

They found Swish hiding in the barn and dragged him out and held him under the pump. He bleated pitifully as the cold water hit him. Lou Emma got the scrubbing brush and worked on his flanks. She stopped, horrified.

"His hair! He's losing his hair!"

Miss Kate dropped the pump handle. They examined the unhappy goat. Big patches of pink showed on his hide. The chin whiskers, Swish's mark of male pride, were a grimy stubble.

"What'll we do?" Lou Emma quavered.

"Keep scrubbing," Miss Kate said grimly. "It's got to come off."

It took more than an hour. Lou Emma and Miss Kate were soaked to the skin. Swish stood with his head drooping, his hide a patchwork. Professor Miller drove up in the Great Smith and jumped to the ground.

"*Sanguine Saturnini!* What happened?"

"Swish got into McKelvys' carbide pit," Lou Emma said, too tired for more.

"And we got him out," Miss Kate said.

"And who got you out?" Professor Miller demanded.

"Lou Emma," Miss Kate said with a bedraggled smile. "Lou Emma and a sack of Bull Durham and a Miss Kate's Original."

Then she fainted.

The doctor had come and gone. Miss Kate had been put to bed, protesting that she was perfectly all right. Swish had been shut in the barn. Maddy had "cooked" supper—bologna, cheese, crackers, and leftover mashed turnips. Lou Emma had washed her hair to be sure there was no carbide that might give her bald spots like Swish. With Maddy she sat on the side steps to get the last sunlight.

"Papa says Swish can't ever run loose again," she reported.

"Papa talked an awful lot," Maddy said. "Mostly, 'Kate I told you—' "

" 'Not to overdo,' " Lou Emma finished. "But how'd Miss Kate or anybody else know Swish was goin' to get in the carbide pit?"

"Grown-ups are s'posed to figure stuff out," Maddy said. "Then they shake their heads and say 'I warned you, Maddy. You should've known.' "

Lou Emma giggled. It was exactly their father's tone and words.

"Well put, Maddy." Professor Miller came out and joined them; they looked at each other guiltily, but he didn't seem cross, only tired and worried. "I am a grown-up, and I have figured out some stuff as you say. So listen, you two."

He sat down between them, an arm around each. The sun was nearly down; the clouds were golden.

This is like it used to be, BMK. *Just us.*

"Look at the sunset, Papa," she said. "Who drives the horses of the sun in the Greek myths?"

"Helios, the sun-god. Those Kansas sunflowers you girls decorated with are named after him, *Helianthus annuus.* He had a son named Phaeton."

"I know." Maddy jumped in to tell the story. "And Phaeton took out the horses all by himself and nearly burnt up the world. Didn't he?"

"That's close enough. I suppose bringing up children was as hard for the Greeks as for anybody—gods or men."

"Papa!" Lou Emma protested. "We're not hard to bring up. Are we?"

He chuckled. "Not really." Then he sobered and

said, "We must, all three of us, keep Kate from overdoing. She works too hard . . . the shop . . . us . . ."

"We will, Papa," Maddy promised glibly.

Lou Emma was silent. It would be easy to promise to do more things, but she knew Miss Kate would not let her. Would it be the truth to say so?

"Lou Emma? How about you?"

"But, Papa . . . But we . . . But she . . ."

"Yes, Lou Emma?"

"Looky! Tommy's runnin' this way like he was chasin' snakes." Maddy ran to meet him. Lou Emma raced after her, thankful that Tommy had saved her from saying whatever it was she would have said.

Feet churning the dust, Tommy dodged the Miller girls, tore around the Great Smith, and came sliding to the steps as if they were first base.

Professor Miller grinned at him. "Message to Garcia, Tommy?"

"Message to Professor Cyrus H. Miller," Tommy said importantly and handed over a yellow envelope. "Dud Grimes gimme a dime to bring it."

"Who's it from?" Maddy danced with impatience.

Lou Emma clutched Maddy. "It's from Aunt Jesse comin' to Kansas, not Colorado."

"No!" Maddy whirled and "died" dramatically on the bottom step.

"Girls, Jesse means well," Professor Miller said as he always did when their aunt's name was mentioned. "Tommy, take charge of these frantic females."

"You betcha." Tommy grabbed one of Maddy's dark braids and a handful of Lou Emma's loose blonde hair and hauled them up tight. They yelled, but he only held tighter.

Professor Miller took out his silver penknife and slit the telegram open. Lou Emma watched surprise and pleasure chase across his face. Then he shook his head, "No," and dropped the telegram into his pocket.

"Don't we get to read it?" Maddy demanded.

"Won't you read it to us?" Lou Emma begged.

Miss Kate came out to the side steps. "What's going on out here?"

"Kate! You're supposed to be in bed."

"I'm tired of bed. I feel fine. What's happening?"

"Papa won't tell us," Maddy said indignantly.

"He's got a telegram in his pocket," Lou Emma said. "That's all we know."

"Is it Western Union rules I have to tell my family?" Professor Miller asked.

"Telegrams are private 'n' personal," Tommy answered. "An' I'm gettin' outa here fast." He let go the girls' hair and ran. Lou Emma and Maddy chased him as far as the corner. When they came back, Miss Kate had the telegram.

"It's a wonderful chance, Cyrus. The girls and I will be fine."

"I am not going anywhere," Professor Miller said with his I-Shall-Not-Be-Moved look. "Rule Number One, remember?"

"Cyrus, this is different."

"Everything is different if you let it be. Bob Barnes can get another man."

"If you don't tell me what you're talking about, I'm going to bust," Maddy announced solemnly.

"Burst," her father corrected. "I don't want to hear that word again."

"But where are you *not* going?" Lou Emma jumped up and down.

"I am *not* going to Colorado Springs, because I am *not* going to lecture at Colorado College on Roman History. We are *not* going to be separated as a family. And while I am on the subject I am *not* going to listen to any more talk."

His words sounded like a door slamming. Lou Emma was not surprised that the sun dropped below the horizon. She looked at Miss Kate for help but got only a shake of her head. Maddy sat on the lowest step and put her head on her knees.

After a few minutes of absolute silence, Professor Miller cleared his throat. "Well, perhaps I have been too harsh. It's only that . . . Confound Bob Barnes! Why did he have to invite me this summer?"

"Because you're the best teacher he could get," Miss Kate suggested.

"Nonsense. Fifty others could do as well—or maybe twenty-five." He looked down at the telegram. "I do wonder who will be there. Colorado College summer lectures are quite a plum."

"You could write and ask," Lou Emma said.

Maddy said, "You could telegraph."

For an instant Lou Emma saw her father waver. Then he shook his head.

"There's no use shilly-shallying. I am not going to leave my family."

"Then let's all of us go," Maddy said. "Could we? Couldn't we?"

Professor Miller touched her shoulder. "Dear child, the railroad fare alone would be more than I'd be paid. And we'd have to sleep . . . eat . . . No. Sorry."

"If you would go and take the girls, Cyrus—"

"KATE!"

"I think I will go back to bed," Miss Kate said. "Be sure your hair is dry before you go up, Lou Emma." Professor Miller followed her into the house.

"I'm going to bed with my hair wet, and get galloping consumption and die," Lou Emma said. "That'll show Papa. He'll cry and cry, and I'll say . . ."

"You can't say anything. You're dead of galloping consumption."

"That's right." Lou Emma slumped in gloom.

From the barn Swish bleated pitifully.

"We forgot to feed him with all the hullabaloo," Maddy said. They tramped out in silence. Swish was a huddled white lump by the manger.

"Do you think he's going to d-i-e?" Maddy spelled.

"No. Miss Kate said if he was going to he would have already. She said he was a Kansas goat and could take a lot of punishment. See, he's eating."

"If he can eat, he can get well," Maddy said. "Say, I'm hungry, too."

"There's some peach pie left," Lou Emma said, "but I couldn't eat more 'n one piece. I feel so terrible about Colorado and Swish and all."

They took the peach pie upstairs and ate it, sitting on the edge of the bed. It was too hot to light the lamp, so they undressed in the dark and crawled across the bed, trying to find a breeze. Maddy dropped off criss-cross and could not be budged. Lou Emma bunched up in one corner, hot and miserable.

In Colorado, it's cool in the summer. There's mountains with snow on 'em. And rivers. It's in our geography.

Below the window was the dark bulk of the Great Smith. Because of Swish's misery Professor Miller had let the auto stay out. The thought of the cool leather upholstery struck Lou Emma. She tiptoed downstairs and out into the night. Far away a dog barked. She had no idea what time it was, and she didn't care, for the leather seats were as she had thought, cool and smooth. For a while she sat at the steering wheel and went through the motions of driving, hearing Tommy's instructions to Miss Kate. Then she slipped lower in the seat and stretched out so that she stared up at the stars.

She ought to go upstairs and get into her own bed. Maddy would have the window side by now, and she would have to take the room side. To get up and move, to go indoors and leave the stars, was impossibly hard. It was so much easier, so much nicer, so much more fun, to stay right where she was. If she could sleep in the Great Smith in Gloriosa, why couldn't she . . . why couldn't Maddy . . . why couldn't all the Millers . . . ?

Was it a dream or an idea? Lou Emma tried to decide, but she closed her eyes and sleep took her. In seconds a little snore burbled from her mouth.

The sun on her face waked her in the morning.

Chapter 8

Lou Emma didn't wonder where she was or how she got there. She knew. The dream or the idea she had gone to sleep with the night before was a plan now as bright, as dazzling, as the sun rising over Gloriosa.

She patted the steering wheel and longed for the nerve to squeeze the horn bulb and wake up the town. "It's your plan, too," she said to the Great Smith. "I'd never have thought of it upstairs in bed. I'll be back, just you wait."

Gathering her nightgown around her, she dashed into the kitchen. Her father was stirring coffee around and around in his cup. Miss Kate was frizzling ham in the skillet. They stared at her, amazed.

"Where have you been, young lady?"

"In your nightgown? Out of doors?"

She didn't stop to explain. "In a minute. Maddy's got to be here."

Upstairs she wasted no time but dashed water onto Maddy's sleeping face. "Get up. Hurry."

"Go 'way." Maddy pulled the sheet around her into a cocoon.

"Get dressed, or I'll pour the pitcher on you."

"Good Granny!" Maddy crawled out, groggy with

sleep. Lou Emma had slid into a minimum of clothes. From surprise or curiosity Maddy dressed and stumbled down after Lou Emma.

"I have something to tell—everybody."

With those words Lou Emma's courage evaporated. A plan new and shiny in the dawn is one thing. To say it out loud to three people is another.

"All right. We're waiting." Professor Miller drank some coffee.

"It's about . . . Colorado." She heard her voice squeak on the last word.

The Professor's cup clinked. "I told you last night—"

"Papa, I didn't know this last night. Please listen."

"I'm starving." Maddy snitched some ham and began to eat it from her hand.

Miss Kate was the only one listening. Lou Emma spoke to her.

"Last night I thought . . . I mean this morning, really. I mean . . . Why couldn't all of us *drive* to Colorado in the Great Smith?"

"Impossible," Professor Miller said.

Miss Kate let the fork bang into the skillet. "I don't see why it's impossible."

Maddy choked on the ham and coughed out, "We could . . . sleep . . . in tents."

"Cook on campfires by the road," Miss Kate joined in.

"Laura drove to Denver," Lou Emma remembered. "If she can, we can."

"The Great Smith's got that little icebox on the running board," Maddy said. "And Wackers won't care if we take their cots."

Miss Kate said, "We can get vegetables and milk and eggs from farmers."

"We can go fishing and cook our fish." Lou Emma added. "And we've got to take an onion. Tommy says if it rains rub an onion on the windshield."

Professor Miller stood up. He was a tall man, but now he looked taller. Nothing they had said seemed to have reached him.

"My dears, I am sorry. We cannot go."

"But—" Three voices cried the same word.

" 'But me no buts . . .' " he quoted. "A train trip to Colorado could be a pleasant vacation. By auto it would be long, hard, tiring. Only last night I told you girls we must take better care of Kate. Driving to Colorado is no way to accomplish that."

Maddy collapsed in her chair and put her head on the table. So did Lou Emma. The beautiful dream of last night had been a dream after all. The Great Smith had let her have the dream; then somehow it had been snatched away. A slow, unreasonable resentment against her stepmother sprouted within her. It grew quickly once it had started, like toadstools after summer rains.

"Cyrus, if you and I were not married, would you take the girls and go?"

"A foolish, illogical question. I won't dignify it with an answer. Now, will you three please stop looking as if the world had ended? Some day I will take you to Colorado in style. Pullman palace car, Fred Harvey meals—"

"I want to go to Colorado overland," Miss Kate said. "The way Lou Emma was talking about. The way my grandmother went to California in Forty-nine."

Lou Emma lifted her head. She forgot her resentment, and it stopped growing.

Professor Miller frowned. "Very few women went West in Forty-nine."

"My grandmother was a very unusual woman," Miss Kate said.

"You never spoke of her before."

Miss Kate said, "Her name was Evangeline . . . Smith. She went in a covered wagon. And it was attacked by Indians."

"Did they scalp her?" Maddy asked eagerly.

"Well, no. Some of the men were killed in the attack. And a tomahawk came right through the wagon cover and almost hit her."

"I wish I'd been there," Maddy said. "I'd have thrown it back."

"I wish we could go in a covered wagon," Lou Emma said.

"I will never understand women," Professor Miller shook his head. "I thought they were fragile, delicate creatures to be shielded from hardship."

"Grandmother Evangeline thrived on hardship." Miss Kate's eyes sparkled. "She even had a baby on the way to California. Great-uncle Mortimer Lucas—"

"I thought her name was Smith," Professor Miller said.

"Smith was her maiden name," Miss Kate answered with dignity. "Naturally she was married when she had a baby."

"Then Lucas was your father's name?"

"You know perfectly well my father's name is Haskell Turner," Miss Kate said. "Evangeline Smith Lucas was my mother's mother. If you doubt me—"

"Not at all," Professor Miller said. "As an historian, I am interested in the trip. How long did it take them, baby and all?"

"I have no idea," Miss Kate said, her head held high. "My grandmother only told us that she loved every minute. She said a covered wagon was a wonderful place to live—all that fresh air."

"I'd think so with those tomahawk holes in the wagon cover."

Are they quarreling? What's going on?

Lou Emma looked from her father to her stepmother. Maddy had lifted her head, too. Then Miss Kate's manner changed completely. She put her hands on her husband's shoulders and looked at him pleadingly.

"Take us to Colorado in the Great Smith, Cyrus. I want to go. The girls want to go. You want to go. I promise I won't overdo."

Lou Emma jumped to Miss Kate's left side. "Please, Papa."

Maddy took the right side. "Please, please, Papa."

The ring of the seldom-used front doorbell startled all of them. Lou Emma ran to answer it and came rushing back.

"It's another telegram!"

"Two in two days," Maddy gloated. "Bet Mosses' never had that."

Professor Miller opened the yellow envelope and read the message, his face expressionless. At last he said, "Kate, I'd like more coffee."

She poured a cup of the strong black brew, and he drank it slowly. Lou Emma thought it was an hour before he finished and said, "Read it out, please, Kate."

" 'Etting coming one-day lecture stop advise you meet him in re textbook stop wire answer collect best regards three girls Barnes.' " She looked up blankly. "Who is Etting?"

"I know," Lou Emma said. "Every time I dust H-O-G I see his name on the back. *Etting, Ed.* It's backwards, and his name's Ed Etting."

"Ed. means Editor," Professor Miller said. "Editor of the *History of Greece* you girls call H-O-G. Dr. Hugo Etting is one of the great classical scholars of this country. I never thought I would meet him. *If* I were going, which I'm not."

"This settles it," Miss Kate said to the girls. "Start packing."

"Kate, I can't let you, not on my account—"

"We're going on my account." She laughed up at him.

Maddy and Lou Emma hugged each other and danced wildly around the kitchen. Then the house wouldn't hold their joy, and they ran outdoors and jumped up and down on the running board of the Great Smith.

"We're bound for Colorado with a banjo on our knee," Maddy sang.

"Colorado or BUST!" Lou Emma flung the forbidden verb to the world.

In his garden, where he was staking tomato plants, Mr. McKelvy grinned and puffed on his pipe.

Word of the Millers' plan to drive the Great Smith to Colorado spread through Gloriosa like a summer cold. No one in town had taken such a trip by auto. Daily the big Sante Fe trains rolled their passengers west to the Rockies, but to drive—to camp out—that was unheard of.

Mrs. Moss and the Baker Electric were entirely forgotten. The *Silver Bugle* ran a story, "The Motoring Millers." The Methodist preacher mentioned them in his sermon. Gifts "for the trip" poured in. Dr. Biddle promised Professor Miller a raise in salary for this boost to the prestige of Eastern Kansas Classical College. Mrs. Wacker heard about it down on her kinfolks' farm where the Wackers were spending the summer and made a special trip to Gloriosa to wish them well and contribute a jug of sorghum.

But for Lou Emma there was a worry no one else shared. What to do with Swish? The once handsome goat spent all his time huddled in the barn, head drooping. He no longer pranced, capered, or entertained with his tricks. Even his bleat had a pitiful quaver in it.

Who was going to feed Swish, water him, keep him out of McKelvys' garden? With Swish in such a state after being hauled from the carbide and losing his hair, no one would want him around. And she could not go off and leave him. All of the plans for going to Colorado were shadowed in her mind by the thought of leaving Swish, sick and alone. *I won't go. I'll stay home.*

"If only Wackers were here," she said to Tommy. "They'd look after him."

"If Ma'd let me," Tommy sighed. "But she told me not even to ask."

"How about Harris?" Lou Emma wondered.

"Gone to Camp Meeting. How about Gracie?"

"She's thick with Adelaide and not speaking to Maddy 'n me."

"Maybe you shouldn'ta pulled him out of the carbide," Tommy said.

"Don't you say such a thing!"

"Well, but—"

" 'Well, but' yourself. I'll find a place for Swish or put him in the Great Smith and take him to Colorado."

At supper she suggested this to her father. His shouted "No!" rattled the dishes in the safe.

Maddy was no help. "Turn him loose and let him take care of himself."

"How'd you like to be turned loose with your hair gone in patches?"

"Oh, piffle!" Maddy said. "You're always sayin' how'd I like to be a goat, or a tadpole, or a frog, or a hootenanny. I'm a people, and I'm going to play croquet."

"It's your turn to dry the dishes," Lou Emma reminded her.

"Do it for me this time. I promised Edna I'd be there, and I'm late now."

Lou Emma agreed, not because of Edna or Maddy's promise but to get a chance to ask Miss Kate what to do about Swish while her father was not around.

"I wish we could put him on a farm," Miss Kate scooped up soft soap. "He's grown now. Too big to be treated like a cute toy."

"I don't want to give him up. You said he was part of our family."

"Yes. But he's changed. He needs more space than we have."

"Everybody liked Swish when he was little," Lou Emma mourned. "And now everybody's down on him, I think he hides in the barn because the sun hurts those bare spots on his hide."

Miss Kate swished the water to make suds, her gold wedding ring winked bright in the dishpan. "I wonder . . ."

"Wonder what?"

"I have a kind of a sort of an idea, Lou Emma. Will you do the dishes while I go see about it?"

"Yes, ma'am." The warm sudsy water felt good. Lou

Emma hadn't washed dishes in a long time. It was fun if you didn't have to do it every meal.

Taking the tape measure out of the catch-all drawer, Miss Kate left the kitchen. Then she popped back in like a pretty brown-eyed jack-in-the-box.

"Everything changes, Lou Emma. The trick is to change along with it."

Puzzling over that remark, which didn't seem to fit Swish or Colorado or the Great Smith or any of the things going on in the Miller household, Lou Emma finished the dishes and poured the water around the zinnias that were drooping in the heat. She rubbed rose water and glycerine into her hands as Miss Kate had taught her to do. The sweet rose scent of the lotion mixed with the leftover smell of fried green tomatoes from supper.

Everything changes . . . The trick is to change along with it. . . .

She asked Maddy, when she came home. "What's it mean?"

"Shoot, when grownups start talking that way I figger it saves trouble not to listen. Let's go upstairs and practice packing our suitcases again."

"NA-NA-NA! Loud and clear it came, just as it had before Swish got into the carbide. "NA-NA-NA!"

Lou Emma wondered if she could be dreaming. She punched Maddy hard.

"NA-NA-NA!" It was Swish's "I'm hungry, come feed me" call.

They tumbled downstairs, and there at the side door

was Swish. He stood resplendent in the Kansas sunshine, his patched hide covered with a green blanket tied with gold-colored ribbons. In bold letters SWISH was written in ribbon, and on his head, speared through his horns, was a small straw hat sporting green and gold ribbons. The girls threw their arms around him, and he stepped on their feet, complained, pranced, and generally acted his old self. Lou Emma brushed happy tears onto the corner of the blanket.

"Oh, Papa, I'm so glad."

"Don't tell me. Tell Kate. She was half the night making this getup."

"It's a miracle," she told her stepmother, "and you did it."

"Don't forget you thought of it. You said the sun hurt his bare hide. Hide or pride, he does seem a lot happier."

Maddy said solemnly, "He's the greatest goat in the world, and he gets the first stack of pancakes."

It was after Miss Kate had gone to the shop and Professor Miller to the college that Maddy got the idea of renting Swish as a pet while they were away.

"It's better'n asking people to keep him free-for-nothing. Nobody 'preciates free things."

"How much rent should we ask?" Lou Emma was big-eyed before her sister's wisdom.

"Dollar per month," Maddy said as if she had been renting goats for years.

"Golly-molly, that's a lot!"

"Only a quarter a week. We can spend the money in Colorado."

They polished Swish's hoofs with shoe-blacking and combed such hair as he had left. Then Lou Emma twined honeysuckle in his chain, and they led him to Assembly Avenue. Maddy made a cardboard sign: PET FOR RENT.

"Let's stand in front of Berkemeyer's. Lots of kids come there."

J. T. and Harris saw them first. Edna came over from the Big Dollar, where her mother had sent her for lump sugar. Gracie forgot she wasn't speaking and joined the crowd. Eddie Gammon arrived from the blacksmith shop with six horseshoe nails made into rings. More and more boys and girls appeared.

To each, Maddy put the proposition of renting Swish. Lou Emma recited the tricks Swish could do: climb steps, stand on a rolling barrel, jump fences—even McKelvys'—and chase the meanest dogs in town. Swish himself showed off in his best style. The green and gold outfit—college colors—was much admired. Every one of the onlookers wanted to rent Swish, but when it came to taking the honeysuckle-twined chain and leading him home each one backed away.

"I'll hafta ask my folks."

Tommy dropped off the back of the ice wagon. "What's goin' on?"

"What do you care?" Lou Emma was still cross over what he had said yesterday. "You wanted me to leave him in that awful pit."

"He's a valuable goat," Gracie said. "I'm pretty sure my folks'll let me rent him. Promise me first chance."

"No promises. First come; first served."

Mr. Berkemeyer came out, saw Swish, and returned brandishing a broom. "Git! All of ya. GIT!"

"Old crosspatch," Maddy said. "Let's stand by the Peanut Machine."

The man with the Peanut Machine was no more hospitable.

"Try the Big Dollar. You buy groceries there," Tommy said shrewdly.

By this time the crowd was big enough to overflow the sidewalk. The owner of the Big Dollar saw them coming.

"You gotta find some place else. Can't have you blocking the door."

Edna Stumpf suggested her father's bank. From there they were shifted to the *Silver Bugle.* The editor came out and beckoned a lanky, moustached man. "Get these kids off the street, Lou."

"Don't seem to me they're doin' any harm."

"Are you the Law, or aren't cha?"

"Yeah, but—"

The editor turned on Lou Emma. "You got a license to rent a goat?"

"I . . . I didn't know. Do we have to have a license?"

"Sure." The editor winked at the Law. "Right, Lou?"

At that instant the door to Miss Kate's Chapeaux

opened, and Miss Kate came out. Never had Lou Emma been gladder to see anybody.

"What's the trouble, Lou?"

"No trouble, Mrs. Miller. Just some kid stuff."

"Renting a goat without a license," the editor grinned. "Can't have that."

Miss Kate looked him straight in the eye. "That's *our* goat and *our* girls. I never heard of needing a license to rent goats. Did you, Lou?"

"Well, Mrs. Miller, it's never came up before."

"Then it'll have to go before the City Council for three meetings and be put to a public vote before it's legal. In the meantime you girls and your friends come in front of my shop. You're always welcome there."

"Aw, Mrs. Miller . . ." the editor protested, but Miss Kate was gone.

Maddy and Lou Emma with Swish took up their stand in front of a display of Miss Kate Originals in autumn colors. They were jubilant at their victory over the editor. For a while it seemed that every boy and girl in Gloriosa was crowding around them, petting and praising Swish. But by noon the crowd had thinned out. Everyone who left promised to come back. The Miller girls rushed home, swallowed ham and scalloped eggplant, skipped dessert, and rushed back. Of all the morning crowd, only Tommy returned.

"I'm sorry about yesterday," Lou Emma said to him as Maddy went inside to confer with Miss Kate.

"Forget it," Tommy said. "Renting Swish is fun."

"*If* we can rent him." Colorado seemed very far away to Lou Emma.

Maddy came back and joined them. "Miss Kate says her business is terrible, too. She hasn't had a customer since morning. She says it goes that way sometimes."

Edna Stumpf drove past with her mother and shook her head sadly. Mrs. Stumpf shook the reins to hurry the horse.

"I wouldn't *let* them have Swish," Lou Emma declared. "She's such a bad cook."

An hour dragged by. Heat, flies, dust, grew worse. At two thirty Maddy took the PET FOR RENT sign, turned it over, and printed on the back: FREE GOAT. Even this brought no takers.

By three thirty gloom was heavy on all three. Maddy suddenly remembered she had promised, *promised,* to go to a meeting of the Croquet Club. She would come back.

J. T. came by to get Tommy to go fishing.

"Go on if you want to," Lou Emma said, hoping he wouldn't.

"Nah, too hot for fish. Nothin' bites but mosquitoes."

They had run out of things to talk about. The sun blasted down and was reflected from the window of the millinery shop. Lou Emma had to admit that Swish did smell—kind of. The high mountains of Colorado shimmered before her like a Promised Land where she was forbidden to go.

Tommy gave a long, low whistle. "Hardy Garrett, himself!"

In the white Stanley Steamer with its red leather upholstery was Hardy, dressed to kill. He had throttled the auto down to the Gloriosa speed limit of six miles per hour, and he drove carelessly, one hand on the wheel, the other arm draped along the back of the seat. As he came closer, he peered, pretended amazement at the sight of Tommy, Lou Emma, and Swish, and brought the Stanley to a purring halt.

" 'FREE GOAT,' " he read aloud. "Who'd pay for one of the critters?"

"All right for you," Tommy said hotly. "Swish is a registered, pedigreed, guaranteed billy goat. Say one more word an' I'll sic 'im on you."

"Excuse me for living!" Hardy said. He tipped his hat toward Lou Emma. "Had a card from Laura. She sent you her best."

"Laura said Swish was the best goat she'd ever seen," Lou Emma said.

Hardy grinned. "Well, Laura's a city girl. Prob'ly never got within sniffing distance of a goat before. Whew! Warm, isn't it?" He fanned himself with his straw sailor.

"I think you're mean," Lou Emma choked. The long day had worn down her defenses. Without knowing she was going to, she began to cry.

"Pick on somebody your own size," Tommy snarled at Hardy.

"Hey!" Hardy pulled on the brake and jumped from the Stanley. "I didn't mean to make you cry, Lou Emma. We're friends. Remember?" He handed her a linen handkerchief that smelled wonderfully.

She wiped her eyes and blew her nose and felt better. Hardy had said they were friends, and she did remember the night he had brought the roses to Laura. He had said, *Good night, kiddo. If I can ever do you a favor, you name it.*

"You said you'd do me a favor Hardy, for me to name it." He looked at her a little doubtfully, but he nodded.

"You've got a farm, and Swish ought to be on a farm now he's grown up. He's the best goat in the world, and I'm giving him to you. Not for just while we're gone but for *always.*"

"Giving him to ME?"

Tommy laughed. "You know it, Sport!"

"You can have his new blanket, and his hat—it's a Miss Kate Original—and be sure he doesn't get in the carbide pit if you've got one." Lou Emma hauled on the chain, twined with wilted honeysuckle.

Swish got wearily to his feet. The day had been hard on him, too. He lowered his horns and shook them at Hardy. The hat wobbled. "NA-AH!"

"See, he doesn't like me. Anyway, I've got to go." Hardy moved back. "Got to see a fellow at Crossroads. Git away, Buster."

"His name's Swish," Lou Emma said. "And you said you'd do me a favor."

"But . . . But . . ."

"I'll boost; you pull," Tommy said. He and Lou Emma hoisted Swish into the Stanley Steamer. Once he was there Swish seemed more pleased than angry. He chewed on Hardy's linen duster. "Na-na-na!"

People began to look toward the Stanley. Miss Kate came out of the millinery shop. The editor of the *Silver Bugle* came out, notebook in hand. Mr. Berkemeyer and the Peanut Machine man peered across the street. Mr. Stumpf waved a cigar and shouted.

Hardy's face turned a blazing red. He glared at the editor, penciling rapidly in his notebook.

"Print this an' I'll sue you, so help me!"

He got into the Stanley and turned the switch. To the cheers of the onlookers the white auto moved down Assembly Avenue. Hardy looked to neither the right nor the left, but Swish put his straw-hatted head over the side and bleated a happy farewell.

Watching the dust cloud as Hardy put on speed, Lou Emma knew that she ought to feel sad; she ought to be crying now, not before. Instead she felt happy and not a single tear wet her cheek.

"Swish's better off," she told Tommy. "He was too big to treat like a—a toy." Somewhere she had heard somebody say that, and it sounded true.

"Yep. He's better off, an' we are, too. Everybody but Hardy, an' he'll get used to it. Oh, brother! I'll never forget his face, long as I live."

"I didn't know Swish was pedigreed, and all that you said," Lou Emma said as they walked toward the Millers' house.

"Well, I don't know he's *not*," Tommy said. "That's good enough for now."

They walked slower and slower, stopping on the bridge to watch the river and the trees mirrored in its surface. Dusty sunflowers edged the road.

"Colorado," Lou Emma said, taking satisfaction in the very word. "I'm really and truly going to Colorado. With Swish safe at Garrett's farm, I'll see the mountains and the rivers and the . . . mountains."

"Mountains," Tommy jeered. "A lot of piled-up dirt an' rocks."

She looked at him, shocked, and saw he was teasing.

"Shut your eyes," he said. She did as he told her and for an instant she thought *he was going to kiss her.* Should she let him, or stop him, or—

"Open up," he called, and when she opened her eyes, he was nowhere in sight. On the bridge rail was a small white package, and there was only a shaking in the willows by the edge of the river to tell what direction Tommy had gone.

Chapter 9

"Promise you won't tell?" Lou Emma whispered late that night.

"Cross my heart." Maddy crossed her heart five times in quick succession.

"You say that for any old thing. This is different."

Maddy thought, then came up with a new promise. "If ever I tell this, under the sun, my teeth will fall out, one by one."

" 'And I'll never play croquet again,' " Lou Emma tacked on.

"I won't say that. It ruins my rhyme, and I don't care what you've got in your hand. I don't *care.*" Maddy flipped the sheet over her head.

Lou Emma waited. At last Maddy jerked off the sheet, cross as two sticks.

" 'I'll-never-play-croquet-again,' " she rattled off. "Now show me."

Moving very quietly, Lou Emma lighted the lamp and turned the wick low. She held out her hand. A silver ring with a blue stone was in it. "It's a birthstone ring. Sapphire for September. Tommy gave it to me."

"Tommy Biddle? When? Why? What'd he say?"

"Today. I don't exactly know why. And he didn't say anything."

Maddy's dark blue eyes were wide with curiosity. "Did he kiss you?"

"Madeline Margaret Miller!"

"Don't jump down my gullet," Maddy said reasonably. "When boys give girls rings, it means they're engaged, and Gracie's sister's engaged, and they kiss each other a lot, Gracie says . . ."

"I'm not engaged, I should hope. And I think you're awful. Gracie, too."

"Did you tell Miss Kate about the ring?"

"No, and you'd better not. You'd hate to give up croquet."

"Oh, I don't know," Maddy said carelessly. "I've beat about everybody in Gloriosa already. Maybe I'll tell Eppie when they get back. She'll drop dead."

"And your teeth will fall out, clunk, clunk." Lou Emma thumped the floor.

"Girls! Settle down!" the Professor boomed up the stairwell.

Lou Emma panicked. "Did he hear? About Tommy and the ring?"

"Sure he heard," Maddy said; then she relented. "He couldn't 've. He just wants us up early tomorrow to start packing the Great Smith."

"Only two more days till we start." Lou Emma blew out the lamp and sighed rapturously. "What d'you think Colorado'll be like? Really?"

But Maddy was asleep or pretending to be.

Turning the birthstone ring around and around on her finger, Lou Emma thought of snow-topped mountains, tall green pines, rippling streams. Then in the midst of all those wonders she saw the small, exquisitely-dressed figure of Miss Jesse Miller and heard her voice, ladylike to the last syllable, saying "My poor little motherless nieces . . ." Clutching Maddy's shoulder, Lou Emma dug her fingernails in deep.

"She'll be there. Aunt Jesse'll be there, too. What'll we do?"

"Lemme 'lone," Maddy said thickly. "How'd she ever know we're there? We don't hardly know it ourselves."

"But—"

"Lemme 'lone."

The Great Smith stood in the shade of the elm tree as the Millers packed, unpacked, and repacked. All day Miss Kate shuttled between the auto and the house. All day the Professor added and then took away books he *must have* to teach properly. All day the girls bickered over packing, and neither would give up a single item she had chosen to take.

"I've got to keep in practice," Maddy brought out her croquet mallet and special ball. "You don't need three hats, for heaven's sake."

"My blue hat's for my blue dress. I can't wear it with my green, so I have to take the yellow straw. The white organdy is the new one Miss Kate just made. I have to take *it*. And besides, look at all the stuff for the Great Smith."

They both looked with disfavor on the stack of tools.

"Tire pump, tire patch, tow rope, block 'n' tackle, can for gas, can for oil, canvas bucket for water, jack . . . Great Granny!" Maddy moaned.

"Every time Papa decides to leave out a thing, somebody comes along and says 'I'd hate to be caught on the road without *that,*' and back it goes. I think Papa's about to give up the ghost. Look at him now."

Professor Miller had opened a book and started reading. Miss Kate stepped around him with exaggerated courtesy. "Excuse me, Cyrus."

"Certainly." He didn't even glance up from the book.

"She'd know better if she'd been married to him long as we have," Lou Emma said.

"I hope the Wacker sorghum stays capped," Miss Kate worried.

"Did you put in the onion?" Maddy asked.

Miss Kate nodded. "Will cream keep in this heat?"

"You could have asked your Grandmother Evangeline," the Professor said.

"If I had that tomahawk she told about, I'd know what to do with it," Miss Kate said. "Cyrus, will you *please* put down that book?"

Maddy giggled. "Rule Number Two: Never Interrupt Papa When He's Studying."

"Your father is not studying. He is hiding behind Rule Number Two to avoid making decisions. He knows we cannot take all this stuff to Colorado."

For Miss Kate to say such things in such a tone startled both the girls into an uncomfortable quiet. Professor Miller looked up.

VOTES
TIRO

"Kate, I am at a bare minimum if I am to teach as I should."

"Nineteen books plus H-O-G to ride in my lap?"

"Don't forget that Dr. Etting, editor of the book you refer to, is the man to thank for this—uh—*wanderjahr*."

Lou Emma winced at her father's icy tone and his use of a German word she, and probably Miss Kate, didn't know. Her stepmother's chin quivered.

Suddenly Professor Miller tossed his book away. "I'm sorry, Kate. The truth is that I have no more idea than a Kansas jackrabbit what to take or what to leave behind—except for books. I'm no pioneer; I'm a simple teacher. Tell me what you want done, and I'll do it."

Miss Kate mopped her eyes. "I'm sorry, Cyrus. I'm the one that's simple."

"Trip nerves," he said. "Nothing to worry about. Just take what can be crammed in and leave the rest. Tomorrow we crank the Great Smith and *go*."

We used to do that way BMK, Lou Emma remembered. *Why can't we now?*

A man in a delivery wagon called to them. "Prof. C. H. Miller? Express package from NOO YAWK."

The package came from Hammacher Schlemmer & Co. It was their famous eighteen-pound Tourist Auto Kit. In it was a note from Dr. Barnes.

" 'Congratulations, Odysseus. Take care of Penelope. Regards, Mentor.' "

Professor Miller laughed as he read it aloud. By the time the Greek names were explored and the compact

Tourist Auto Kit had replaced the stack of miscellaneous tools, the Millers were happy again. "Trip nerves" faded away.

Now Miss Kate began to discard things with both hands. Maddy put her croquet ball and mallet back in the barn, along with a VOTES FOR WOMEN sign she was planning to tie to the Great Smith. Professor Miller reduced his books to ten. Lou Emma gave up two hats and took the yellow straw plus a blue ribbon.

They ate a hasty clean-out-the-icebox supper and went to bed, each one telling the other to go to sleep "right away" and be up before sunrise.

Maddy was asleep two minutes after the "Amen" to her prayers. Lou Emma turned and twisted and envied Maddy, snoring beside her. Inside the pillowcase was the birthstone ring. She put it on, and went over every detail of Tommy's giving it to her. What he said, and what he did not say. And what Maddy said. . . .

How dark it was with only the stars. The street lights went off at eleven when the electric power stopped. That had been a while ago, so it must be midnight. The word chimed, cold and solemn. The side door creaked. *Burglars?* Lou Emma gasped and then caught a glimpse of white on the ground below. *Ghosts?* She slipped to the window ledge and saw Miss Kate in her long white dressing gown, putting some forgotten thing on the front seat of the Great Smith. But instead of going back inside, she stood there, her hand on the square glass side lamp. The night was so still Lou Emma heard her stepmother's deep-drawn sigh.

The very way Miss Kate stood, head bowed, leaning on the big red auto made Lou Emma want to run downstairs and hug her. "Forlorn" was an old-fashioned word seen only in books, but it was the one that came into Lou Emma's mind. For the first time since her father had married, she wondered if being a stepmother was much fun.

I'll go tell her I'm glad she married us. I'll thank her for fixing it so we could go to Colorado. We'd never have got there without her. I'll—

But as she thought happily of all she would say, the side door creaked again. It was too late. Miss Kate had gone inside.

The gray light that comes before dawn made the familiar yard a strange mysterious place. The grape arbor was a dark cave. Stars glittered in the bottomless pit of the rain barrel. The kitchen lamp shone a sickly yellow.

Loaded to the mudguards, the Great Smith waited for its passengers. The black Pantasote top was raised for protection against the sun. Two spare tires were lashed to the back. Oilcloth-wrapped suitcases were strapped to the sides. The canvas water bucket was slung over the spare tires, where it dripped slowly. A chunk of ice had been put into the icebox on the running board, and it dripped fast. The cookbox was in the center of the back seat between the Miller girls; a tablet was on it for playing tick-tack-toe. Cots and the tent were piled on the floor, reaching to seat level. The Tourist Auto Kit was on top. Professor Miller walked around the Great Smith and shook his head. "I never thought we could do it. Get in, girls. Time's wasting."

They crawled in, taking the places they had agreed on yesterday: Maddy behind her father; Lou Emma back of Miss Kate. At once Maddy wanted to trade. When Lou Emma turned stubborn, she began to fuss.

"I'm hungry. We didn't have oatmeal."

"You hate oatmeal," Lou Emma said. "You always say you hate it."

"I hate it, but I'm used to it. And I'm used to sitting on the other side, and—"

"Papa, what am I supposed to do with my feet?"

"Unscrew them at the ankles and put 'em in your pocket." Professor Miller took out his watch. "What's keeping Kate? It's four fifteen. We ought to be on the road. Four sixteen."

"My feet are on the corn-meal sack," Maddy said.

"Don't! I packed the eggs in there," Lou Emma squealed.

She was too late. Maddy scooped up a mixture of raw eggs, shells, and corn meal, and threw it into the yard. She wiped her hand on the tent. "Gooooosh!"

"Four twenty," Professor Miller said gloomily.

Out the side door stepped Miss Kate wearing a long pongee motoring coat, the sleeves shirred at the wrists. Her hat was a full-gathered cap with a stiff visor, tied on with a flowing veil of pale green crepe de Chine.

The Millers applauded, Lou Emma longer and louder than either of the others. The memory of Miss Kate last night, weary and forlorn, nagged at her.

Why didn't I go tell her then what I wanted to? Now's too late.

Back of her goggles Miss Kate smiled. "I'm glad you like my outfit, but don't wake the neighbors."

"They'll never see a prettier sight at four twenty-one A.M.," Professor Miller said as he went to crank the Great Smith.

"Is it that late?" Miss Kate settled herself in the front seat, holding away from her a drippy jar of stewed apples Mrs. McKelvy had brought over "for the trip." "Let's get out of sight so we can eat these and not carry them."

"Throw 'em out," Maddy said. "I don't like stewed apples."

"They'd haunt me all the way to Colorado. It's the first thing she's ever given us, and we've got to eat them. Try one slice."

Lou Emma took one and made a face. "Not enough sugar."

"What'd you expect?" Maddy asked smugly.

"Couldn't we eat them right here in our own yard?" Professor Miller leaned wearily on the hood of the Great Smith. "I'd like to get started before noon."

"She said 'for the trip,' and she's sure to ask exactly where we ate them." Miss Kate sighed. "Oh, Cyrus, do drive out by way of the post office. I wrote Jesse last night and put the letter on the front seat."

Maddy reared up from the back seat. "Did you tell her where we're going?"

"Why—yes. I thought she should know how to reach us, in case—"

" 'In case' of what?" Maddy wailed. "She'll be over to Colorado Springs like a duck on a June bug, and it'll be all your fault."

Lou Emma threw in with Maddy. "She'll say we're dressed wrong and where are the caps she knit us last Christmas, and mine's in the missionary barrel on the way to the Fiji Islands. She'll ruin *everything!*"

"I didn't intend—" Miss Kate looked scared by the hullabaloo.

"Sanguine Saturnini!" Professor Miller slapped the hood, and the Great Smith reverberated. "Do you girls want to go on this trip, or don't you?"

Maddy collapsed on the tent and said meekly, "We want to go. Please."

"Please. We want to go." Lou Emma reversed the words.

"Very well." Professor Miller looked at them sternly. "I don't want to hear any more of this talk. Colorado is a big state. It is unlikely that we will hear anything from Jesse, but if we should—"

"Yes, Papa," Lou Emma said.

"Yes, Papa," Maddy said. "We will. We promise."

"Promise what?" Then he held up his hand. "No, don't tell me. It would take too long. Kate, will you forgive our girls' rudeness and retard the spark?"

With a pat for each girl, Miss Kate pulled the lever.

We weren't rude. Grown-ups want kids to tell the truth, but when they do, they're rude. Do you pull that thingamajig up or down to retard the spark? Tommy would tell me, but Papa would give me a lecture on gasoline engines.

The engine responded to the Professor's heave with a satisfying roar. The chassis quivered. The hand brake creaked. The Great Smith's big wooden wheels rolled forward . . . bumped over the culvert . . . stopped at the post office . . . then rolling faster and faster, the six-miles-per-hour speed limit forgotten, took the Millers toward the edge of town . . . toward Colorado.

It was astonishing the way Gloriosa disappeared. A town of five thousand plus a college, it dropped behind as if it didn't exist. Leaning out, the Miller girls waved good-bye at the tower of Old Main looming up from the campus. As they rattled over a bridge, Maddy spied a cluster of faded confetti.

"That's from the Three-State Auto Race," she told her sister.

Struggling for foot room, Lou Emma missed the confetti. "It seems like a long time ago. I can hardly remember it, except for Laura." She gave up the struggle and propped her feet higher than her head on the Tourist Auto Kit.

Maddy slid down and propped her feet on the back of the front seat.

"If Aunt Jesse could see us now!"

"Shhh. Don't mention her name. She's already caused us enough trouble. And you said she wouldn't know we were in Colorado when she was. You *pill!*"

"Lissen," Maddy said. "When you wake me up in the middle of the night, don't ever believe a word I say. Promise?"

"I'd just as well promise that as anything else," Lou Emma said. "You won't remember it anyway."

On either side of the road were Osage Orange hedges. Kansas law now said they must be trimmed to no more than four feet along the highway, but Gloriosa farmers hadn't yet heard about it. The hedges towered over them like two high green walls. Then the hedges dwindled. Professor Miller called over his shoulder:

" 'But westward, look, the land is bright.' "

The line of poetry vibrated in Lou Emma's head like a plucked guitar string. She whispered it over and over. Ahead the western sky was blue, cloudless, and brimming with glorious light. The world looked as it might have on the day of Creation. Meadow larks rose from the fields and flew whistling ahead of the Great Smith. Purple thistles and blue spiderwort crowded among the golden sunflowers.

A few rods ahead a man stood, holding a horse's head and gesturing to them. The Professor slowed the Great Smith to a crawl.

"Go slow, but git past as fast as you can," the man shouted.

The road was so narrow that Lou Emma could see

the rolling whites of the horse's eyes. Foam ridged his flanks. She was thankful when they got by.

"Horse-and-buggy roads," her father said. "Some day . . ." It was the Good Roads Boosters' dream—paved roads everywhere. It was crazy, but . . .

In 1910 the road was marked by two deep ruts, made years before by the steel wheels of farm wagons. Auto drivers had no choice but to drive in these six-inch ruts and wind from side to side as the wagons had chosen to go. Farmers were assessed so much road work per year. Townships furnished a horse-drawn road scraper to dig out the ditches, and a King drag to break the big clods into little ones. After a rain all auto driving would stop for two or three days. The Millers were lucky that no rain had fallen. It made the dust bad, but dust was better than mud any day.

After much study Professor Miller had chosen the route of the New Santa Fe Trail. It was clearly marked in the *Touring Guide* that Dr. Biddle had presented to the family. Along the road would be painted poles with a white band, eighteen inches broad, and the familiar cross and circle of the Santa Fe Railroad in the center.

Back in Gloriosa they had set the odometer—a mysterious dial on the Great Smith's dashboard—at absolute zero. It was the duty of the one who sat by the driver to hold the *Touring Guide* open, read the mileage on the odometer, check the listed landmarks, and keep the auto on the right road. Professor Miller scoffed at any possibility of getting lost:

"As long as we use logic—and the *Touring Guide*—we'll know where we are at all times."

Outside the known territory of Gloriosa, Miss Kate opened the *Touring Guide* at the marked page. She held the stewed apples away from the book.

"Four corners, turn left. Cross R.R., turn right. Next mile impassable in wet weather. Waycross 9.6 Bear right to bridge. Cross with care, loose boards."

Maddy groaned. "It sounds horrible."

"Like Pilgrim's progress through the Dismal Swamp," Lou Emma said.

Miss Kate read on: "Irregular four corners. 16.3 Jog right. 22.5 Jog left. Ford creek if not in flood."

"What'll we do if it is in flood?" Maddy asked but got no answer.

"Watch for stone windmill. 23.1 Bad dog at farmhouse." Miss Kate took off her goggles, and apple juice smeared the *Touring Guide*. "We'll have to stop and eat these apples, Cyrus. They're all over everything."

"They'll go down better at twenty miles per hour." He increased the speed.

"All right, girls. It's up to the females. Eat fast and don't drip."

Lou Emma took a slice. "They're not so bad."

"We're hungrier," Maddy said. "Gimme some more."

As they finished the last slice, the road forked. "Which way, Kate?"

Licking her fingers, Miss Kate opened the *Touring*

Guide; then she shook her head. "I guess I've lost my place. We were on page 87, but I don't know what page we're on now."

"We're not on *any page*. We're in the Great Smith, and we can't possibly be lost, and I asked you to throw out those apples at home."

"I think the next town is Hawkeye, Cyrus," Miss Kate said meekly.

"The name of the town is unimportant. It's WHICH WAY," he shouted.

"There's a man you could ask." Maddy pointed to a distant field.

In grim silence Professor Miller cut off the engine, disentangled his long legs from the baggage, and stalked toward the field.

"What's he so mad about?" Lou Emma wondered.

"My father hated to ask directions; I guess your father does, too. You take this chance to stretch your legs, and I'll study the *Touring Guide*."

Rubber-legged from having their feet higher than their heads, the girls staggered around a bit, then took off on the high center of the road. It was fun to run after sitting still. The air was sweet from a field of alfalfa in flower. Elderberry blossoms like white lace promised a harvest of fruit. A small box turtle walked confidently west. Lou Emma scooped him up. His bottom shell was yellow with brown markings.

"Every turtle ever born is marked different," Lou Emma said with awe. Tommy had told her this, but quoting Tommy to Maddy brought too much teasing.

"Turtles aren't born they're hatched, crazy." Maddy aired her knowledge.

"Let's take him to Colorado! He can be our mascot, like our toad last summer at Chautauqua." Lou Emma saw her father and ran back to him.

"Look Papa, we've got a MASCOT," Maddy yelled when they were within hearing distance.

It never failed. Maddy always got her nickel's worth in first.

"Isn't he darling?" Lou Emma waved the box turtle like a flag.

" 'Darling' is not a word I would use for a turtle, but he is quiet, and that's more than most of your pets are. Get in. We have to turn around."

"What for?" Maddy dodged the spank her father aimed at her.

"Because we missed Hawkeye by miles. I jogged right when I should have jogged left. Now we turn around and look for a red barn and a strawstack."

Turning the Great Smith on the narrow road was quite a trick. Twice Professor Miller killed the engine. Lou Emma nudged her sister and whispered, "Miss Kate's a better driver."

"Shhhh. Wait'll his birthday." Then Maddy said loudly, "What'll we name our good old turtle mascot? How about Tommy Turtle?"

"No," Lou Emma said. "How about Plutarch II after our toad last year?"

"Tarquinius Superbus, the last king of Rome," Professor Miller suggested.

But Miss Kate won by thinking of T. G., short for *Touring Guide.*

"We need a guide," Maddy said. "We've already been lost once, and Papa said we couldn't possibly get lost."

"Not lost," Miss Kate said. "Just on the wrong page."

"Excelsior!" The Professor shouted. "The yellow barn and the red strawstack!"

Lou Emma knew that his cross spell was over, now that he was mixing his colors to make them laugh. Maybe Papa had 'trip nerves,' too. Anyway he whistled as he drove, asked riddles, pointed out strange shapes in the clouds, and suddenly stopped and declared it was noon, and he was hungry.

"Hungry?" Lou Emma marveled. "I never heard you say that before."

"I never drove to Colorado before."

They spread a tablecloth on the ground and set out food. Fried chicken, deviled eggs, ham sandwiches, whole tomatoes, and a slightly squashed cake Mrs. Biddle had had Hilda make them "for the trip."

"Everybody was glad we left town," Maddy said, licking icing from her lips.

"Let's hope they'll be glad when we get back," Miss Kate said.

"Let's forget all about them and enjoy the moment," Professor Miller advised, and to Lou Emma this was the best way to do.

Except for Tommy, except for the birthstone ring.

They ate until eating any more was plain greediness

and went on eating anyway. Maddy gave T. G. a chicken heart. Lou Emma capped an ant hill with the white of a deviled egg and watched the black ants by the hundreds gang up to remove it. Miss Kate found a four-leaf clover under the tablecloth. Professor Miller took an old much-marked copy of the *Odes of Horace* from his pocket and read aloud.

" 'At the fit hour 'tis sweet to unbend . . .' "

Lou Emma forgot the ants and moved nearer to Miss Kate, who stroked her hair gently. Maddy sat in rare quiet. On and on, her father read, and it came to Lou Emma that she had never been as happy as she was right now, this minute. If only she could stop time and stay forever in this grassy pasture. Then in her memory she heard Miss Kate saying *Everything changes . . . The trick is to change with it.*

"But I don't want to change," she said aloud, and turned hot with embarrassment as the others looked at her. "Keep reading, Papa. Please."

But the spell was broken. Her father tucked the book back in his pocket. "Time to go," he said. "Time and the New Santa Fe Trail wait for no man."

By midafternoon the temperature in the back seat of the Great Smith must have been over a hundred. Waves of heat rippled in the clear air.

"My clothes are stuck to me." Maddy wriggled. "I wish I was made like T. G. and could carry my clothes on top of my back."

"T. G. can't ever change clothes. He's got to wear

brown and yellow all his life. S'pose he really liked blue best—or purple."

"Purple-turtle, purple-turtle, purple-turtle." Maddy made it a singsong. "Golly-molly, I wish we'd have a flat tire so we could get out an' walk."

Swissssh, thud-thump. The Great Smith slewed out of the ruts.

"But I didn't mean it! I was just talking!" Maddy quavered.

"Then you shouldn't 've," Lou Emma said. "But how'd you do it?"

"What are you gabbling about?" Professor Miller asked, climbing out of the Great Smith and surveying the flat tire on the right rear wheel.

"Nothing," they both answered, and Maddy added, "Sir."

"We have to change this tire and patch it. 24.8 miles to the next town. Go get some rocks to put under the wheels so I can jack up the rear end."

Searching for rocks, Lou Emma looked stealthily at her sister. "How'd you do it? Tell me, and I'll never tell, honest."

"But all I did was say— You heard me say—"

"Did you cross your fingers? Or look over your right shoulder?"

"You know I didn't. You saw me. All I did was—"

"Hurry up with those rocks!"

"Look!" Lou Emma lifted some ragweed away. An ancient wagon wheel was half hidden in the dirt. "I bet that came off a covered wagon."

They hurried back and dumped some rocks by the flat tire. "There's a wheel off a covered wagon over there," Maddy said impressively.

"Maybe your grandmother—" Lou Emma said to Miss Kate.

"I don't think these rocks are big enough," Miss Kate said.

"This is the start of the road to California," Maddy insisted.

"It could be off Evangeline Smith Lucas' own wagon," Lou Emma said.

"I suppose . . . it could . . . ," Miss Kate said unhappily. "I suppose."

"Drop your grandmother and get me the tire iron," Professor Miller shouted, as he slowly raised the rear end with the jack. "Wedge some more rocks under those front wheels, girls. GET CRACKING!"

They flew to do what he told them and came back staggering under the weight of the boulders. Miss Kate had the Auto Touring Kit spread out on the roadside and handed her husband tools as he called for them.

Sweating and swearing in Latin, he wrestled the tire from the rim. The Great Smith stood awkwardly on three wheels, like a rooster in the rain. With the tire off, they took the tube from the casing and searched for the puncture. A horseshoe nail was embedded in the casing; twisted into the thin canvas and rubber, it had turned back to puncture the tube. It took pliers to get it out.

"Now we'll patch the tube," Professor Miller

announced. Lou Emma and Maddy tried not to act as if Tommy had taught them how this should be done, but their father was too absorbed in the business to notice. "Girls, pump 'er up."

They took turns with the tire pump, and with listening for the hiss of escaping air that would tell them where the hole was. Maddy found it and had the honor of spitting on the spot, rubbing the spit around, and seeing the tiny spit bubbles that made her discovery certain.

"I've got special spit," she said.

To Lou Emma went the job of putting on the cold patch. They half filled the tube with air then and stuffed it back into the casing. Once more Professor Miller wrestled it onto the rim and turned the wheel around until the valve stem could be reached by the tire pump. The family lined up to pump the tire to its capacity. Up-down, up-down, they labored. Faces red, arms tired, hands grimy.

At last Professor Miller nodded. "That's enough."

Gingerly he let the wheel off the jack. They held their collective breaths, waiting, but it stood, tight and inflated. The girls removed the rocks as he repacked the tools. Straightening, he looked at his watch.

"One hour and fifteen minutes. We'll have to do better than that."

"We could," Maddy whispered, "but we had to be polite."

Miss Kate shook her head and put her finger on her lips.

I wish we'd brought Tommy, Lou Emma thought. *He'd sure be handy.*

Back on the road they hit a steep grade. The Great Smith's radiator began to boil. Wrapping his handkerchief around his hand, Professor Miller twisted off the radiator cap. A geyser of steam and water erupted. He sent Lou Emma to the back of the auto for the canvas water bucket. It was empty! A tiny hole and a trail of drippings showed what had happened.

"What'll we do?" she asked, half-scared to get the answer.

"I . . . don't . . . know."

Slowly the boiling radiator stopped. The only sound from the Great Smith was an occasional uneasy gurgle. The Millers sat in silence.

Then Miss Kate said, "Cyrus, would it run on tea?"

"I suppose so. If we had tea, which we don't. Or do we?"

"I brought along a jug for this afternoon. I thought it might be refreshing. Two quarts."

Professor Miller turned completely around and addressed the girls. "Hip-hip-hooray! Hip-hip-hooray! Hip-hip-hooray! KATE!"

They joined in with all their lungs, though Lou Emma tried to say "Miss Kate" and got laughed at.

Out came the brown jug, sweating coolness, and very slowly so as not to crack the engine block, which was still hot, Professor Miller poured the tea into the radiator. As the last drop went in, Miss Kate laughed.

"I just remembered, I almost brought chocolate milk instead, but Mrs. McKelvy asked me for any leftover milk we had as she was making cottage cheese."

"Thank goodness for Mrs. McKelvy," Lou Emma said, "but we don't have to give three cheers for her, do we?"

"No more cheers," her father said, "until we see how the Great Smith likes Orange Pekoe." He cranked the auto, and it went off purring on its journey.

"Let's write a letter to the people at Topeka that make the Great Smith and tell 'em about tea," Maddy said.

"Later," her father cautioned. "Let's find a farmhouse with a well and add some more water, quick. Two quarts is hardly a nip for this engine."

He turned the Great Smith into a grassy lane. Beside a weatherbeaten barn, a woman in a sunbonnet was shelling corn for some hens. Behind her was a windmill and a trough brimming with water. As they stopped, she pointed to a sign on the windmill: NO WATER FOR AUTOS. Then she turned her back.

"If that's not the hatefullest—" Maddy stormed.

"Shhh," her father said and got out of the Great Smith.

As she watched him walk toward the woman in the sunbonnet, Lou Emma gripped Maddy's arm in fear. "She might shoot Papa. She might put him in jail."

"Don't worry," Miss Kate said. "Cyrus can charm a bird out of a tree, if he puts his mind to it."

Swinging the water bucket, he circled around and came up facing the sunbonnet, smiling. He rocked back and forth on his heels, chatting, as if he were an old friend. It was no time at all until he was pumping water into the leaky canvas bucket and filling the Great Smith's radiator to overflowing. The woman in the sunbonnet followed him to the auto.

"The mister says you're Colorado-bound," she said amiably. "Seems like a long ways. I know a woman in Colorado, but I disremember her name. She's got buckteeth."

"If we meet her, we'll tell her how good you were to us," Miss Kate said.

"Oh, it ain't nothing. Like I told the mister, water's free an' b'longs to the Good Lord, but autos killed five hens, two shoats, and drivers tore down our fence to get pry poles to get outa the mud, so we made that sign."

"I don't blame you," Miss Kate said. "I would, too. Thanks again."

"You're welcome. But if I's you I wouldn't figger on driving tomorrow. It's gonna rain cats 'n' dogs 'n' red-tailed crawdads."

The girls giggled. Then they looked at the blue sky. "Rain?"

"Rain?" Professor Miller said.

"Yep. Old cat moved her kittens this mornin'. Benny the rooster crowed at sunset. An' I heard a hoot owl at daybreak. Stands to reason, don't it?"

"Thank you for the water." Professor Miller shook her hand cordially, covering up that he had not answered her question. "And good-bye."

Off they drove, trailing thanks out the back and waving to the woman, who stood waving to them. Then Maddy punched her father's shoulder.

"Is it really going to rain?"

"Certainly not. Mere superstition."

"Mrs. Wacker can tell about rain by her bunions," Lou Emma said.

"Her bunions come from wearing her shoes too small. What connection can that have with rain, Lou Emma? Use logic, logic."

Miss Kate spoke from the front seat. "Turtles crawl before rain."

"Et tu, Brute," he quoted with a groan. "Where do we turn?"

"Page 93. 'Turn left by green house.' But the only house is yellow."

"Yellow and blue make green. Maybe you're only seeing half the house."

But this was lost in the girls' shout of discovery. There, painted on a telegraph pole, was the first sign of the New Santa Fe Trail. It stood out boldly, and Lou Emma felt a sense of security on looking at the cross and circle she had seen so many times back in Gloriosa.

The woman with the sunbonnet was forgotten and the game of locating painted poles began. Even the driver played it, though the Great Smith swerved dangerously whenever Professor Miller was the discoverer. Other roads to the west also had signs painted on the poles. The Golden Belt was a broad yellow band. The Pike's Peak Ocean to Ocean Highway had red and white bands. It was Maddy's favorite. Sometimes when the road swerved away from the railroad and there were no telegraph poles the Good Roads Boosters painted the signs on rocks, trees, or barns.

As dark came on, they found a level place for the tent and prepared for the night. The cots were balky, but Professor Miller got them up, and Lou Emma spread covers while Maddy and Miss Kate fixed supper. On a small campfire—"My father said never build a fire bigger than your hat"—Miss Kate made coffee. The smell of it was as cozy as in their own kitchen in Gloriosa. They had tin cups of coffee with lots of cream and sugar, for the cream would be soured by morning and had to be used. Even the girls had coffee. They toasted leftover ham sandwiches on long sticks. Butter sizzled and dripped into the fire. Far off a hound dog bayed, and the lonesome sound made the camp seem safe and warm.

"We really are pioneers," Maddy said.

"Like Miss Kate's grandmother," Lou Emma said. "Tell about her again."

"No more talk," Professor Miller stood up and stretched. "Time to get to bed. How far did we come today, Kate?"

After a few seconds of bending over the *Touring Guide* Miss Kate looked up, her brown eyes big with wonder. "Nearly a hundred miles: 87.2."

"As the crow flies?" Lou Emma liked the old words.

"No. As the Great Smith bounces. Now get to bed, girls. Tomorrow's not far away."

In the tent Lou Emma took out the birthstone ring and put it under her pillow. She liked to think of it there, blue and shiny for her alone. The last thing she saw through the tent opening was her father and Miss Kate sitting on the cookbox, the firelight flickering on their faces.

It was a quarter past midnight when the rain began.

Chapter 10

"My cot's the only dry spot in the world." Lou Emma looked out at the streaming rain. Maddy had deserted her own cot because of a leak in the tent and was rooting her way in beside her sister.

"The Sahara desert's dry," she said.

"It's too far off from Kansas to count. Move over!" She shoved Maddy.

"I think it's slacking up," Miss Kate said.

"Why don't you people get a book and settle down?" Professor Miller looked up from the book he was reading.

"I can't read on an empty stomach," Maddy said.

"I'm starving," Lou Emma said.

"I never heard of anyone who starved overnight," her father said. "Feed your mind, not your stomach. Here's *Caesar's Commentaries.*"

Lou Emma looked at the book. "I'd rather starve."

"Very well, but be quiet about it. Remember, we are *all* responsible for leaving the cookbox out in the rain, and the icebox open."

"It really is slacking. There's a break in the clouds," Miss Kate said.

"There's some birds flying. That could mean something," Lou Emma reported.

"It means they want to fly." Professor Miller snapped his book shut. "I think you'd really rather believe cats, roosters, hoot owls than logic."

"But it rained," Lou Emma said stubbornly.

"Because of a juxtaposition of meteorological conditions."

Maddy winked at her sister. "Let's give 'im you-know-what."

Lou Emma took a deep breath. "In promulgating your esoteric cogitations—"

Maddy took over. "—and articulating your superficial sentimentalities—"

"—and amicable, philosophical, psychological observations—"

"—beware of platitudinous ponderosities," Lou Emma ended in triumph.

Miss Kate stared. "Where did you get that?"

"From me, unfortunately," their father said. "It's only 'say what you mean and don't use big words,' but they have never let me forget it."

"It's really stopped raining now," Maddy said.

"Let's go, Papa. If birds can fly, we can drive. Maybe."

"Maybe not. Look at that road." He took up his book and began reading.

The ruts were parallel rivers. The mud was a quagmire. Overhead the clouds were breaking, and a patch of blue sky widened. All at once the sun came out, and the girls and Miss Kate cheered; Professor Miller only turned another page. By noon not a cloud was in the sky, but the only cheerful member of the party was T. G., who breakfasted on a drowned grasshopper and a forgotten apple core.

"I'm going exploring." Miss Kate put down her tatting shuttle.

"Me, too." Maddy tore up the tick-tack-toe game.

"Remember, I won," Lou Emma said, coming too.

They squished around in the wet grass, Miss Kate with her skirts outlandishly high. T. G. was dunked in the pool of rain water that had collected in the icebox and proved he could swim. They buried a drowned bird and put muddy wild roses over its grave.

Miss Kate looked up suddenly. "There's a team and wagon!"

Professor Miller heard it, too, for he came out of the tent.

Plodding slowly through the mud, the team came opposite the tent. The driver lifted his hand. "Wet 'nough for ya?"

"Sure is," Professor Miller said. "How's driving?"

"Not bad, if you can find bottom."

"How far's bottom?"

"Don't know. Ain't found it yet." The team plodded past.

The Millers watched in silence. Then Maddy said, "He's moving, isn't he?"

"Yes, but he's driving a light wagon, and he has a team."

Lou Emma said, "The Great Smith has thirty horsepower, fifteen teams."

With one accord they turned and looked at the red auto. Compared with the wagon it seemed big, powerful, and able to do whatever was asked.

"Want to try it, Kate?"

"I'm ready whenever you are, Cyrus."

The girls jumped and shouted, and started rushing to pack. They soon found that putting the soaked tent back where it had been yesterday was like trying to stuff a whale into a goldfish bowl. When it was finally done, there was barely room for them under the Pantasote top. Then chains had to be put on the back wheels. The engine responded to the first cranking, and the chassis vibrated with power. Slowly, slowly but surely the Great Smith moved from the campsite out into the road.

"We're moving," Maddy squealed.

"Cross your fingers," her father called back.

"If we said that, he'd say it wasn't logical," Lou Emma whispered. But she and Maddy crossed their fingers and held their breath as long as they could.

Squish. Swoosh. The auto settled into the ruts. The water had run off now, but the mud it left was slicker than a pair of greased pigs. Swoooosh.

The mud flew in all directions. The elegance of the Great Smith's red paint turned to a drab coating. The steering wheel had a life of its own. No matter how hard the Professor held it, it turned this way and that. The engine raced; the chains bit into the mud and inched them forward. The odometer measured one mile . . . two miles.

Maddy peered over the side. "Kansas is the biggest mud pie in the world."

Lou Emma looked out her side. "Knee-deep, knee-deep, jug-a-rum." She tried out Tommy's frog talk and thinking of him slipped the birthstone ring on her finger, then put her hand in her pocket as Miss Kate glanced back.

All at once a terrible clatter began. Clank! Clank! Clank! Metal was striking metal.

"Oh, Papa, what is it?"

"One of the cross-links on the chains broke, and it's hitting the mudguard. I hope that's all it is. How far to the next town?"

"About four miles. Arvin, Kansas. Pop. 768. No garage." Miss Kate's voice faltered a little on the last two words.

"We don't need a garage. A blacksmith could fix the cross-links. Or I could with a little baling wire. If we can make four miles—"

Another cross-link snapped. Clank-smack! Clank-smack!

A little rise in the road was ahead. In the deep ruts there was no traction. The wheels spun, and great sheets of muddy water rose and fell. The windshield was caked with mud. Professor Miller leaned from the side to see. Mud speckled his face; his goggles were useless.

With terrific effort the Great Smith groaned up the rise, but the pull made the engine boil. Puffs of steam came from the radiator cap.

"Have to fill the radiator." The Professor pulled on the brake.

"Cyrus! The mud!"

"Can't be helped." He slid down into the black ooze. It was ankle-deep.

Slogging back to get the canvas water bucket, fortunately still full, he dribbled water into the steaming radiator. Once again they started forward. The slight downgrade eased the engine's labor, but now the Great Smith began to skid. Not fast, not spinning, but slowly, certainly, the big red auto headed for the ditch.

"Look OUT!" the Miller girls screamed.

"Look out yourselves!" their father yelled back.

T. G. slid across the tent and into the front seat. Miss Kate screamed and flung him back. Maddy fielded the box turtle, and handed him to Lou Emma as the Great Smith lurched into the ditch. The wheels turned, but there was no motion forward. Every turn dug them in deeper.

"Papa, we're in up to the hubcaps," Maddy leaned out and reported.

"We'll have to get out and push," he said. "Girls, take off your shoes and stockings. No, Kate, not you. I want you in the auto. Can you do as I say?"

"I'll . . . I'll try to, Cyrus."

"Very well." He gave her a short lesson in driving autos out of a ditch. "Do you understand? Race the motor. Engage the clutch when I shout. Ready, girls?"

"Yessir." They were barefoot, and trying not to laugh as their father told Miss Kate all the things

Tommy had already told her. They stepped from the running board into the warm ooze of the mud. Deeper and deeper they sank, to where the mud was cool, and it slithered up over their ankle bones.

"It's between my toes." Lou Emma shivered with delight.

Maddy churned her feet up and down. Bubbles of air burst with a loud sucking sound. "I bet I could go down to China."

"I'll take the right side; you girls take the left. When I tell Kate to engage the clutch, you shove against the mudguard as hard as you can."

They skated through the mud to their appointed place. Lou Emma skidded and grabbed Maddy for balance. Her hand left a muddy track on her sister's sleeve. Maddy bent low to get the most strength in her push. Her braids hit the mud.

The racket of the racing motor began. Up . . . up . . . up . . . it became a deafening roar. Braced against the Great Smith, Lou Emma felt her bare feet going deeper, searching for bottom. The smell from the exhaust made her cough.

"Now!" Professor Miller shouted.

Miss Kate pushed down on the clutch pedal and pulled the throttle low. The big wheels spun. Gobs of black greasy mud flew backward, plastering all three pushers.

"Ugh!" Maddy staggered from her post.

"Gagh!" Lou Emma spit mud. "My mouth was open."

But the Great Smith had not moved from the ditch.

"Try it again, Kate." The Professor was intent only on the auto. He had no idea how he looked. The long linen duster was a sheet of mud; his face, though higher above the surface than the girls' faces, was sprinkled with mud gobs.

"Papa's got the black smallpox," Maddy jeered.

"Papa's got a polka-dot mask on," Lou Emma said. "And look at your duster! Miss Kate'll have to dye it black."

He looked down and laughed. Then he scooped up a handful of mud and threatened to throw it at them.

"If you throw, we will." Maddy got a fistful. Lou Emma reached for a soggy Osage orange and rolled it in the mud.

"Pax." Professor Miller dropped the mud, tried to wipe a clear space around his mouth, and came out spitting. "Kansas tastes terrible."

"What's going on?" Miss Kate craned from the driver's seat. When she saw them, she fell back against the seat and laughed until she had to wipe her eyes with the crepe de Chine veil. "If Dr. Biddle could see you now!"

"Or Aunt Jesse," Lou Emma said.

"She'd die dead," Maddy said with satisfaction.

"Come on in, Kate, the mud's fine," Professor Miller invited.

"No, thanks. We need one clean Miller for contrast."

"It really is fun." Lou Emma squirmed her feet down farther. "I hate to be a little bit dirty, but I like bein' dirtier 'n anybody else in the whole world."

"Back to your posts," their father ordered. "We've got to get out."

Over and over the wheels spun, but not one inch did the Great Smith move. Each time it settled a little farther into the ditch. The running board was level with the mud. Professor Miller took the hatchet and went to cut brush to put under the back wheels. The girls took T. G. and found a log by the roadside and sat down to rest from their pushing. T. G. came out of his shell and waddled down the log, east to west. Whenever the girls turned him around, he sprawled and kicked until he was headed west again.

"He knows the way to go," Lou Emma said. "I'm glad he's our mascot."

"Fine mascot! Getting us into a loblolly like this!"

"He wasn't driving." Lou Emma took up the box turtle, let him kick in mid-air, and put him down. "I've just thought of something."

"Well, don't try to rent T. G. for a pet," Maddy warned.

"That was your idea, and you know it. This thing I thought of is out of the Sunday School lesson for last Sunday, so it's bound to be good."

"Wasn't it mean of 'em to have the Willing Workers' picnic while we're away?" Maddy said. "I'll bet Adelaide was at the bottom of that. Fried chicken, and Mrs. Biddle promised two of Hilda's devil's food cakes."

"Stop it." Lou Emma heard her stomach growl.

"The lesson was about Noah's Ark. Genesis 8:8 was the memory verse."

"Watermelon in the afternoon," Maddy mourned.

"The memory verse was, 'Also he sent forth a dove.' "

"Fried dove might be good," Maddy said.

"Well, we don't have a dove to fry. . . . I mean to send forth. You've got me all mixed up. But we do have T. G."

"Fried box turtle? Gagh! I won't eat it. Anyway T. G.'s our mascot."

"Nobody wants to fry him. I'm talking about sending him *forth,* like Noah sent forth the dove. And the dove brought back an olive branch."

"What'd we do with an olive branch?"

"If an olive branch is good enough for Noah, it's good enough for me," Lou Emma said in exasperation. "I found T. G., and I'm going to *send him forth.*"

After some more argument, Maddy agreed, but once she had, she began to have plans of her own. Finding a fairly clean handkerchief in her pocket, she put the letters SOS on it with pencil, poked T. G.'s left hind leg through a hole in the corner, and gave him a pat on the shell.

"What'd Noah say when he let the dove loose?"

"The Bible didn't say."

"He's bound to 've said something." As usual Maddy had taken over Lou Emma's plan. Now she made passes over the box turtle and chanted, "Go forth, T. G., and bring us help. And be quick about it."

"I don't think you should 've said that last. Noah wouldn't 've."

"How'd you know? Maybe he said, 'Hurry up, dove, or I'll wring your neck and bring back some fried chicken while you're bringin'.' "

Lou Emma felt that this might be sinful talk, but she giggled anyway. " 'And devil's food cake,' " she added. She put T. G. and his handkerchief on some thick grass. After a long minute he began to move, dragging his white flag with him, slowly and confidently going west.

Professor Miller came back with an armload of brush, and they wedged it under the wheels. Once more Miss Kate gunned the motor, but now a stinging rain of brush struck the pushers. A sumac branch grazed Lou Emma's chin and drew blood.

"No more of that," her father said as he dabbed peroxide on the place. "I'm going to walk into Arvin for help. You girls stay with Kate."

"Look, Papa, look!" Maddy pointed dramatically up the road behind him.

A man driving a high-haunched team of mules came toward them. "Howdy. Figgered you folks'd be about ready for a mite o' help."

It was the man who had passed them in his wagon, back at the campsite. He announced his name. "Harvey L. P. Stuckey. And my team, Jenny an' Jump."

"But how did you know we'd be stuck, Mr., uh, Stuckey?" Miss Kate asked.

"City folks ain't got the patience to wait out these rains. They got to get on the road. Me an' Jenny an' Jump, we haul a half dozen out after every rain."

Lou Emma was indignant at the criticism but pleased to be called "city folks." She watched as Mr. Stuckey hooked a trace chain to the tow rope that came in the Auto Tour Kit. When he said the word, the big mules leaned into their collars and pulling steadily brought the Great Smith onto the high center of the road. Then the Millers scraped as much mud as they could from themselves and their clothes, and got back into the auto. With Professor Miller at the wheel, and Mr. Stuckey standing on the running board, Jenny and Jump hauled the Great Smith about a mile to where the road was a little less muddy. Lou Emma was thankful for the Great Smith's sake that they passed no one who knew them; it must be terrible to be an auto hauled by *mules*.

"Think you c'n make it?" Mr. Stuckey said.

"I think so. Now, what do we owe you?"

"Not a thing. Glad to help out."

"But we'd like to pay you." Professor Miller put his hand in his pocket.

"Whatever you say, mister. Dollar . . . or so."

Lou Emma watched as her father put two one-dollar bills in Mr. Stuckey's hand where they were at once swallowed up and placed in his overalls' pocket.

Money sure goes fast on a trip.

As her father went around to crank the Great Smith, Lou Emma jumped from the back seat and ran over to

Mr. Stuckey at the side of the road. "Did you see a box turtle when you came after us? A little small box turtle with a handkerchief on his left hind leg?"

"Well, Sis, I guess I seen a dozen box turtles today, but I never looked to see if none of 'em was carrying handkerchiefs. Maybe so."

"Hurry up, Lou Emma!"

"Thank you, Mr. Stuckey. And thank Jenny and Jump."

By the time Lou Emma scrambled back in beside Maddy, she felt it was right and fair to say that Mr. Stuckey had seen T. G.—at least, *maybe*.

Arvin, Kansas, Pop. 768, was a compact town with two blocks of stores and a white clapboard two-story hotel. A long porch with rocking chairs ornamented the front. Half a dozen men sat rocking, occasionally spitting over the railing.

"Drummers out of Kansas City," Miss Kate said knowledgeably.

"I hope they have a dining room and a good hot supper," Professor Miller said. "A little longer, and I'd 've eaten Jenny and Jump, bless their high-priced help."

"If after a rain, he hauls out a half-dozen autos a day at two dollars each, he's making a lot more than most farmers," Miss Kate said.

"Well, we live and learn. Now let's go in and get supper."

"We can't go in all over mud, Papa," Lou Emma said.

"They wouldn't let us in." Maddy wriggled a mud-covered leg out the car.

"The girls are right, Cyrus. We'll have to take a room to get cleaned up, and if we do that, we might as well sleep here and start fresh tomorrow."

The girls began to babble happily. Neither one of them had ever stayed in a hotel. Maddy was sure that none of the other Willing Workers had, and she was already planning how she would tell them about it if they dared to mention the picnic.

Professor Miller looked at his muddy duster. "You go in and get rooms, Kate."

"Rule Number One," Miss Kate said. "We'll all go together."

Their adjoining rooms were on the second floor. At the end of a long hall was—wonder of wonders—a bathroom. It served the entire floor, and Miss Kate warned the girls to be quick about getting cleaned up. But the big white tub with its flow of warm water and the elegance of the lavatory were too much luxury to hurry over. Three times as they splashed, scrubbed, and dabbled, an unknown person rattled the door and went away grumbling.

The birthstone ring Lou Emma had put on just before the first cross-link broke was caked with mud. No one, not even Miss Kate's sharp eyes, could have noticed it on her hand she was sure. She rubbed it on the cake of Fairy soap, soaked it, brushed with a nailbrush, and at last set it on the windowsill.

"Miss Kate'll make you give that back," Maddy said. "Ella Johnson back-in-Ohio's mother made her give back a ring just out of a Crackerjack package."

The door rattled again. "You kids!" It was a man's voice and mad!

Smothering giggles in towels, the Miller girls tried to hurry. They buttoned each others' backs, but the buttons and the buttonholes kept coming out wrong. At last they rushed out the door, but Maddy had forgotten one garter and had to go sidewise, holding up her stocking as she ran, and Lou Emma left her slippers unbuttoned and lost them three times. They collapsed on the lumpy bed, out of breath from laughter.

The dining room had an enormously high ceiling decorated with pressed metal squares. Tables were set for ten. There were white tablecloths, only a little stained now as they were changed every Sunday. At each place a napkin folded in a fancy design was tucked into a water glass.

"Do we have to fold 'em back like that?" Maddy muttered.

"Sure. Notice how so's we can do it right," Lou Emma said.

A waitress stalked over to their table. "Rozbifrozporksteakanunions."

"Roast beef," Professor Miller said. Lou Emma marveled at his understanding.

"The same," Miss Kate said.

"The same," Lou Emma said.

"Not me," Maddy said. "I want that last you said—nunions."

The waitress blinked. "Howzat?"

"My daughter wants steak and onions," Professor Miller translated.

Maddy's face fell. Lou Emma knew she didn't like steak and onions, but nothing would get her to admit it now. Could she change plates with Maddy? Or would that hurt the hotel's feelings?

"Coffeeteaormilk?"

"Iced tea for everyone." Professor Miller simplified matters.

The waitress disappeared and came back with a tray as big as a wagon wheel. It was loaded with dinner plates of meat and potatoes, glasses of strong iced tea, and what looked like dozens of small oval birdbaths filled with corn, peas, stewed tomatoes, green beans, cabbage, and slithery okra.

After starving all day, Lou Emma thought she would wolf the food down, but once it was in front of her she felt queasy. The smell of the cabbage in the oval dish went all through her. She shuddered and pushed it away. Maddy was staring at a mound of fried onions heaped on a slab of fried steak.

"I'm going to be sick," Maddy whimpered.

"No, you're not." Miss Kate spoke pleasantly but firmly.

"Me, too," Lou Emma said. "I can't eat anything, or I'll—"

"No. Sip some tea . . . eat a bite of bread . . . swallow slowly . . . sip some tea . . . take a taste of corn . . . swallow slowly. . . ." As Miss Kate talked, she did exactly what she was telling the girls to do. Cautiously they followed her example.

The bread filled the watery spaces in Lou Emma's mouth and kept her from swallowing nothing all the time. The corn was good, right out of the field. The tea was strong, but she liked it. The queasiness went away; her appetite came back. She cut off some roast beef. It took a lot of chewing, but it had a safe, familiar flavor. BMK roast beef was her favorite Sunday dinner to cook.

"Halvers?" Maddy asked, pushing over her plate.

They divided their two kinds of meat, and Lou Emma took a few onions to show the hotel that somebody liked them.

The waitress came over and spoke to Miss Kate.

"There's a lightning-rod salesman got a room by yours, and he found this ring on the bathroom windowsill. He thought it might b'long to you folks."

She held out the birthstone ring. Lou Emma's backbone turned icy.

"No, it's not ours." Miss Kate took the ring and looked at it.

"He said to ask the folks with the girls that hogged the bathroom so's he couldn't shave—if you'll excuse me saying so."

"I'm sorry the girls took so long." Miss Kate smiled and handed back the ring. "Tell him it must belong to some other girls."

If Lou Emma let the waitress go, she would never see the birthstone ring again. If she spoke up and claimed it, Miss Kate would make her give it back to Tommy. Mothers, stepmothers, all grown-ups everywhere, thought rings from boys were poison—or something. Even Crackerjack rings. She didn't need Maddy to tell her.

"If nobody claims it, I'll give it to my girl," the waitress said.

Hot dislike of the unknown girl burned in Lou Emma.

"Was she born in September? That's a birthstone ring, for September people. It's awful bad luck for anybody else to wear it."

Lou Emma could feel the surprised looks of her family focused on her. She took a bite of okra, punishing herself with the slithery stuff. *Why did I make that up about bad luck? It's a lie. No, it's a fib. NO, it's a lie.*

"My girl was born in April. I wouldn't want her to have bad luck." The waitress shifted the ring to her other hand, not knowing whether to go or stay.

"Lou Emma," her father said, "do you know something about this ring?"

She ate more okra. Tiny pink seeds slipped from her fork.

"Louisa Emmaline?"

"It's my ring; I was born in September. Honest I was."

"I know when you were born, but I don't know where you got the ring."

"Tommy Biddle gave it to me," she said in a low voice.

"Why didn't you tell us about it?"

"I . . . I . . ."

Miss Kate said, "We've all been so busy with the trip, there's hardly been time. I'm sure Lou Emma intended to tell us."

She grabbed at the straw her stepmother offered. "I did. I really did. Intend to tell you, I mean. Only everybody was so busy all the time."

"But to take a ring from a boy—" her father began.

Lou Emma interrupted. "Tommy's not a boy. He's our first friend in Gloriosa."

"—and to conceal it in this way."

"I intended to tell you. Miss Kate said so; you heard her."

Looking at the waitress, Professor Miller said, "A misunderstanding. It seems to be Lou Emma's ring, after all."

"Shoot, mister, you can't tell me nothin' about girls. Raised five and startin' in on granddaughters. They give you lots of trouble, but they're worth every bit of it." She handed him the ring and hurried away.

Shaking his head, he passed the ring to Miss Kate. "This is your department."

"It's a pretty ring." She looked at it admiringly. "Take better care of it, Lou Emma."

"I will, I promise." Her eyes swimming with gratitude, Lou Emma waited while Miss Kate slipped the birthstone ring on her finger.

It was fun to walk up and down Arvin's Main Street and feel superior because they were "city folks" from Gloriosa. It was fun to sit on the porch and talk to the waitress' daughter who was born in April. It was fun to decide which man was the lightning-rod salesman who had been cheated out of a shave. Even the lumpy bed was fun, because it wasn't their bed but was part of their first night at a hotel.

"It's sure been a long day," Maddy said, punching her pillow. "The rain, and T. G., and Jenny and Jump, and all."

"Taking a bath in a bathtub, and eating supper, and getting the birthstone ring back. We ought to have a memory verse for this day."

"You make one up." Maddy yawned. "I'm too sleepy."

"I already did," Lou Emma said. "Here it is: 'We sent forth a turtle.' "

Chapter 11

"Let's pretend yesterday never was." Maddy looked at the sunlight streaming down on as much of Arvin, Kansas, as she could see from the bed.

"We can't. If we do, then we'll have to say T. G. is still in the back seat, and he can't be because we sent him forth." Lou Emma wriggled to fasten her back supporters to the very top of her long cotton stockings. "These stockings have shrunk, or I've grown."

"We've both grown." Maddy bounced out of bed. "Aunt Jesse wouldn't know us if she met us in the middle of Colorado. We were little kids in Ohio."

"Big enough to come to Kansas. And to run the house, BMK."

"Well I for one don't think you're big enough to get a ring from a boy." Maddy looked at her sister disapprovingly.

"Tommy's a friend," Lou Emma insisted. "Your friend as much as mine."

"Then why didn't he give me a ring?"

There was no ready answer, so Lou Emma went back to Maddy's earlier remark. "Aunt Jesse would, too, know us. We haven't grown all that much."

But it was hard to get Maddy off the subject. "Papa wouldn't 've let you keep that ring, BMK."

"There's the bell for breakfast. Let's skedaddle."

The waitress hurried over to them. She seemed like an old friend now. Her girl's name was Maude, and she had more freckles than Tommy Biddle.

"HamneggsbaconneggsMaudesaysHello."

Proud to translate, Lou Emma said, "Tell Maude hello from us. We'd better wait for Papa to order."

"Not me. Ham and eggs. Eggs with their eyes open," Maddy said.

"The same," Lou Emma said.

"Coffeeteaormilk?"

"Coffee," Lou Emma ordered boldly. The waitress frowned.

"Yourfolksletcha?"

"Sure." Maddy tossed her dark braids.

"Lots of sugar 'n' cream, please," Lou Emma said. The waitress left.

"Why'd you say that?" Maddy fumed. "She'll think we're babies."

"Why'd you say 'eggs with their eyes open'? What's it mean?"

"I heard a man say it." Maddy pointed with her spoon.

"Copycat." Lou Emma said with outward scorn, but inwardly she wished she had heard the man and ordered that way first. "Here's Papa an' Miss Kate."

"We ordered coffee," Maddy said quickly to head off any fuss. "You let us have it night before last."

Professor Miller shook out his napkin. "One of the problems of rearing children is that a parent is never permitted to do a thing once. It must be done for time and eternity."

"It's too nice a morning to worry about eternity," Miss Kate said. "Coffee twice won't hurt the girls, but twice is plenty."

"Yes, ma'am," Lou Emma said meekly.

"I don't like it anyway," Maddy said.

Their breakfast arrived. Slices of fried ham and eggs fried on one side only, the yolks a bright, staring yellow.

"Is that all 'with their eyes open' means?" Lou Emma asked.

"Sure. I knew it all the time." Maddy peppered her eggs heavily.

Mounds of German fried potatoes were on the table, hot biscuit, and a center dish of comb honey. The Millers ate heartily and in silence.

As they left the dining room, the Professor spoke to the owner of the hotel. "Think we can get on the road today?"

"Yep. Y'see, Arvin's on a hogback. Rain dreens off quick. Some towns you'd of been swamped for a week. Come back 'n' see us."

"Backnseeus." The waitress waved good-bye.

"You come see us," the Miller girls called. "And bring Maude."

On the road again, mud flaked from the Great Smith as they bounced over chuck holes. There had been little rain past Arvin, and the road was passable. Miss

Kate studied the *Touring Guide;* the Professor whistled Yale's famous "Boola, Boola." The girls propped their feet high and chewed on beeswax from the comb honey.

"Everything's new every day on a trip," Lou Emma mused.

"Back home the stuff that you did wrong on Monday's still hanging round on Tuesday," Maddy agreed.

In Gloriosa I was mad at Miss Kate. Now I can't remember why. She said I could wear the birthstone ring all the time, not just sneak it out.

"I love my love with an A." Maddy started a word game. "Because he's Adorable. I hate him with an A because he's Awful. I'm going to take him to Alaska and feed him on Apples."

"I love my love with a B. . . ." Lou Emma took her turn. Far down the alphabet she knew T would be on her turn and that Maddy was trying to trap her into saying, "His name is Tommy." She had Thad, Timothy, and Theodore all ready.

The painted poles of the New Santa Fe Trail were frequent now. Each time one was located Miss Kate gave out jelly beans all around. Maddy traded hers for licorice, and her tongue turned black.

At Peabody they bought gasoline at the livery stable. As the man poured it from a can into the tank under the front seat, he told them that the state once operated a silk farm in the town. There was still a grove of mulberries for the silkworms to feed on. Lou Emma couldn't believe it. Silk was from China.

"It's true," Miss Kate said. "My grandmother had a piece of the silk."

"Your Grandmother Evangeline?" Maddy leaned forward.

"That had a baby in the covered wagon?"

But Miss Kate had opened the *Touring Guide,* and Professor Miller was whistling "Boola, Boola" so loudly no one could be expected to hear the questions.

The day grew hotter as they rolled into Newton where the big Santa Fe railroad engines puffed and snorted. At Hutchinson the garage man told them about the salt mines and gave the girls chunks of rock salt as souvenirs. Lou Emma kept licking hers on the sly until she got so thirsty she had to take a drink from the canvas water bag. Outside Noblesville they ate a cold lunch. Professor Miller took a cat nap under a cottonwood tree instead of studying H-O-G. At Sylvia they had a flat tire.

But that was only the beginning. At Zenith they had another and took a chance at getting to Stafford with only one spare. Between the two towns one of the thin tires, overheated and overloaded, burst with a noise like a shotgun blast. The Great Smith lurched, slithered, and came to a halt inches away from a deep ditch. The last spare went on and lasted about three miles. They limped in to Kinsley on the rim.

"There's the hotel," Lou Emma said hopefully.

"I love hotels," Maddy said, one night having convinced her.

Miss Kate shook her long-visored cap. "Three

dollars a night is too much. We said we were going to camp, and we'd better stick to it. Rule Number Three, everybody."

It was clear dark before the man at the Sunflower Garage patched all the tires and persuaded the Professor to buy a new one to replace the blowout. Getting the tent up by lantern light plus the light from the Great Smith's acetylene head lamps was not easy. But once it was done and they were cooking supper over the campfire, the pleasure of camping out returned. Maddy and Lou Emma begged to be allowed to sleep in the Great Smith for one night.

"I suppose it's all right," Miss Kate said. "We'd be here close."

"We'll be safe," Maddy said. "I'll look after us."

"I'm the oldest," Lou Emma said. "I'll look after us."

They dragged the covers up and spread them in the back seat. It was fun to poke heads out the side into the starry night and watch for falling stars. Little sounds in the grass and brush near the Great Smith sounded just scary enough to be fun. Lou Emma went to sleep first while Maddy was still telling the ghost story of Rawhead and Bloody Bones.

Clutching hands around her shoulders waked her.

"Wake up," Maddy quavered. "What's that?"

A long-drawn eerie sound that ended in unearthly yelping came from the darkness. Again and again it broke loose, seeming to come from all sides.

"Rawhead and Bloody B-B-Bones," Maddy whimpered. "Coming after us."

"It c-c-can't be. That's only a st-story."

"How do you know?" Maddy burrowed her head under the covers.

Once more the sound rose and fell and ended with its screeching yelps.

"I'm going after Papa," Maddy's voice mumbled through the covers.

"Hear the coyote, girls?" Miss Kate called from the tent. "We used to have them on the farm. They were always stealing chickens."

"Coyote?" Lou Emma asked, remembering that Tommy had killed one and collected a bounty on it to help buy Swish. If Tommy could kill one, maybe it wasn't anything to be scared of. Not terribly scared. If Miss Kate knew what it was . . .

"Get up, Maddy. It's nothing but a coyote."

"Are you sure?" Maddy came out of the covers, slowly, the way T. G. did. "But . . . what's a coyote?"

"I don't know really," Lou Emma said, "but it steals chickens, and I'm not going to be scared of a chicken thief."

"Me, neither," Maddy sat up and looked around. "Here comes Miss Kate."

"They make a terrible racket," their stepmother said, walking through the dark as if she were back in her millinery shop. "But they're really cowards."

Once again the coyote's crying shivered along Lou Emma's backbone, but it didn't seem terrible any longer. Miss Kate popped her head inside the auto.

"You two look snug as bugs in rugs," she said,

tugging the cover so it would be divided evenly. "If the coyote comes closer, throw a pillow at him."

"Shoot-a-mile," Maddy said scornfully. "Let 'im come. We don't care."

In the morning as they looked out from the Great Smith, Maddy and Lou Emma decided that the trees were smaller and the hills were flattening out. On one side was the Arkansas River, the *Touring Guide* related. Before noon they came to Spearville, near where Coronado crossed the river in 1541.

"Why'd he come to Kansas, clear from Spain?" Maddy asked.

"Quivera," Professor Miller said and refused to explain, telling Maddy to look it up.

"It's a trip," Maddy said. "We're s'posed to have fun, not look up stuff all the time. If you were something besides a teacher, we wouldn't have to."

"It's because I'm a teacher that we're going to Colorado College," her father said.

"It's because you're a *good* teacher," Miss Kate put in. "And you're going to write a good textbook. And—Jelly beans!"

The painted pole she had spied was right outside of Dodge City.

"The West begins here," the Professor said flatly.

Maddy and Lou Emma looked around, but they saw nothing more exciting than a bony hound dog nosing across the road. When the dog jumped a jackrabbit, they were more interested.

"Six bits on the rabbit," Maddy whispered.

"You haven't got six bits," Lou Emma whispered back.

"If I had, would you bet on the dog?"

"Girls, stop buzzing and listen," Miss Kate said. Professor Miller cut off the engine and began to talk.

Papa ought to write a book about Kansas. He makes it so . . . lively.

It was no longer 1910 as he talked: the busy city ahead of them on the plains disappeared. In its place were the buffalo hunters, the gamblers, the gunfighters, the freighters, the soldiers. Far away, Lou Emma thought she heard the bellowing of the herds of Texas longhorns—three hundred thousand cattle in one season—and the shots and shouts of the cowboys as they came roaring into Dodge. He told about the Masterson brothers, Ed and Bat, who tried to tame the town, about Wild Bill Hickok, and Wyatt Earp, and many more.

"I wish we'd come here then," Lou Emma sighed.

"No Great Smith then." Her father patted the steering wheel. "And there was one year money was so tight they used buffalo bones for cash. You'd like that?"

"Oosh, goosh, no," Lou Emma said.

Five miles beyond, they came to old Fort Dodge. Once the commanding officers had been Custer, Miles, Sheridan. Now it was an army veterans' home, sleepy and peaceful, where old men whittled in the sun. A mile farther on, they saw some shade trees big enough to sit under and eat cheese and crackers washed down with buttermilk bought from a nearby farm. For dessert they had ripe, ripe, running-down-the-chin peaches. The Professor took out a book; Maddy challenged Miss Kate to checkers. Left on her own, Lou Emma wandered back down the road.

The soft dust held many kinds of tracks, including the marks of the Great Smith's tires. She teased up a doodlebug with a ball of spit, mixed with dust on the end of a grass stem.

Grasshoppers ticked in the dry weeds. Turning her back on the Great Smith, Lou Emma looked toward the West and felt that her father must be right. It did begin here. The treeless plains, the arching endless sky.

In the tall grass at the roadside she caught sight of a grayish-white stone. Pushing through the ragweed, she found a lone gravestone. The top was rounded, and words were carved on the front. Kneeling in the grass she read:

"EDWARD DORRIS. DIED JULY 21, 1865. AGE 31

Edward thou hast gone to rest
In this far country of the West.
Brothers and friends, we mourn and weep.
Thou in the tomb dost sweetly sleep."

A swelling in her throat could not be swallowed down. How foolish to cry for a man you didn't know, dead long ago. And yet . . . and yet . . .

"Don't cry, Lou Emma." It was her father on his knees beside her.

"I'm not crying. I'm just—Oh, Papa, it's so lonesome."

"Death is always lonesome," he said, stroking her bowed head. "But think about the Santa Fe Trail the way it was in the old days. Wagons coming and going, troops from the Fort, Indians . . ."

"Was he in history, Papa?"

"Lou Emma, for every General Custer or Wild Bill Hickok there have to be a thousand Edward Dorrises. These are the people who do the work, the soldiers that fight the battles, the homesteaders that settle the country. They're the stuff history is made of. Their names may be forgotten, but their work won't be."

"I won't forget his name," Lou Emma said and gave a swipe to her eyes with the back of her hand. Before they left, she pulled some cardinal flowers and laid them on the top of the gravestone. The fierce sun wilted them in moments, but from the side of the Great Smith Lou Emma watched the spot of red color as long as she could see it. When it disappeared, she waved good-bye.

"Dodge City to Garden City 52.5 miles, less five miles to the Fort," Miss Kate calculated. "Can we make Garden City this afternoon?"

"Certainly. I don't see any turtles crawling to predict rain."

"By the way, where is T. G.?" Miss Kate looked back.

"Him?" Maddy asked as if she had never heard of T. G.

"We haven't seen him for a while," Lou Emma said truthfully.

Professor Miller said, "Sounds to me as if you threw him out."

"Oh, Papa! We wouldn't do that."

No more was said from the front seat, but in the back seat Maddy nudged her sister. "Why don't we just out 'n' out tell him what we did?"

"I don't know." Lou Emma struggled for the real reason. "I hate for grown-ups to know everything I do 'n' think 'n' breathe."

"Cimarron, Ingalls, Charleston, Pierceville—" Miss Kate stopped as she read out the list of coming towns. "Why I've got a cousin in Pierceville. Cousin Jennie Coonrod. We'll spend the night with them."

"Four people? Dropping in uninvited?" Professor Miller said.

"You don't know Cousin Jennie. She'd be hurt if we didn't drop in."

The Coonrods appeared to be as delighted to have company as Miss Kate had said they would be. They were a big family living in a big rambling unpainted house a few miles outside of Pierceville. They took the Millers in with open arms, fed them, bedded them down, and sent them on their way next morning loaded with gifts of food.

At the fence, where Maddy and Lou Emma got out

to open and close the gate, a dozen horses galloped past, manes and tails streaming in the wind. In the distance a herd of cattle grazed. As they closed the gate, Maddy suddenly grabbed Lou Emma's arm.

"Know what? We've spent the night at a *ranch.* A real live *ranch.*"

They raced back to the Great Smith and poured questions over Miss Kate. "Was it a ranch? Really? Like in that book *The Virginian?* And they're your own kinfolks?"

"Yours, too," Miss Kate said. "Rule Number One. Why, I guess it's a ranch. Cousin Ed has about a thousand acres, counting what he leases."

"A thousand acres?" Lou Emma gasped.

"Jerusalem my happy home! Pass the jelly beans," Maddy said.

The sandy land of western Kansas made driving easier. The road ran due west, arrow-straight. Twenty miles an hour and the Great Smith hummed happily. At thirty the engine began to boil. Waiting for the engine to cool, the girls got out for a leg-stretcher. Up jumped a jackrabbit.

" 'Humpin' - jumpin' - jackrabbits!' " screamed Lou Emma in Tommy's favorite words.

"Catch 'im!" Maddy shrieked.

The jackrabbit flipped his black-tipped ears, put on a burst of speed, and disappeared from sight. The girls were left huffing and puffing.

"That story about the Tortoise and the Hare, that's

in the *First Reader,*" Lou Emma said. "I don't believe it. T. G.'d never catch up with that jackrabbit."

"Aw, people write stuff like that to fool kids when they're little. It's like Santa Claus and storks and Easter Bunnies."

"Oo-*oo*-gah!"

They ran back to the car. By now the Great Smith had begun to seem like home. Out on the plains of western Kansas, Lou Emma had a need of one fixed point to keep from being swallowed up in the immense distances around them. The big red auto provided that, for it carried the people she cared for most. The back seat where she and Maddy "lived" was very much like their bedroom, BMK. It was a rat's nest of rocks, books, apple cores, crumpled tick-tack-toe games, broken pencils, faded wild flowers, and graham cracker crumbs. Daily the girls told each other they would clean up, but there was always something to do that was more fun. And always something new to see.

Yellow ant hills a foot high of yellow clay grains. Wide-winging hawks. Banks of orange day lilies. Prickly-pear cactus with its million thorns. Prairie chickens darting across the road. A rattlesnake that coiled and rattled in a dry stream bed. And early in the morning as they left the Coonrod ranch a deer fled across in front of them.

So the back seat stayed a mess. Miss Kate didn't clean it up the way she did their room. Not even when Rule Number Three was broken into umpty-nine pieces did she say a word. Everything on a trip was different.

"You've got that silly Tommyish look on your face," Maddy accused her sister. "Whenever you think about him, you look like a simp."

Lou Emma said Tommy was a million miles out of her head. But, of course, now that Maddy had brought up his name she began to think about him.

The birthstone ring had been much admired by one of the Coonrod girls. *Solid silver,* she had said, her eyes round in her round face.

Did solid silver make a ring more important? What about solid gold? Miss Kate's wedding ring was solid gold. Had Tommy really meant something special when he gave her the ring? *Then why didn't he say something special?*

"Painted pole!" Maddy screamed in her ear. And there it was, on Lou Emma's side, where she ought to 've seen it first. The New Santa Fe Trail was leading them right to the edge of Kansas, but Lou Emma had to admit that if they depended on her for directions they might end up in . . . Gloriosa.

Garden City was the next town. Then on a good dragged dirt road they drove through a series of windswept towns: Holcomb, Deerfield, Lakin—and past Lake McKinnie—into Kendall, and at last into Syracuse.

Syracuse was blessed with a Harvey House. As they drove near the railroad station, they heard the loud clanging of a triangle, struck by a man wearing a long white apron and a chef's cap. It was suppertime, and the Santa Fe train had stopped to give its passengers a chance to eat. Suddenly the Millers were out of the Great Smith and hurrying with the train passengers into the Harvey House.

It was fun because it wasn't planned. Even the slightly grubby look of the Millers compared to the passengers on the Santa Fe didn't make them feel bad. Actually, they felt a little superior, like veterans of a war to those who were only "play soldiers."

The black-uniformed, white-aproned waitresses fairly flew through the room. Orders were taken and returned with a speed that was unbelievable. The glistening china and the heavy silverware felt awkward after tin spoons and "fingers-were-made-'fore-forks" meals.

Miss Kate had broiled liver and bacon. Maddy could not understand it. "You mean you're paying *money* to eat *liver?* They'd have to pay me."

Seventy-five cents was the price of the meal, but Maddy had heard it was a rule of the Harvey Houses that any child who sat in a high chair was served for half-price. She wanted to try to fit herself into the high chair, and only her father's stern "No" stopped her.

The food was hot, good, and served in the best style. In spite of the train outside on the tracks, there was no air of hurry. A wire from two stations ahead had warned the restaurant crew how many might be expected. The head waitress, known as the "wagon boss," inspected every table and even every rosebud in its silver vase. The only thing that went awry when the

Millers were there was the entrance of a late passenger *without a coat.* This was strictly against Harvey House rules, but they were prepared, and the "wagon boss" handed the man a black alpaca coat before the astonished eyes of the Miller girls.

"Perfectly correct," the Professor said to get ahead of their remarks. "A man's coat is a civilizing influence. Suppose he wanted to dine without trousers?"

The triangle banged; the train whistled; and the Santa Fe passengers filed back to the long cars. The Millers finished their supper almost alone as the waitresses set up the tables for the next train.

Back in the Great Smith, Miss Kate wondered if dining in luxury was going to spoil them for camping out.

"It was real nice," Lou Emma said, "but—"

"Me, too," Maddy said, not waiting for her to finish. "I like our way best."

They drove on to Coolidge, Kansas, and the sun was still in the sky, the clouds pink and gold. There was a pleasant grove of trees near the edge of the town. Professor Miller stretched his fingers, cramped from holding the wheel. This was the longest stretch of driving the Millers had done. He cut off the engine.

"Shall we camp here?"

"I know how tired you are, Cyrus," Miss Kate said, "but it's only two miles to the Colorado State Line."

"Let's go," Maddy shouted.

"Let's go NOW." Lou Emma jumped up and down.

"All ABOARRRRRD," the Professor mimicked the

conductor of the Santa Fe. "This train leaving now for ColorADO. Kate . . . retard the spark."

Settling herself in the back seat, Lou Emma said, "Whyd' you say that all the time? Miss Kate's not going to forget."

This brought on a lecture as to what would happen if the spark were not retarded. Broken wrist . . . arm . . . shoulder. Maddy groaned.

"Papa, you've talked more'n two miles worth already."

"We could be in Colorado this minute," Lou Emma said.

Very deliberately Professor Miller lighted the acetylene lamps, lest darkness should overtake them. Darkness came quickly on the plains. Only then did he crank the Great Smith, and off they went, Miss Kate leaning toward the odometer so as not to miss the magic moment. The speedometer needle reached for thirty, quivered, fell back, reached thirty, and *stayed.* Recklessly the Great Smith hurled them forward.

"Faster." Maddy leaned from the back seat.

"Faster," Lou Emma shouted from her side. The warm wind whistled past her ears. The horizon was endless. The world was spinning around the sun, and the Great Smith was spinning around the world.

The sky went from pink to flaming red. The red ball of the sun dropped suddenly out of sight. The Great Smith hit a chuck hole, jerked out of the ruts, and the *Touring Guide* bounced from Miss Kate's hands. She scrambled for it in the bottom of the front seat and came up with her nose almost on the odometer. She threw the *Touring Guide* into the air and shouted:

"Colorado! Hooray! Colorado!"

Professor Miller braked hard. The Great Smith raised a great cloud of dust and swerved to the right. He switched off the engine, and the sudden quiet rushed at them. In the quiet Lou Emma heard her father's words.

"We've made it, Kate. Thanks to you."

A sour taste in her mouth and a twist of inner pain brought back to Lou Emma with a rush the feelings against Miss Kate she thought she had left behind in Gloriosa.

We could've done it, BMK. *He's forgotten coming in the Great Smith was my idea. He's forgotten our own mother. She'd have done it, too.*

"Well, girls?" Professor Miller asked.

Maddy had jumped out into the road. Lou Emma put her face against the back of the back seat and did not answer. Miss Kate patted her ankle, and she jerked it away.

The silence lasted too long.

"What's going on?" Professor Miller turned clear around.

Still Lou Emma didn't answer. It was lucky that at that moment Maddy thrust her face back into the auto; in the dim light her lower lip curled down.

"It's exactly like Kansas," she said. "Not one smidgin different."

Chapter 12

Very early, before the others stirred, Lou Emma slipped out of the tent to look around. Maddy was wrong, dead wrong! Colorado was *not* exactly like Kansas.

For one thing, Colorado was colder. She shivered, and wondered where she had packed her sweater. For another thing, that small creature slipping through the grass was no jackrabbit. Back in Kansas she and Maddy had counted 267 jackrabbits in one day's travel, so she felt she knew what they looked like, and this was a different animal, a different shape. A black-tipped tail flickered around some bunch grass, and Lou Emma began to run on tiptoe so as not to scare the whatever-it-was. But the sun was not up; the light was dim; and all of a sudden she stumped her toe on a mound of dirt and went down on the bare earth.

She wasn't hurt; she knew she wasn't hurt. All her legs and arms worked. But under her ear was a chittering, chattering racket below the ground. Something was making an almighty fuss! As she scrambled to her knees, she saw that right across from her, on the mound where she had tripped, a small indignant face had popped out. Its bright eyes, twitchy whiskers, and prominent teeth were on the mound level; then they began to rise, and below them a grayish tan furry body stretched upward nearly a foot tall. The creature and Lou Emma stared at each other, both astonished. Then Lou Emma laughed and stood up, rubbing her knees, and quick as a wink, the creature disappeared.

"Lou Emma! Thank heavens, you're all right!"

It was Miss Kate hurrying across the prairie. In seconds her arms were around Lou Emma. The sweet scent of rose cologne was in her hair. The lingering resentment Lou Emma had carried over from the night before suddenly went away. She smiled at her stepmother.

"Did you see it? I don't know what it was, but it *fussed* at me."

"All I saw was you, down on the ground, and I thought—" Miss Kate gave Lou Emma a little squeeze. "Never mind what I thought. But don't let anything happen to you; I couldn't stand it."

It must have been the sun that jumped up over the horizon, for Lou Emma saw the world turn bright and glittering. She pointed at the mound.

"He was right there. But there's another—and another—and another—"

From where they stood the ground to the west was dotted with mound after mound, and as if on signal a small furry sentinel popped up on every top and began to bark, chitter, squeal, and squeak.

"Prairie dogs," Miss Kate said. "And those mounds are their houses. Go call Cyrus and Maddy. This is a sight to behold."

As the light grew stronger, the prairie dog town came into full view. There must have been fifty mounds. Up and down popped the owners of the mounds, chattering at the intruders, talking to each other, and diving out of sight as soon as any of the Millers came close.

"I'm going to catch one," Maddy decided. "Can I keep it, Papa?"

" 'May I keep it?' Yes, you may keep all that you catch. Kate, let's make breakfast."

Over and over the girls sneaked up on a prairie dog, but they caught nothing but dust for their trouble. They tried using a laundry bag as a net, but it didn't work any better. All at once they saw a "prairie dog" stationed on a mound take wing and fly away.

"Jerusalem!" Maddy dropped the laundry bag. "Did you see that?"

"We ought to catch that one and take it back to EKCC for Science."

"Uh-uh. They'd put it in a bottle. But let's go tell Papa."

"—and it flew away," Lou Emma said. "It had wings."

"Sounds like a burrowing owl." Professor Miller handed them tin plates of Spit-in-the-Eye—bread with a hole in the middle and an egg fried in it. "They share homes with prairie dogs. They're night hunters, and the prairie dogs are day hunters, so it makes a good arrangement."

"Like last year you taught History in daytime and Astronomy at night."

"Or like Moss's Ice and Coal," Miss Kate contributed. Then she said, "Before Lou Emma found the prairie dog town, I was adding up the grand total of miles we have come. We are now four hundred, sixty-four and six-tenths miles from Gloriosa, Kansas."

The Millers sat with something like awe silencing them. Every single mile the Great Smith had carried them safely. They had seen the sun rise and set, eaten food grown on the land, sweated in the heat, and dug out of the mud. They had talked to strangers and left feeling acquainted.

Miss Kate put the open *Touring Guide* aside and bowed her head. The sun touched her brown hair with radiance. She said: "Bless the Lord, O my soul, and all that is within me, bless His holy name."

Three "Amens" followed her words.

Holly was their first Colorado town. Sugar beets were a new sight for the Millers. The big coarse green leaves stretched in long rows. By the railroad tracks they saw the sugar mills that towered over the town.

"See, it's different from Kansas," Lou Emma said.

"Salt in Hutchinson, sugar in Holly. What's the diff?"

"Put salt in the cocoa, and you'll find out."

Another thing different was the way the roads ran. In Kansas they were arrow-straight. In Colorado they wound around by the lay of the land or the needs of the ranchers. Fences crossed the roads, and gates had to be opened, *and closed.*

There were buggies, wagons, and men on horseback but few autos. Out of Amity they caught up with a Winton Six and ate its dust until it turned off at Granada. Near Grote a Premier roadster whirled past them; the veiled and goggled occupants waved and laughed. On the back of the Premier was a banner: EXCUSE OUR DUST. Not only dust but gravel struck the Millers in the face, and the Great Smith's windshield got a deep pockmark in the glass.

Professor Miller swore in Latin and shook his fist. Miss Kate said the driver should be jailed. The girls spent the next five miles inventing other punishments for him. But when they found the Premier outside Lamar, broken down in the ditch, they stopped to help. Autos were too few and far between to leave a fellow driver in the lurch—even if he had thrown gravel in their faces.

Lamar had cement sidewalks, a library, and five hotels. The man at the Grange Garage said there were fifty autos in Prowers County, and he predicted a hundred in five years. He warned them about the road out of La Junta. "Scrub timber, range country. Carry extra gas, water, an' tires."

"We keep going uphill," Lou Emma said. "We go up and up, but we don't ever come down. There's just another hill."

"Mountain country," her father said. "We've been climbing since Dodge City. The Great Smith knows it, if you don't."

"I want mountain mountains," Maddy sketched a jagged outline. "When'll we see 'em, Papa? What'll they look like?"

"Teddy Roosevelt said, 'The Rockies beggar the English language.' A history teacher couldn't describe them if a President couldn't."

"A prize for the first one to see the mountains." Miss Kate held up a sack of jawbreakers bought in Lamar. "Winner take all."

It wasn't the jawbreakers Lou Emma wanted; it was the sight of the mountains, the *really* mountains. She leaned from the Great Smith and stared ahead. Maddy leaned from the other side. Clouds were low on the horizon. Time after time Maddy shouted, "Mountain!" but each time it was only a cloud.

"I can't tell a mountain from a molehill," she admitted.

Lou Emma's eyes ached with the distance and the dust. She was glad when they stopped in Las Animas for a leg-stretcher. As she and Maddy walked around, a man pointed out an ancient stagecoach in a livery barn. "Horace Greeley rode in that, back in 1859. Ever hear o' him?"

"Yessir. He said, 'Go West young man and grow up with the country.' Our father teaches History, and he told us—"

But Maddy dragged her away. "If you get Papa and that old coot together, we'll never get to Colorado Springs. I want to see the mountains, and I want to see 'em first, first, first."

But Lou Emma wanted to see them first, too. As they got back on the road again, it seemed to her that she would rather beat Maddy at this than at croquet.

To the south the clouds were darker. It might be about to rain. Surely not before she saw the mountains. *Go away,* Lou Emma willed the clouds. *Go. Now. Scat.* But no matter how she willed them away, the clouds remained. She blinked her eyes to rest them from staring.

High, high, the dark clouds towered; low, low, they came down to rest on the edge of the world. They looked solid enough to touch . . . to climb.

To climb? To climb?

Lou Emma looked north to clear her vision; then she looked south. The clouds hadn't moved one single bit. They must be . . . they had to be . . . She licked her lips and opened her mouth.

Maddy, watching Lou Emma, shouted, "MOUNTAINS!"

The Great Smith came to a throbbing halt. The Millers stared at the Spanish Peaks. Far, far to the south they reared their massive shape against the horizon. A blue-purple haze surrounded them. They looked exactly as mountains should.

"Good for Maddy. She saw them first," Professor Miller applauded.

Miss Kate handed Maddy the sack of jawbreakers, looking at Lou Emma as she did so. There was a question in her look, but Lou Emma pretended not to see it.

I won't be a tattletale. Why did I sit here like a ninny?

"I won, I won, I won!" Maddy jammed jawbreakers into her cheeks until she looked like a prairie dog with mumps. "I won, I won," she kept mumbling.

"Did you?" Miss Kate asked.

"Didn't she?" Professor Miller turned to his wife.

"I said it first. I said—" Then all at once Maddy spit the jawbreakers into her cupped hand and threw them from the auto. Tears welled in her eyes. "Lou Emma saw the mountains first. All I did was see her see them."

She emptied the sack of remaining jawbreakers into Lou Emma's lap.

"Good for you, Maddy," Miss Kate said. "Good!"

But Maddy was not ready to be comforted. Still crying, she said, "I stole your mountains, Lou Emma. I'm sorry, honest I am."

Love for Maddy came rushing back, taking the place of the anger she had felt a moment before. Lou Emma gave her sister as much of a hug as she could manage, and the jawbreakers rolled all over the floor.

"Don't cry, Maddy. There's a lot of mountains. We'll go halvers. You get the next batch."

It was enough, she knew now, to have been the first one to see the mountains. Winning can be inside as well as outside. She retrieved a jawbreaker from a tin cup; it was orange-flavored, her favorite. Miss Kate smiled at her, and that was better than the candy.

They crossed the long bridge over the Arkansas River and camped that night near Rocky Ford.

"Cantaloupe for breakfast," Professor Miller promised.

The famous Rocky Ford melons were right in season. Sweet, luscious, fragrant, they seemed to spread their aroma over the whole town. The Millers ate and ate, and bought more to carry along. Miss Kate scraped out the seeds of the melon voted the *very best* to carry home to the McKelvys for their garden.

On the stretch between Rocky Ford and Nepesta they got into a song-fest. Maddy started with "Forty-nine Bottles Hanging on the Wall," and insisted that each bottle be taken down and hung up again. Lou Emma who had trouble with the simplest tune tried an old song Mrs. Wacker had taught her, "They Say It Never Rains in Kansas." Remembering the mud, they made a joke of it until she wouldn't even try to sing it any more. Miss Kate knew all the verses of "Clementine" and kept them busy with the sad tale of ". . . a miner, Forty-niner, and his daughter, Clementine. . . ."

As they started the last mournful chorus, "O my darling, O my darling, O my darling Clementine . . . ," the right front tire blew out. For almost two days they had had no tire trouble. Professor Miller blew out his breath.

"Our last good tire. How far to Pueblo, Kate?"

"At least thirty miles."

"Jumping Jupiter! I wish I'd kept count of the tires I've patched. Everybody out."

The Professor wearily set the jack. The girls

brought out the rocks to wedge under the wheels. They carried these with them now, for good rocks were often in short supply in prairie country.

The sun was blistering hot. The metal on the Great Smith could have fried eggs. Patching tires had long ago lost its novelty. Lou Emma cast about for something to pass the time. She looked at the rat's nest of the back seat.

"I'm going to clean this out."

Maddy stuck out her lower lip, prepared to resist. "What for?"

"Cat fur to make kitten britches," she snapped, knowing the old smart-aleck answer would only make Maddy madder. On her side of the auto she began to reach in and throw things away, careful not to come near the jack.

Away went the wilted wildflowers, saved for a "collection" that never existed. Away went seven apples cores and five peach stones. She had saved the peach stones to carve them into rings as the old soldiers did at Fort Dodge. Maddy picked up a peach stone and threw it at a goatsbeard plant, scattering the winged seeds to the wind.

"Here's the rock salt from Hutchinson." Lou Emma licked it. "Tastes like Lot's Wife."

"Nobody in the Bible tasted her that I know of. What's that?"

"Bread 'n' butter. We fixed it for T. G."

"Smell it. I bet it's a peanut-butter sandwich from our supper at Ingalls, Kansas."

"Smell it yourself." Lou Emma tossed the rock-hard morsel to Maddy. To her horror her sister began to eat it. "Stop! It's dirty."

"Tastes good."

"It's prob'ly poison."

"S'pose the Great Smith really was a covered wagon, like we talked about at home? S'pose we ran out of food? I'd eat it then, wouldn't I?"

Miss Kate, standing by her husband said, "I think I'll walk down the road a ways. I need the exercise."

Lou Emma watched her stepmother go. "You made her leave, talking about covered wagons. Miss Kate can't *stand* covered wagons." She reached into the auto and began throwing away again.

"Stop!" Maddy grabbed her hand. "That's my rock."

"It was on my side." Lou Emma pulled loose and threw the rock. Maddy rushed after it. "Say, there's my cactus. I thought it was lost."

"It's *my* cactus," Maddy said. "I've still got splinters from it in my thumb." She went to her side of the Great Smith. "I'm going to clean up, too. If I don't, you'll throw out half my stuff and swipe the other half."

Lou Emma didn't answer. She had found the small white box that held the birthstone ring. A shell-shaped fossil was inside. A *brachiopod,* her father had told her; it came from the great sea that had once covered western Kansas. She was going to take it to Tommy.

The Professor finished the tire and straightened to ease his back. "All done, girls. Hop in, and we'll pick up Kate."

They started for the back seat, but he said, "Get in the front with me, Lou Emma, and retard the spark."

"Yessir." She climbed into Miss Kate's place as her father walked forward.

Only half of what he said had penetrated her thoughts about Tommy.

Maddy, who could almost read her sister's mind, began to sing, very softly: *"Tommy was a Welshman, Tommy was a thief, Tommy came to my house and stole a piece of beef. . . ."*

"You stop that!" Lou Emma turned, furious. "And it's not 'Tommy' in the song, it's 'Taffy' and you know it and—you make me sick."

She jerked herself around just in time to see her father whirl the crank.

With a coughing snarl, the thirty horses of the Great Smith kicked. The engine bucked against itself; the crank jerked backward. Professor Miller staggered away, his right arm limp, his face a sickly white.

In that split second, time stopped, and from some part of her memory Lou Emma heard her father's directions in full:

"Get in the front with me, Lou Emma, and retard the spark."

"Papa!" Maddy screamed and went tumbling from the car.

But Lou Emma, horrified at what she had done, sat rigid. She couldn't even look at her father. Far down the road she saw the pongee coat and the visored cap Miss Kate wore. She squeezed the horn bulb.

"Oo-oo-GAAAAAH!"

Then she jumped from the Great Smith and ran down the road.

"Come quick," she choked out to her stepmother. "I broke Papa's arm."

"Don't run, Kate," Professor Miller said hoarsely as they got near enough to hear him. "Don't run."

"Hush." Miss Kate took hold of his right arm that he had cradled in his left. She moved it slightly. He groaned, and sweat popped out on his forehead. Maddy was crying, but Lou Emma had no tears, only dry-eyed misery.

"I did it, I did it." She said like a parrot with only one sentence.

"Stop talking about yourself. It's your father we must think about," Miss Kate said sharply. "Find my green scarf. *Quick.*"

As if cold water had been flung at her, Lou Emma gasped, stopped talking, and walked to the front seat of the auto. The green scarf was there, neatly folded, on top of the *Touring Guide*. She handed it over.

Why would she care about a scarf with Papa hurt?

With strong quick hands Miss Kate tore the scarf, end to end. The silk screamed. She bound one half around Professor Miller's arm, not stopping when he groaned but going right on as if she didn't hear him. The other half she fashioned into a sling to hold the injured arm, tying it at the neck. Then she spoke to the girls. "We've got to get him to a doctor."

Maddy wept louder than ever.

"Can't drive," Professor Miller said. "Should've taught you, Kate." He shook his head unhappily. "Should've . . . should've . . ."

For the first time Miss Kate faltered. It was Lou Emma who stepped in front of Miss Kate and spoke to her father slowly, distinctly, as if he were a small child or a deaf person.

"Miss Kate can drive, Papa. Tommy taught her how. It was supposed to be a birthday present for you, next week. It's come early, that's all."

He looked puzzled, frowned.

"Kate can drive? And all the time I was telling her what to do when we were stuck in the mud, she knew already?"

Miss Kate took his good hand. Her face was flushed. "Yes, Cyrus, I knew already. But it was for your birthday. Please don't be angry."

"Angry?" he said at last. "I was never so thankful in all my life. Best birthday present I ever had."

They helped him into the front seat. Miss Kate took the wheel.

"Maddy," she said, "you may crank this first time."

But Maddy struck the hood with her clenched fists. "The Great Smith broke Papa's arm. I won't touch it. I hate it. I hate every bone in its body."

"Illogical." Professor Miller's lips were white. "My fault."

"No!" Lou Emma cried out. Then she said to Miss Kate, "I'll take first turn cranking. I can do it."

But the crank looked menacing, hanging loosely at the front of the engine. Up close there was something scary about the big brass-rimmed radiator and the head lamps glaring like angry eyes. A smell of hot metal and oil breathed out. Gingerly she took hold of the crank.

Miss Kate leaned from the auto. "I've retarded the spark, Lou Emma. Be sure to remember what Tommy said about not putting your thumb under."

Tommy's name gave her confidence. Tommy had taught her; he wouldn't teach her wrong. She gripped the crank handle, thumb carefully on the outside of her handgrip. She tugged upward, straining at the crank; then shutting her eyes, gritting her teeth, and putting every ounce of strength into her arm, she turned the crank . . . over. It caught on the first try. The engine coughed. Miss Kate adjusted the gas flow, the familiar four-stroke chug-chug-chug-chug began.

"Good work," Miss Kate called as Lou Emma climbed in behind her. For an instant she felt a flash of pleasure, but a glimpse of her father's face, set against the pain of his arm, made her burrow in the back seat where at last she began to cry.

They spent the night at a hotel in Pueblo. The doctor in Avondale said the Professor had a simple fracture but he'd be better off for a night in bed. He put on a splint, complimented Miss Kate on the green-crepe sling, collected three dollars, and called in the next patient.

It was a long, long night for Lou Emma. Her father had told her to stop worrying, and he had told her he knew she was sorry, and he had told her that most people who crank autos get a broken bone in the course of time. But still the burden of what she had done weighed heavily on her. Especially with Maddy sleeping the sleep of the unburdened just beside he .

If Maddy hadn't sung that song about Tommy . . . If Miss Kate hadn't walked down the road . . . If Papa'd said it over just once more . . .

There was no use in all this, she told herself sternly. There was nobody else to blame. It was like playing hide-and-seek when suddenly you find all the hiding places are taken up, and you run from one to the other, and there's no place—no place at all.

The hotel was near the enormous plant of the Colorado Fuel and Iron Works. All night long, wagons rumbled past; the smoke stack belched black clouds; and the eerie light of the blast furnace flickered on the dark sky.

Suppose Papa dies!

She sat up in agony, her arms wrapped around herself. From far away, as far as Fort Dodge, she remembered the gravestone of Edward Dorris beside the Santa Fe Trail. She remembered the words cut on it: "Edward, thou has gone to rest / In this far country of the West . . ." How easy it was to say "Cyrus" instead of "Edward." Do people die of broken arms? "A simple fracture," the doctor had said. But he might have been trying to fool them or to "spare the family," as she had read in a book someplace.

And it's all my fault.

A gentle tapping at the door, hardly more than the scratch of a kitten, brought Lou Emma out of bed. She ran through the dark room and flung the door wide. A gas jet burned in the hall, and in its dim light she saw Miss Kate.

"Is Papa . . . dead?"

"Good heavens no, Lou Emma. Whatever made you think—" Miss Kate came into the room closing the door behind her. "He's asleep and snoring. The doctor gave him something to make him sleep, but then I couldn't sleep because I was afraid of bumping into his arm, so I remembered you had a rocking chair in here, and I . . . Lou Emma, surely you didn't think . . . ?"

In her misery Lou Emma was aware of arms around her and the scent of rose cologne. In spite of the warmth of the night, she was shivering.

"I d-d-d-don't know what I th-th-thought. I was so sc-sc-scared. And it was my f-f-f-fault."

"Get under the covers right now." Miss Kate led her to the bed and poked her in, unceremoniously rolling Maddy out of the cocoon she had made from the bedclothes. Once she had Lou Emma tucked in, she pulled the rocking chair over by the bed and sat down. Little by little Lou Emma's shivering stopped. "There. That's better."

The dark was all around them, except for the line of light under the door and the flickers from the blast furnace. It was easier to talk in the dark. Lou Emma reached for Miss Kate's hand and found it reaching for hers.

"Why did I do it? I love Papa. Why'd I hurt him?"

"You didn't mean to. You weren't thinking. That's all."

"If anything happens to Papa, I'll—"

"His arm is going to get well. It's mending right now, this minute."

"But it was my fault."

"Yes, but now it's over. Stop punishing yourself."

There was a long silence.

Lou Emma sighed. "I'll try."

"Good. Now go to sleep. I'll sit right here by you."

Squeak-uh-squeak went the rocker, *squeak-uh-squeak*. It lulled Lou Emma into a doze, but each time sleep came near, she jerked awake.

"I can't sleep. Everytime I do, it happens all over again. Miss Kate, would you talk to me about when you were a little girl?"

In a low voice, so as not to wake Maddy, Miss Kate began.

"We lived on a farm in western Kansas. . . ." She told about her mother, her three pretty sisters, and her father, and about how she was always "his girl." The rocker squeaked comfortably. Miss Kate told about pulling tail feathers from the prize rooster to trim doll hats; she told about the pet skunk that followed her to Sunday School and got in a fight with a dog under the church. "Phew!"

Lou Emma giggled sleepily. Miss Kate told about climbing into a boxcar on a dare and how the train started up and her father had to drive nine miles to bring her home.

"Was he mad?" Lou Emma wondered.

"Of course he was. And it was right in the middle of haying, too."

Squeak-uh-squeak went the rocker. Outside the wagons rumbled, but that was no longer frightening, only a part of the night.

"Still awake?" Miss Kate whispered.

"Mmmmmm," Lou Emma mumbled. "Some."

"I had a little Indian pony named Dan. Once my

father sent me on Dan to put out some salt for the steers he had on grass in the north pasture. The gate was barbed wire and hard to close. I left it open, thinking I'd close it on the way back."

" 'On the way back,' " Lou Emma echoed to show that she was awake.

"Dan got to racing jackrabbits, and we had so much fun we came home the other way. It was late, and I went to bed right after supper. In the night I waked and thought about the gate only—I went back to sleep."

She was quiet so long that Lou Emma roused herself to say, "Wha' happened?"

"Well, the steers got out, and got into some green cane and ate it. They died of bloat. Every single one. *My father's whole year's work.* I cried and cried. I must have cried for a week, and one day he said . . ."

"I'm awake, Miss Kate. Please tell me."

"Well, he said, 'Kate it's time you buried those steers. Stop hauling 'em around by their tails.' That's all. But I stopped crying, and I've remembered it all these years. I try not to haul dead steers around."

"Yes, ma'am," Lou Emma said. Then she found Miss Kate's hand again. "I remember your father at the wedding. He was real nice."

"Just like your father," Miss Kate said. "Now go to sleep."

This time Lou Emma slept.

Chapter 13

Colorado Springs was a welcome sight. Six hundred and forty-three and eight-tenths miles the Great Smith had brought the Millers, and they were ready to get out and stay in one spot. As the girls had predicted, Miss Kate was a better driver than her husband. From Pueblo they had come through sagebrush country to the town of Fountain, and now they were approaching the rise that would become Mount Washington. Past that, they saw the great green lift of Cheyenne Mountain.

"Glorious!" Miss Kate waved a gauntleted arm.

"Look out!" Professor Miller said for the tenth time.

"The air!" Miss Kate breathed in, deep.

"Don't breathe, Kate. Just drive."

"There's too much to see to take time to breathe," Lou Emma said.

She was right. Everyplace they looked was something new, exciting, and as different from Gloriosa as chalk from cheese. General William J. Palmer had located Colorado Springs at the very foot of the Rocky Mountains. Pike's Peak, called "the Peak" as if no other existed, rose above it, and the whole great range of mountains rolled back into the distance so that grandeur and beauty were everywhere in sight. From all over the world people had come there to live. At one time Colorado Springs was nicknamed "Little London." One of the boasts of the city was, "Three hundred and ten days of sunshine each year." Another was, "More millionaires per capita than any other city in the United States." Gold from the mines of nearby Cripple Creek poured into Colorado Springs bringing beautiful homes, elaborate estates, wide streets, parks, and the finest system of trolley cars in the world. These trolley cars were a gift to the city from Winfield Scott Stratton, one of the millionaires, who had started as a three-dollars-a-day carpenter.

But climate and money were not all. Colorado Springs was proud of its culture, and that included Colorado College. Men and women from Boston, Philadelphia, and New York who had come to live in General Palmer's "Fountain Colony" brought with them Eastern ideas of education. Western get-up-and-go combined with this had brought about a college with high standards and a lively faculty. At Colorado College, art and music were encouraged, and so was science. To promote learning, a museum was started, and one of its features was an eighty-two-foot skeleton of a whale, donated by Mr. Stratton. Visiting professors in many fields were brought in, and some of them liked the college so much they stayed on as permanent residents.

On the morning that the Millers arrived, Miss Kate as if by plan drove the Great Smith straight to the finest of all the sights the city could provide: the view of the Peak at the end of Pike's Peak Avenue. There stood the new Antlers Hotel with its twin towers, and high above it, rubbing the top of the world, it seemed, was Pike's Peak. Its massive red-granite shoulders rose far above timberline and stood out against the blue, blue sky—everybody's idea of a mountain.

Miss Kate killed the Great Smith's engine.

After a moment of silence Professor Miller said, "Roosevelt was right. There's no way to describe the Rockies."

Words came into Lou Emma's mind and fell away again. It was better not to talk, but to look and try to hold the sight forever.

Maddy said, "Glory hallelujah!"

Miss Kate pushed back her goggles. Tears were running down her cheeks. "I d-don-t know wh-why I'm cr-crying. I'm so h-happy."

"Sanguine Saturnini," the Professor growled in pretended anger. "I drive six hundred miles, change a hundred tires, fight mud and dust, break my arm, and *she* cries over a mountain."

"It's so b-b-beautiful," Miss Kate sobbed happily.

Behind them the chime of bells sounded. Lou Emma and Maddy popped their heads out of the Great Smith. Bearing down on them was an olive-green trolley car, an eight-wheeler, sides open to the sun and

wind. A motorman in uniform braked the trolley, nearly touching the Great Smith. He kept the bells chiming while the conductor came around to Professor Miller.

"Mister, please ask the lady to move offa the tracks."

"Gladly, but right now she's in tears over your mountain up there."

"I'll move"—Miss Kate sniffed—"but it's so *beautiful.*"

The conductor grinned. "Take your time, lady. And don't worry about cryin'. It's the altitude."

In this way Lou Emma and Maddy first heard the excuse given for anything in Colorado Springs that needed excusing—"It's the altitude."

Mopping her eyes, Miss Kate moved the spark lever to the right, and the Great Smith started. She had discovered this simple means of starting without cranking if the engine had been idle only a few minutes. Off they drove, the girls waving to the people in the trolley car behind.

Bicyclists whizzed around the Great Smith. Up ahead they saw the Mining Exchange Building and the First National Bank. Either one, Maddy said, was bigger than all the buildings in Gloriosa rolled together. Trees shaded the sidewalks. Ladies in fine summer dresses, topped with big hats and parasols, strolled along. Surreys, phaetons, runabouts, and hacks were pulled by horses, but there were autos, too. Colorado Springs listed 811 autos in 1910.

Lou Emma looked wide-eyed at the people around

them. There was a vacation air about the whole town. "Everybody's having a good time," she said.

"Somebody must be working hard to make this whole place run," Professor Miller said, but Maddy shook her head.

"If they're working hard, it sure don't show."

"Doesn't," he corrected.

"We're on vacation," Maddy said. "Grammar *don't* count."

As Miss Kate didn't mind asking directions, she soon had them on their way to the college. Wide, smooth Cascade Avenue had a speed limit of eighteen miles per hour—three times what it was in Gloriosa. Every driver felt honor-bound to try out the limit of his auto on North Cascade. Maddy urged more speed on Miss Kate, but a French Panhard rolled by them, and a Hupmobile zoomed past and left them gasping in its dust.

"Papa'd never 've let that dude pass him," Maddy said.

Lou Emma wiped dust from her eyes. "No, but Miss Kate drives so smooth. I don't feel like a bag of jelly the way I do with Papa."

"Colorado College!" Professor Miller called back to the girls.

The college was built on a bluff overlooking Monument Creek. It had been started in three rooms in 1874. Now it had nine buildings and more planned for the future. There was Palmer Hall, named in honor of its donor, the General, who had also given the land for the campus. Palmer Hall was two stories high, squarish in shape, and built of peachblow sandstone with a green tile roof. The other buildings in sight were also of peachblow sandstone, but they sported red roofs. There was Coburn Library, Cutler Hall with its bell tower, Perkins Hall where music drifted from the open windows, Hagerman Hall built for the men students, and the four buildings of the Women's Quadrangle. The Miller girls were awed into quiet by the size of the place. EKCC had one building; Auden College had had three. The unspoken question between Lou Emma and Maddy was, *How's Papa going to get along?*

But if the Professor was worried, he didn't show it. Hampered by his sling, he got together a few books, papers, and a sheaf of notes made on the trip, and marched off to meet President William Frederick Slocum, whistling "Boola, Boola."

"Now let's find the place where we have rooms." Miss Kate took out a slip of paper and read, "The Wrenn's Nest, Mrs. America Wrenn, Prop. Room and board. College people preferred."

"Sounds snippy to me," Maddy said.

"Shhhh," Miss Kate hushed her. "Don't start finding fault before you get there. Here are the directions. 'Turn east at Miss Henry's Private School, go three blocks on Tejon Street . . . turn . . . turn . . .' Goodness, I hope we find it."

"There's a man. I'll ask him." Maddy jumped from

the auto. She came back filled with indignation. "He calls Te-jon Street Te-hone. He can't know anything. I'll find somebody that does."

"Never mind," Miss Kate said. "We'll start looking on our own."

After a little backtracking, they located the Wrenn's Nest. It was within easy walking distance of Colorado College. A rambling frame and stone house with glassed-in sleeping porches, built-on rooms, and a fence covered with sweet peas in blossom. On the front lawn was a big rose arbor. In its shade sat a half-dozen ladies in rocking chairs.

Mrs. America Wrenn met the Millers with an outpouring of welcome that was a little like a bath of molasses. She marveled at their bravery in driving from Kansas, threw up her hands in dismay over the Professor's broken arm, admired the girls' long braids, asked Miss Kate if they were kin to the Millers in Louisville—"connections of my late husband, very prominent"—and talking every step of the way, led them to the second floor.

"More blankets if you need them; breakfast at seven, dinner at twelve thirty, supper at six, sharp. No Sunday supper on account of the help. Fire in the fireplace in the parlor every evening. Dr. Pettigrew has a wonderful collection of Red Seal records for the Victrola. No ragtime, *please.* Croquet ground in the back yard. Trolley service to any place in the city only four blocks away. Even with an autoMobile a trolley's handy."

"Yes, indeed. It sounds very nice." Miss Kate tried to stem the flood, but Mrs. Wrenn was not through talking.

"Now, Mrs. Miller, come right down and meet our ladies. Lovely people, *lovely*. Wives of professors. You'll enjoy them I'm sure. Cambridge, Mass.—Harvard, you know. And Johns Hopkins, and the University of Michigan. Dear Miss Magruder's a little deaf, but brilliant, very brilliant, never married, writes poetry. And what is Professor Miller's college?"

"Eastern Kansas Classical College," Miss Kate spoke with great distinctness. "Gloriosa, Kansas."

"Oh, yes, I remember. Yes—yes—" Smiling and repeating "yes," Mrs. Wrenn left them. They heard her calling, "Mitchell, come help with the trunks."

"Wow!" Maddy plopped on the bed. "My ears are ringing."

"Trunks?" Lou Emma asked anxiously. "Should we've brought trunks? And who's Mitchell anyway?"

"We didn't need trunks," Miss Kate said. "Go find Mitchell, whoever he is, and let me freshen up before I meet that rocking-chair brigade."

As they started away, she called them back. "Girls, always be proud you're from Kansas."

They marched downstairs as if broomsticks were up their backs.

"I dare 'em to say a word," Maddy scowled. "One—word—"

"One syllable," Lou Emma said. "Kansas is better 'n they are any day."

The rocking-chair brigade, as Miss Kate had named them, sat expectantly under the rose arbor. Some were crocheting; some were tatting; some simply sat. Their eyes were on the front door of the Wrenn's Nest. Seeing them, Lou Emma stopped inside to push back her hair and straighten her stockings.

Maddy wrinkled her nose. "Who cares what they think?"

"Nobody. But we want to be a credit to Miss Kate. And Papa. And Kansas. *And* your petticoat's showing."

Maddy shrugged, but she hitched her petticoat up out of sight. Suddenly she grabbed Lou Emma. "Somebody's in the Great Smith!"

They ran pell-mell to the big red auto, forgetting the ladies under the rose arbor. A boy of about fourteen sat behind the steering wheel.

"Vroom, vroom." He twisted the wheel. "Rootin' tootin' galley-hootin'."

"Get out of our auto." Maddy stamped her foot.

From the high point of the driver's seat the boy looked down. Lou Emma's heart did a slow flip-flop. He was without a single doubt the best-looking boy she'd ever seen. Dark curly hair, green eyes with dark lashes, smooth, tanned complexion without one freckle, and white teeth that lighted his smile. He smiled now.

"Hello," he said. "I'm Mitch Cunningham. Is this your go-buggy? I just tried it for size. Don't get huffy."

"You've got no business in our auto," Maddy stormed.

Lou Emma pinched her. "Don't let him get your goat." To the boy she said, "Mitch? Is that the same as Mitchell?"

"One and the same, kiddo. But only old Merry-bird calls me that. Want to know what makes me call her that? Merry-bird, Mrs. America Wrenn. Get it?" He flipped the spark lever up and down as he talked.

"Don't do that," Maddy said. "You're likely to ruin something."

Mitch went on flipping the spark lever. He gave Lou Emma a wink. "I heard you and your folks came from some jerkwater college in Kansas."

Lou Emma stiffened. "Jerkwater yourself."

"Dare you to say that again." Maddy squared off.

"Say, you're a couple o' fizzers. And your old man's a prof. What's his razzamatazz?"

Neither girl knew what to answer.

"What's he teach?" Mitch explained with exaggerated patience.

"History, Greek and Roman." Lou Emma felt sure of herself.

"And he's writing a textbook," Maddy added.

"All of 'em are." Mitch shrugged. "Textbooks are a dime a dozen around the old Merry-bird's nest. My Pop's in Pol. Econ., and he's writing *A Life of Adam Smith.* Old Pettigrew's from Harvard, and he's got a plan for proving Shakespeare was Bacon or he wasn't; I dunno which. But look out for Miss Magruder in Lit. She writes poetry and reads it out loud. Gaaagh!"

Suddenly Mitch descended from the Great Smith.

As he hit the ground, he bowed and *clicked his heels.* "How do you do, ma'am?"

He spoke to Miss Kate who was looking like a fashion plate in green voile with a white lace collar. She smiled at him. "You must be Mitchell. Mrs. Wrenn said you'd help us with our suitcases."

"Happy to do so." Mitch spoke with such grown-up elegance that Lou Emma's knees turned weak. "I was admiring your automobile, Mrs. Miller."

"Thank you. It was made in Kansas, you know. Topeka. Not far from our home in Gloriosa."

"Yes, ma'am," Mitch spoke respectfully, picking up the oil-cloth covered suitcases. "I've never been to Kansas, but I hope to go sometime."

Lou Emma and Maddy looked at each other with bugged-out eyes and followed along without a word.

Dinner at the Wrenn's Nest was family style. Lou Emma was amazed at the platters and bowls of food, but she soon saw that the helpings were carefully counted, and there was no margin for extras. Latecomers had skimpy fare. The rocking-chair brigade made a big fuss about Professor Miller's "poor broken arm." Because they were the only boarders who had driven to Colorado, the Millers were celebrities from Breaded Veal Cutlets to Floating Island.

After dinner Mitch asked the girls to play croquet. Maddy jumped at the chance, confident of winning. He beat her easily.

"But I always won at home," she said, bewildered.

"Kansas style, kiddo." Mitch grinned. She took after him with her mallet, and he said he was sorry. "It's the altitude. Couple of days, and you'll be the winner again."

Just then Miss Kate called the girls to come upstairs. They found their father looking serious. Lou Emma sat down by him on the bed; Maddy sat on the floor and leaned against his legs.

"Tell us quick. Don't keep us in suspenders," Maddy said, trying to make her father laugh. But he shook his head.

"I've come up against a problem I never even considered. This arm that's broken is my right arm. If you will permit a pun, it's also my *write* arm. I find I can't write on the blackboard, correct papers, or even take the class roll."

"But I can," Miss Kate said eagerly. "I never went to college, but I've run a business, and I write a good clear hand. I can do what you tell me to."

"Kate, I didn't bring you to Colorado to lock you in a classroom."

"But we can do things after class," she insisted. "And another thing—I'd never fit into that rocking-chair brigade. And I don't really want to try."

"Old hens," Maddy said.

"They're not that bad," Miss Kate said. "But I . . ."

"Old Wrenn's hens," Lou Emma said.

"Girls, don't gang up on me," Professor Miller begged.

"The way they went on over you at dinner," Maddy

sniffed. "And Mitch's mother giving you her Floating Island, 'For extra nourishment for broken bones.' "

"The doctor didn't say a word about Papa having extra Floating Island," Lou Emma said. "Mrs. Cunningham just wanted Papa to notice her."

"But what about you girls if I take Kate away?" the Professor worried.

"We can look after ourselves when we get used to the altitude," Maddy spoke up.

"We can go lots of places on the trolley cars," Lou Emma said excitedly. "It'll be fun. It'll be like it was BMK."

Maddy pinched her sister's leg.

"BMK?" Professor Miller frowned. A painful silence filled the room.

"It means Before Miss Kate," Miss Kate said.

"Lou Emma you DUMKOPF!" Maddy pinched really hard this time.

Sick at what she had done, Lou Emma stammered. "I didn't mean . . . I mean I . . . Oh, Miss Kate, how'd you know it meant that?"

"It wasn't hard. It's not such a bad way to say things. After all, my life is divided into different parts, too. There's BMG—Before the Miller Girls."

Maddy laughed, but Lou Emma squirmed in misery. "I'm sorry. Honest."

"I'm sorry, Kate." The Professor took his wife's hand.

She laughed. "Humpin'-jumpin'-jackrabbits, to quote Tommy. If we stand around being sorry all afternoon, we'll miss Colorado. Where do we go *now?*"

Lou Emma felt the guilt roll off her back. Miss Kate wasn't mad. She knew Lou Emma hadn't meant any harm.

"Mrs. Cunningham says the first thing to see, after the Peak, is the Garden of the Gods," Professor Miller suggested.

"Hmmm." Miss Kate considered. "She must be a smart woman, the way she took to you. How about the Garden of the Gods, girls? Get your sweaters and crank the Great Smith, and we'll be off before you can say, 'Hurrah for Kansas.' "

"And Gloriosa," Maddy said.

"And Eastern Kansas Classical College," Lou Emma said.

They drove west on Colorado Avenue, then turned north. The Garden of the Gods was acres of red sandstone curiously carved over millions of years by wind, rain, sun, and snow. It was a favorite picnic spot, and visiting families in buggy and surrey were enjoying it, along with the Millers. A crowd was gathered around the famous Balanced Rock—four hundred tons of sandstone delicately balanced on a point that looked no larger than a coffee cup. A man had climbed to the top, and a woman was taking his picture with a box camera.

Lou Emma shuddered. "You wouldn't catch me up there."

"I think it'd be fun," Maddy said. "When that man gets down—"

"Drive on, Kate," Professor Miller said. "I do not want to be responsible for unbalancing the Balanced Rock."

They got out of the auto, admired the huge Steamboat Rock, the lifelike giant Baked Potato, and tried to see the features of King Arthur on Horseback. Maddy thought it looked more like President Taft, but Lou Emma favored William Jennings Bryan. At the Devil's Pulpit Maddy delivered a "sermon" until her father sternly told her to hush. There were many, many more rock formations with strange names. The grass was bright green; the rocks warm red; and the holiday spirit was everywhere. Far above them Pike's Peak seemed to smile on their pleasure. About four o'clock a brisk shower hurried them into the Great Smith, but it was gone almost as soon as they got there, so they ventured out again.

They marveled over Chief Manitou, the Elephant Rock, the Setting Hen, and the Scotchman—who reminded the girls of Mr. McKelvy. They drove slowly toward the entrance only to be stopped by the majestic Gateway Rocks that rose more than three hundred feet in the air. At the top of one of these pillars of stone was the wind-carved pair of Kissing Camels. Kneeling, and seeming to lean toward each other, the camels were the easiest to see of all the many other named rocks. There was even a dark spot for an eye in exactly the right place.

Miss Kate sat down on the running board. "I just want to sit here and look my fill. It's the most amazing place I've ever seen."

Professor Miller took his *Odes of Horace* from his pocket and began to read to her. Lou Emma wandered away and began talking to a girl from Omaha, Nebraska, who had a birthstone ring with a green stone for October. It was a gift from her aunt, she said.

"A boy gave me my ring," Lou Emma said, enjoying her superiority.

"What's his name?" the girl leaned toward her.

Lou Emma started to say, 'You wouldn't know him, anyway.' She started to say, 'Tommy Biddle.' But to her own astonishment she said, "Mitch, Mitchell Cunningham gave it to me."

Why'd I do that? she asked herself frantically. *What'll I do now?*

There was a shrill whistle, and the girl from Omaha scampered back to her family. Lou Emma saw them getting into a surrey.

I don't even know her name, and I told her a lie.

She walked slowly back to the Great Smith.

"Where's Maddy?" Professor Miller closed his book.

"I thought she was with you. Maybe she went back to Chief Manitou. She liked him."

"I hope she won't be long," Miss Kate said. "We have just about time to get to the Wrenn's Nest for supper."

The afternoon light was fading. The picnickers were packing their baskets to go home. High on the Gateway Rocks the swallows that built mud nests there were returning for the night. Twittering flutelike calls came to the listeners as the birds darted after flying insects and wheeled and turned in the air.

Watching the swallows, Lou Emma became aware of a bright red spot of color, redder than the sandstone would ever be.

Maddy's sweater! Forty feet up.

Twice she opened her mouth before a sound came out.

"Maddy's up there!" She pointed.

"Ye gods and little fishes! What'll she do next?" her father said.

Then thin and fluty, like the bird notes of the swallows came Maddy's call. ". . . stuck . . . can't . . . get . . . down. . . ." And louder, "Help!"

"Oh, Cyrus, we've got to help her. She may fall," Miss Kate said.

"She got up; surely she can get down." Professor Miller cupped his good hand around his mouth and shouted, "Come down. Now!"

The booming echoes made the swallows fly faster.

"Help . . . help . . ." Maddy's cry was thin and muffled.

"Kate, go for help. There's got to be somebody who knows what to do," Professor Miller said. "Lou Emma, you and I'll stay here and try to keep Maddy quiet."

Off Miss Kate drove in a whirl of dust. Professor Miller called up to Maddy: "DON'T MOVE. STAY WHERE YOU ARE."

But to Lou Emma it seemed Maddy had moved: *she was slipping.* Professor Miller rushed to the base of the rock wall and tried to climb, but with one arm useless he couldn't get anywhere. Chills chased through Lou

Emma. It was up to her, and she knew it, but she was scared—scared.

"Papa, you'll hurt your arm trying. Let me."

Inside she was saying, *I can't. I'm scared. I can't.*

Her father looked at her, and she knew he knew she was scared, but he said, "Go on. Get near enough to talk to her if you can. Tell her we'll have her down in a jiffy. Tell her—Oh, confound this arm!"

"Give me a boost up," Lou Emma said.

He braced himself against the rock wall, cupped his good hand for her to put her foot in, then helped her to step to his shoulder. There was a foothold not far above his head in the rock. Lou Emma got up to it.

It's all backwards. Maddy's the climber. She knows how. But me . . . I'm scared . . . scared . . . scared. Her teeth began to chatter.

But she kept on climbing.

The Gateway Rocks had been climbed before. Footholds, handholds, had been gouged out. A stone knob helped here, a tough bit of brush there. She kept going.

Now she was close enough to see Maddy looking down.

"Hold on," Lou Emma quavered.

"All right," Maddy quavered back.

One more heave, and her foot found a crevice that felt safe. Her head was level with Maddy's slipperless foot. Now that she had reached Maddy she didn't feel thankful or proud of her climbing or anything but plain *mad.*

"What's the matter with you, you crazy galoot? What'd you get stuck up here for? Don't you know we'll be late for supper?"

"The rock I was on broke, and my slipper came off, and that started me to slide. And I don't know where my foot oughta *be.*" Maddy was half crying as she looked pitifully at her sister and whispered, "I'm scared. Real scared."

"Nothing to be scared of," Lou Emma scolded. "Miss Kate's gone for help, and Papa says for us to stay right here and they'll have us down in a jiffy. I've got a good hold here. Put your foot on my head, if you want."

"I'm scared to move," Maddy wailed.

"You're not either. Do what I tell you." A pair of cliff swallows darted at the girls. Lou Emma shouted at them, "Shoo—scat—scat."

Maddy gave a weak giggle. "Scat's for cats, not birds."

Slowly she got her foot to move, bringing it down on the crown of Lou Emma's head. It settled there snugly. Lou Emma could feel the bones of Maddy's foot through her stocking. The head-foot bridge made them both feel better, as if the danger were all at once divided by two.

Lou Emma leaned her cheek against the still-warm sandstone. The anger that had given her courage drained away. She dared not look down. Instead she stared at the blue sparkle of the birthstone ring on her hand. *I don't know what got into me to say that. If I ever get down . . .*

A trickle of sandstone came down from above. Was the rock crumbling? Far away she heard the chug-chug-chug-chug of the Great Smith. Her father shouted, but she couldn't hear what he said. The Great Smith must be closer; the rock walls echoed the engine sound. Miss Kate wheeled through the turns and twists of the dirt road. Once she blew the horn, and Lou Emma wished she could wave, but she didn't dare.

There were shouts and scramblings below. They'd better hurry—hurry. Her hands were numb and slippery with sweat. The weight of Maddy's foot on her head was heavier, almost too heavy.

Suddenly a man's face was close. He spoke to Lou Emma. "Lemme put this rope around you. Lean out a mite. Don't be scared."

"My sister," she gulped. "She's been here longer 'n me."

"We'll get her, too. Don't get the fidgets. I've been pullin' kids off these rocks since who laid the chunk."

She felt the rope go around her and tighten under her arms. Then she was being taken down a ladder she hadn't even known was there. Somehow Maddy was down, too, and they were laughing and crying together. Miss Kate had her arms around both her stepdaughters. Professor Miller was thanking the men.

Miss Kate said, "I'm so thankful you're not hurt. So thankful."

"I was sure scared," Lou Emma said. "I was as petrified as any Kissing Camel ever was."

"You weren't too petrified to climb up there. It's

braver to do a thing you're scared of." Miss Kate hugged Lou Emma again.

For what might be the first time in her life, Maddy said, "I was scared, too. Awful, awful scared. If Lou Emma hadn't come, I'd have fallen for sure."

"Don't say that." Lou Emma shivered.

"I have to say it." Maddy was solemn. "You saved my life. Thank you kindly, Louisa Emmaline."

"You're welcome." A wave of blushes burned Lou Emma's face.

They got into the Great Smith, and as they drove from the Garden of the Gods and turned onto Ridge Road, Professor Miller spoke to Maddy.

"Can you tell me why you did such a foolish, dangerous thing?"

"Why, Papa, I wanted to see if the Kissing Camels were really kissing. You always told us not to take things for granted, but to investigate for ourselves, so I thought—"

"That will do. I knew I'd be sorry I asked, but I couldn't resist it." He turned back to Miss Kate. "Look out for a drug store, Kate. We're much too late for any supper at the Wrenn's Nest, so I propose to have a chocolate malted milk with an egg in it, and if it costs a nickle extra, hang the expense!"

"Me, too," Miss Kate said.

"Me, too," Lou Emma said.

"Me, too," Maddy said. "Only I want strawberry."

Chapter 14

The next morning Lou Emma bounced out of bed, and bounced right back in. It was cold! Never before could she remember being cold on her father's birthday. When they left Gloriosa, the temperature was up to a hundred every day. She snuggled in beside Maddy, who as usual had two thirds of the covers.

"Wake up," she hissed. "It's Papa's birthday."

Maddy didn't move.

"Wake up. I've thought of something mean to do to Adelaide."

Maddy's eyes flew open. "What?"

"Send her a postcard and say, 'Sleeping under three blankets.' "

Maddy yawned. "That's not worth a one-cent stamp. When I'm mean, I want to be good and mean. What'd you say first?"

"I knew you were awake. I said, 'It's Papa's birthday.' Did you finish hemstitching your handkerchief for him?"

"No, it takes years. Did you finish?"

"Yes, and I put an initial on it, but it doesn't look too good. The *M* is sort of broken-backed. We'd better give him a different kind of present."

Maddy was for doing anything different, and she agreed that they should look for something that very morning. The truth was that Lou Emma had led her into this agreement, because she had decided to give the handkerchief with *M* on it to Mitch. What Maddy didn't know wouldn't hurt her—or their father.

Miss Kate rapped on the wall as a signal that they should get down to breakfast. The second time out, the room didn't seem so chilly, but Lou Emma hurried to get dressed, and she was the first one downstairs.

Bowls of stewed prunes were spotted along the table. She liked prunes, but not in such quantity. Mrs. Cunningham arrived and smiled at her.

"Hello, Miss Early Bird. I wish I could get Mitch up before nine."

"Yes, ma'am," Lou Emma said, feeling downright countrified at being up so early. She was glad when Maddy came in to keep her company.

Other breakfasters hurried in and ate in silence. Professor Miller divided his time between a large bowl of oatmeal and instructing Miss Kate in her new duties. When he went to get his books, she turned to the girls.

"I'm as nervous as a settin' hen on a clutch of duck eggs!"

"Don't listen when Papa talks about education," Lou Emma told her from long experience. "Remember what Mrs. Biddle said, 'Teachers are the worst paid when they ought to be the best paid.' "

Miss Kate struck her hand against her forehead. "I

nearly forgot. Here's a quarter for each of you. Make it go as far as you can. Here's Cyrus. Good-bye."

A quarter? Each? Lou Emma and Maddy stared after her.

"Jumping Jehosophat!" Maddy said.

"She didn't even tell us how to spend it," Lou Emma said. When Aunt Jesse gave them money, she always laid out the way to spend it to the last cent.

"Let's go right to town and buy Papa's birthday present," Maddy said.

"Let's get slicked up first," Lou Emma said. She was half hoping Mitch would come down before they left. "We'll have to ask Merry-bird how to go."

"She takes too long. Let's just go."

Dressed in their almost-best, the girls started to leave the Wrenn's Nest.

"Well, little girls, off on a spree?" It was Mrs. Wrenn, but she hurried into the kitchen before they had to answer.

"Ugh. 'Little girls,' " Maddy said. "I'm glad we didn't ask her. She wouldn't know straight up."

"We ought to know where the trolley stops," Lou Emma worried.

"It stops at the corner. Same as in Cleveland or Topeka."

"Which corner?"

"Any corner. All we have to do is find the car tracks."

Lou Emma shoved Maddy, and Maddy shoved back, and all at once they were running for no reason at all but the joy of the clear cold air, the bright blue sky, the immensity of the Peak, and the flowers blooming everywhere. Panting hard, they skidded to a stop and leaned against each other.

"Wha's wrong?" Maddy puffed. "You're outa breath."

"You, too. Don't lay it on me."

"It's the altitude," Maddy said. "Mitch said it was the altitude."

"Mitch won't ever get up till nine A.M.; his mother told me."

"She's a pill. But he's—"

"He's what?" Lou Emma looked into her sister's face.

"Listen!" Maddy screamed. It was the chime of the trolley bells.

"This way!" Lou Emma ran to the right.

"This way!" Maddy ran to the left.

Around the block they met, just as the olive-green trolley car wheeled up to the corner. It was a summer car with seats running crossways. A woman got off, giving the Miller girls time to race up and climb on. They held out their quarters to the conductor, and from each quarter he gave them back two shiny new dimes—and a wink. They settled back on the comfortable seats, got their breath again, and felt as if they owned the town.

The trolley car bounced just enough to make the ride seem fun. On either side the streets were wide and busy. Off a ways they caught a glimpse of the red-tiled roofs of Colorado College, and both of them waved.

"I know the college yell. Mitch told me," Lou Emma said.

"You've got to tell me. Rule Number One," Maddy demanded.

"I never thought Rule Number One—Oh, well." And Lou Emma recited, " 'With a Vevo, With a Vevo/ With a Vevo, Vivo, Vum, Vum/Johnny get a Rat Trap Bigger than a Cat Trap/Cannibals, Cannibals, Siss Boom Ah—"

"Colorado College, Rah, Rah, Rah." Maddy deflated her by reciting the end. "They're all alike. EKCC, Auden, even Yale."

"Why'd you ask me if you know so much?"

"I wanted to see if you'd tell me. You won't tell me stuff about Tommy and now you're starting the same way with Mitch." Maddy let the trolley stop and take on a load of passengers before she went ahead. "You're sweet on Mitch."

"You stop that! If you say that again, I'll tell Papa on you."

"You'd better not," Maddy said. "I heard him tell Miss Kate that that Cunningham boy was a little too smooth for his taste."

"That's hateful!" Lou Emma flared; then she choked back her anger. Maddy had already made her say more about Mitch than she meant to. Next thing she'd be telling her sister about the girl from Omaha and the birthstone ring.

"Oughtn't we be getting to the stores?" Maddy asked, looking out.

"Maybe it's a ways farther." Lou Emma glanced at Pike's Peak. It was up there all right, but it seemed to be a little out of place. "Looky, a creek."

The motorman chimed the bells and announced that the bubbling stream beside the tracks was Cheyenne Creek. The water was clear as crystal. Ferns dipped into the stream. A fisherman on the bank waved at the girls.

"It's pretty." Maddy bounced in time to the bouncing of the trolley. "Colorad-o's pretty, everyplace it's pret-ty."

"It's pret-ty," Lou Emma bounced with Maddy. "But I don't remember any creek from yes-ter-day. Do you? Down-town?"

"No, but there's the Peak. We can't be wrong if we see the Peak."

They looked at the mighty mountain. Now it was over their shoulders.

"It's moved," Maddy shrieked.

The conductor hurried to them. "Something wrong, little ladies?"

"Pike's Peak. It's moved," Maddy said.

"It ought to be *here.*" Lou Emma pointed dead ahead. "And it's *there.*"

The conductor scratched his head. "It's *there* all right. S'pose you little ladies tell me where you aimed to go this morning?"

"Down to a store close to the Antlers Hotel," Maddy said. "To get a birthday present for Papa."

"You got kind of turned around. This car's headed

for Stratton Park. There's a sign on the front, but maybe you missed seein' it."

"Didn't you look?" Maddy asked Lou Emma.

"I thought you looked. You said—"

"Oh, well," the conductor soothed them, "it's easy not to see a thing that's right under your nose. Now we're just about to the Park, and it's a fine day. Cars run every quarter hour. If I's you, I'd go to the Park and enjoy it."

He moved on, giving them a friendly wave.

"We'd better do what he says," Lou Emma decided. "Aunt Jesse says always ask a man in uniform if you get lost."

"I'm not lost," Maddy insisted. "Pike's Peak is."

"Stratton Park," the conductor called. The trolley emptied, and after a moment's hesitation Lou Emma and Maddy got off and followed the others into the Park.

Stratton Park was made for enjoyment. Winfield Scott Stratton had spent money with both hands to make it the finest, happiest, freest place possible. It ran south for hundreds of acres at the base of Cheyenne Mountain. There were swings, picnic tables, benches, fountains, lakes, and an elegant bandstand where concerts were given. Lou Emma and Maddy wandered through the Park and felt that it was in a special way their very own. Hadn't they found it by themselves? If it had been a mistake at first, they declared it was "on purpose" now and Maddy put three sprigs of kinnickinnick on the foot of the statue of Mr. Stratton who had died in 1902. "Thanks," she said, and Lou Emma added, "Thank you *very* kindly."

But scenery and swings were not all of the pleasures of the Park. One of the main ones, brand-new to two girls from Kansas, were chipmunks. Bright-eyed, striped, with tails neatly curved, chipmunks raced down the paths, scrambled on the benches, and dug in the flower beds. One approached the Miller girls and put up his paws as if to beg.

"Wish we had something to give 'em," Lou Emma said.

"Could we buy peanuts?" Maddy looked at her two dimes.

"Better not. We've got to buy Papa's present."

"Then we'd better do it now," Maddy said. Money always burned in her pockets, and she knew she couldn't hold out long against the itch to spend.

"There's a souvenir stand by the entrance. Let's look there."

It seemed as if anyone could buy anyone the right present at the souvenir stand. There were dishes with Pike's Peak painted in wild colors, spoons from Colorado and every other state in the Union as well, burros made from iron with cloth packsaddles, fool's gold from the mines at Cripple Creek, and every kind of paperweight the mind of man could imagine. They had almost settled on a boot carved from wood with a tiny round glass lens in the sole that showed Pike's Peak if put up to the eye when they saw the exact thing they wanted. It was a pillow stuffed tight with pine and balsam needles. Painted on the pillow top was a weeping Indian maiden and the words, "I Pine for You and Balsam."

They giggled over the puns, smelled hard of the piney fragrance, and only then did they ask the price.

"Fifty cents," the woman said, buffing her nails.

"Fif-ty cents?" Maddy inhaled. "Are you sure?"

"Sure's death 'n' taxes," the woman said cheerfully. "Want it?"

Lou Emma returned the pillow to the counter and backed away.

"Not today," Maddy said and joined Lou Emma. They sighed in unison.

"Higher'n a cat's back," Lou Emma said. "Not really worth it."

"We could make one as good," Maddy said. "If we had pine an' balsam an' paints an' Miss Kate would give us some cloth."

"We'll have to look for something cheaper," Lou Emma said. "We've got forty cents, and it'll cost a dime to get back to the Wrenn's Nest. Could we ask Papa to have his birthday tomorrow?"

Maddy was scandalized. "You can't swap birthdays around."

The trolley was approaching, and they joined the people waiting to get on. Both of them were feeling down in the mouth, and it was a real comfort to see "their conductor" coming toward them, collecting fares.

"Have a good time?" he asked. "Find your Papa a present?"

"Yessir," Lou Emma answered the first question.

"Nossir," Maddy answered the second. "We didn't have enough money."

"Well, nothin's free but salvation around these parts," the conductor said. "Take the price to ride the Cog Train up Pike's Peak. It's sky-high."

"I wish we could go," Maddy looked longingly at the Peak.

"Why, right here you little ladies got the biggest bargain in the Springs, five cents for a ride to Stratton Park."

"Maddy, he's right," Lou Emma said, "and I just got an idea what we can give Papa for a birthday present. Stratton Park!"

The conductor grinned. "Want it wrapped in tissue paper?"

On the palm of Lou Emma's outstretched hand was one dime and one nickel. "I've got fifteen cents, and so has Maddy. We can invite Papa to ride the trolley to the Park for his birthday present. And Miss Kate and us, too."

Maddy looked at her in disgust. "Why don'tcha learn to add? That comes to forty cents, and we've only got thirty between us."

Lou Emma drooped. "You're right; I'm wrong. Golly-molly, I thought we could do it."

"You can." The conductor leaned toward them, his face beaming. "I'll be on this run till seven tonight.

The ride out to the Park for you and your family'll be my treat. Only don't gab around about it! It could mean my job."

"We won't tell a soul." Lou Emma perked up.

"And we'll pay you back," Maddy said.

"Nope. My treat." He winked and left them.

"The best birthday present I ever had, next to Kate's driving," Professor Miller declared as they waited for the trolley to take them back to the Wrenn's Nest.

Lou Emma and Maddy looked at each other in congratulation. It had worked out fine. When they got on, they had introduced Miss Kate and Professor Miller to "our conductor," and he had rung up the four fares in great style, complimenting Miss Kate on how much the girls looked like her. The Park was even more wonderful when the girls displayed it to their parents. They had sneaked slices of bread from the dinner table for the chipmunks, and Miss Kate coaxed one clear up her arm to her shoulder. The Colorado Midland Band played a concert for a Sunday school convention, and Lou Emma said it might as well be for them, too, because they belonged to the Willing Workers.

As they rode back, Maddy's sharp eyes spied a tiny plume of smoke on the side of the Peak. She showed it to her father.

"Must be the Cog Train," he said. "I hope we can take that trip."

Miss Kate shook her head. "Mrs. Wrenn said five

dollars for adults and two fifty for children. Maddy's the only one who's still a child—still twelve, I mean."

"Me? A child? Why, I'm bigger'n Lou Emma any day in the week."

"That'd be seventeen fifty for us," Lou Emma said, right in her arithmetic for once. "Why, we can come to Stratton Park for only twenty cents. Pike's Peak can't be so much better just because it's standing up on end."

The conductor gave her a nod. "That's right, little lady."

It took some doing before Lou Emma found the right time to give Mitch the handkerchief. She had a speech made up and rehearsed, but when the moment came, she stuck the tissue-wrapped handkerchief into his hand and said, "Here. I made it."

Then she ran upstairs, unable to bear watching her gift unwrapped.

Did Tommy feel this way about the ring? Is that why he ran?

Maddy called her down to walk to the post office. This had become part of the routine of the day. Each one mailed a postcard, and asked at the General Delivery window for "any mail for Millers." Once their father had a letter from Dr. Biddle, and twice Miss Kate had letters from Etta Mahaffey about Miss Kate's Chapeaux. So far that was all. But today there was a heavy white envelope with Greystokes-in-the-Pines engraved in one corner and inked in "Miss J. Miller, Care of J. Mayfield." The letter was addressed to "Miss

STRATTON
PARK

Louisa Emmaline Miller and Miss Madeline Margaret Miller." It took two stamps.

Lou Emma balanced the letter carefully on her thumb and little finger. "Are we going to open it? It's to us. Miss Kate wrote *her,* but she writes *us.*"

Maddy wrinkled her nose. "Miss Kate oughtn't to've tattled."

"Don't haul dead steers around by the tail," Lou Emma said and refused to explain what she meant.

"Let's not open it till we get back to Merry-bird's. That way whatever Aunt Jesse's got to say won't be real till then," Maddy said.

Lou Emma wasn't sure about this, but she didn't want to hear from Aunt Jesse either, so she put the letter in her pocket as they went down Weber Street. Mitch appeared from nowhere and joined them. Lou Emma was scared he would mention the handkerchief in front of Maddy, but he gave her a wink and she felt safe.

Mitch's so smart, so good-looking. Why'd Papa not like him?

They started to turn at a street with many glassed-in porches.

"Uh-uh," Mitch said. "Dead Man's Row. Lungers."

So many people came to Colorado Springs with lung disease that talk like Mitch's was common. Still it made Lou Emma uneasy. Nobody could help getting sick, and her father said lots of them got well. But to say so to Mitch was beyond her, though not beyond Maddy—not by a long shot.

"You ought to be ashamed, Mitchell Cunningham. I'm going to walk down this street, and I'm going to speak to every person I meet."

"Suit yourself," Mitch said. "You won't catch me— Coming, kiddo?"

He looked at Lou Emma with his black-lashed green eyes, and she went weak in the knees. But she heard herself say, "I'd better stay with Maddy."

They watched Mitch cut across a yard, jump a border of marigolds, and go out of sight.

"Now you've made him mad," Lou Emma said mournfully.

"Who cares?" Maddy said. "He made me mad, too. C'mon."

They walked on down the street, and true to her word Maddy nodded and smiled at every person she saw, until Lou Emma was ready to run from embarrassment. She was thankful when they came to the turn for the Wrenn's Nest. Maddy took a look at the rocking-chair brigade and said, "You go on. I'm going in the back."

Before Lou Emma could protest, Maddy was gone. She wanted to run, too, but instead she walked stiffly forward, conscious of every item of clothes she wore, every hair on her head. To her horror Mrs. Cunningham called her over.

"Such a nice little seamstress," she cooed. "You ladies should see the handkerchief she made my Mitch. Hemstitched and initialed."

Lou Emma begged the ground to swallow her, but it

didn't. In her misery she took out Aunt Jesse's letter and turned it around and around.

"We've been to the post office," she mumbled.

"Did your mother teach you to sew?" Mrs. Pettigrew asked. "I understand she does . . . sewing."

"She owns Miss Kate's Chapeaux," Lou Emma said stiffly. "*Chapeaux* is French for hats."

"I believe I *did* know that," Mrs. Cunningham said.

But Lou Emma was past caring. "Miss Kate's Chapeaux is the best millinery shop in Kansas. Originals start at thirty dollars."

"Money, money." Mrs. Pettigrew gave an artificial sigh. "Dr. Pettigrew feels that the modern woman is money-mad. Unfeminine."

Lou Emma was so angry that the letter slipped from her hand without her even noticing. Mrs. Cunningham picked it up and made no bones about reading the engraved return address.

"Greystokes-in-the-Pines?" She looked questioningly at Lou Emma.

"Our Aunt Jesse's up there," Lou Emma said. "It's from her."

She was aware of the murmur as the name of the famous hotel went from one rocking chair to the other. There was a sudden difference in the looks she got, even in the voices. "Are you going to Greystokes?" Mrs. Pettigrew asked.

"Maybe." Lou Emma tried to sound as much like Maddy's "I-don't-give-a-hoot" voice as she could. "Maybe not. If Miss Kate wants to."

"One of the three finest hotels—" she heard.

"Our Regents' president stayed there, but of course we—"

"Never able to afford a meal there, let alone a day—"

"There's your mother, dear," Mrs. Cunningham said. "Tell her we miss her in our little circle. Perhaps she will join us one day."

"Yes, ma'am. No, ma'am." Lou Emma backed away.

The bell rang for dinner, and everybody hurried to the dining room.

Mitch pulled Lou Emma into the dark little library. "What'd my old lady say?"

"Why'd you tell her? Why'd you show it to her. I hate you. I—"

Mitch grinned. "You're cute when you get mad, Lou Emma. C'mon, stay mad."

She stamped her foot. "I—hate—you—."

Suddenly he turned serious. "She asked me where I got it. You wouldn't want me to tell my mother a lie, would you?"

Like the walls of Jericho, Lou Emma's anger fell down. "No. I'm sorry."

"Forget it." Mitch snapped his fingers. "You been to Manitou yet? Soda Springs Park? It's kind of fun. Next Monday. I'll meetcha at the trolley stop. Nine thirty."

"Mitch-ell!" his mother called. "Din-ner!"

He was gone, and Lou Emma was left gasping. He was asking to take her out. Mitch Cunningham! Next Monday, and this was Friday. She wondered if she could last that long.

Chapter 15

When Miss Kate and Professor Miller came from the college, they were in high spirits. President Slocum had announced that Dr. Hugo Etting, editor of the famous *History of Greece* would arrive for three lectures on August twelfth.

"We should celebrate," the Professor said. "What's nearby, unseen, inexpensive, and worth writing a postcard about?"

"Pike's Peak," Maddy said. "Only not 'inexpensive.' "

"Stratton Park," Lou Emma said. "Only not 'unseen.' "

"Seven Falls," Miss Kate said. "Mrs. Wrenn said—"

"Is Mrs. Wrenn running a boardinghouse or a sightseeing bus? From the size of the pork chops it's hard to tell."

"Now, Cyrus, she has to make a profit," Miss Kate defended the landlady.

"Not at every meal," Professor Miller said. "But let's go to Seven Falls and see the sights. I feel like exploring."

As they started out to the Great Smith, Mrs. Cunningham stopped Professor Miller at the door. Lou Emma waited, her teeth clenched.

If she tells him I'm a good little seamstress, I'll hit her. I will.

But Mrs. Cunningham had other things on her mind. "Marvelous that you're going to Greystokes, Dr. Miller."

"Professor. I have never finished my doctorate."

"Only a matter of time." Mrs. Cunningham dimpled and blinked her eyes. "We're all *so* excited to know that you—and Mrs. Miller and the girls—are going to that heavenly place. Don't forget us when you rise so high. Promise?"

Professor Miller looked puzzled. "Seven Falls is hardly that high."

"Of course I meant Greystokes. You're such a *tease*."

But Miss Kate was calling. "Cyrus—Lou Emma—hurry—"

"Later, Mrs. Cunningham. Sorry to hurry, but—Coming, Kate."

Shooing Lou Emma ahead, he rushed through the door and got into the Great Smith and wiped his forehead.

"What is that addlepated woman talking about?"

"You shouldn't call her addlepated. She thinks you're wonderful." Miss Kate shot the Great Smith forward, barely missing a tandem bicycle.

"Kate! Not so fast. I have no idea what Mrs. Cunningham means."

"I know," Lou Emma said. "It's about a letter from Aunt Jesse to me 'n' Maddy that's upstairs in my green-dress pocket."

"And we're not going to drop it in the river like that other time," Maddy said.

"But what does Mrs. Cunningham know about it?"

"She's an old snoop," Maddy said. Lou Emma had told her about the rocking-chair brigade during dinner, using Pig Latin. "An eal-ray oop-snay."

"At least tell me what Jesse said," the Professor insisted.

"We don't know. We haven't read the letter," Lou Emma explained.

"We weren't ready for it to be real, so we didn't read it," Maddy said.

"Kate, have you any idea what these two mean?" He appealed to his wife.

"Of course. I never open bills from the millinery wholesalers first thing in the morning. I wait till I've totaled the cash in the evening."

"You don't owe the wholesalers any less, do you?"

"No, but I feel better, and I can deal with it better. See?"

"I certainly don't see. Most illogical thing I ever heard of. As for Jesse, when you girls do open the letter, remember she means well."

"Yes, Papa," they said. "We know."

They drove south on Tejon Street, which Maddy now pronounced Te-hone as if she had never had other ideas. Angling west, they found Cheyenne Road. This took them around Stratton Park to a road that forked where the North and South Cheyenne canyons split off from the mountain. At the entrance of South Cheyenne Canyon was a tollgate. They left the Great Smith there, for no autos were allowed to enter, and paid the toll for four on foot.

Soon they were deep between the granite walls. It was as if some great knife had slashed into the very heart of the world. The walls were so high on either side—two thousand feet, a fellow traveler told them—that the people and the burros wandering up and down dwindled to almost nothing. Voices were hushed, footfalls quiet.

At one side of the canyon floor a stream rippled over a bed of water-rounded stones. The stream wandered across the road, and the Millers crossed it on mossy rocks, holding each other's hands and watching the amber-colored water lap around their feet. On the sand bars along the banks, tall blue pentstemons bloomed along with yellow mountain parsley. Creamy evening primroses were already opening their petals, because the sunlight had gone from the canyon floor.

Mountain jays and juncos flew about the trees and quarreled over the leavings of a picnic. An eagle or a hawk soared so high in the blue above that he came and went from sight. Chipmunks chattered, gray squirrels barked. Back of all the other sounds was the rush of falling water that came closer with each step they took.

Now they were at the foot of Seven Falls, looking up . . . up . . . up. The glistening wall of water was white and blue and silver. It fell three hundred feet to the canyon floor. Seven times it turned in its falling, and each time, each separate fall, increased in beauty.

The Millers stood, hand in hand. The fine mist from the falls touched them, drifting like a silvery veil. For a moment no one spoke.

It was Maddy who broke the spell. "Humpin'-jumpin'-jackrabbits!"

The others laughed, but Lou Emma had a sudden qualm as she thought of Tommy's freckle-dotted face.

S'pose he met that girl from Omaha. S'pose she said . . . and he said . . . No!

There were wooden steps built alongside Seven Falls. They had handrails and platforms here and there, for the climb was almost straight up—or so it looked. But other people were making it and talking as they came down.

". . . worth every step."

". . . nothing like it in Iowa, I'm bound to say."

". . . sat right there and wrote *Ramona*."

The Millers started the climb. Up and up and up they went. Halfway up Lou Emma was sure she couldn't make it, but three fourths of the way she knew she must. To stand at the very, very top was a victory she had to have. Professor Miller went first and made them rest at every platform. Miss Kate came next and climbed steadily, breathing through her nose. Then came Lou Emma who had spurts and starts of energy, and last Maddy who fussed at everybody else's slowness but couldn't get up steam enough to pass them.

At last they stood at the very, very top. And it was a victory. Lou Emma wanted to shout, "Hallelujah!" but she didn't have breath enough. Below them was Seven Falls, and out of the mist shone a rainbow.

A man who had climbed just behind them pointed out the *exact spot* where Helen Hunt Jackson got the idea for *Ramona* and where she came day after day to write her novel of the persecution of the Indians. It was easy to understand how anyone might get an idea in such a spot, but to sit day after day on a rock and write. . . . Lou Emma wondered about it and at last asked her father.

"I find writing hard enough with a table and chair. But the important thing is the book. Go to the library tomorrow and get it and read it."

She might have known asking him would end with her reading.

They strolled about on the cleared area, then climbed again to Inspiration Point. Seven thousand feet, a sign told them, and a breathtaking view.

"All that goes up must come down," the Professor said, and started them back to the steps.

Going down made the backs of Lou Emma's legs ache, but she looked at the faces of people coming up and felt superior to them. Leg aches didn't matter.

"Is it worth it?" puffed a large woman at the third platform.

"It's worth every step," Miss Kate told her.

"And there's 290. I counted 'em," Maddy said.

On down they tramped, heels hitting hard and

breath coming short. "It can't be the altitude," Lou Emma reasoned. "We're coming down, not up."

"Altitude's all around Colorado," her father puffed. "Up or down or sideways. We started climbing at Dodge City, Kansas. Keeps on to the top of the Peak."

"Oh, Papa, will we get to go? On the Cog Train?"

"We'll see, Lou Emma."

After supper they gathered in the girls' room, and Lou Emma opened Aunt Jesse's letter.

"She does want us to come see her. Come to Greystokes-in-the-Pines, have dinner—six o'clock dinner—and spend the night." She reported it with awe, thinking of Mrs. Cunningham and the others who had been impressed with Greystokes.

"Well? Is that all?" her father asked.

"No. She says the Mayfields want us to come, too. That it's a great experience to be at Greystokes, and we mustn't miss it. And to be sure and remember that they *dress for dinner.*"

"That lets me out," Professor Miller said. "No dress clothes."

Miss Kate smiled. "I packed them, Cyrus, just in case."

He looked pained. "Eve led Adam astray. Now you, Kate."

"Adam shouldn't 've blamed Eve." Maddy bristled. "It was as much his fault as hers."

"I'll press your clothes, Cyrus," Miss Kate said.

"We can only come the day she asks us," Lou Emma went on. "Because the Mayfields have a very full social calendar and they have been very kind to include her family and we must realize this and not be late."

" 'Hallelujah, I'm a Bum!' " Professor Miller quoted with a snort.

"Now, Cyrus, your sister means well," Miss Kate reminded him.

Maddy laughed, but Lou Emma looked up, worried. "Oh, Papa, the day we're asked for is August twelfth, the day Dr. Etting comes."

"Tell him to beat it," Maddy said. "I want to see Greystokes."

"Couldn't he come another day?" Lou Emma asked.

"My dears, is it logical to come six hundred miles to meet a man and run away when he arrives? Particularly when Bob Barnes has asked Etting to take a look at my book? Sorry, I can't go to Greystokes-in-the-Pines. But you can."

"I don't want to go without you." Maddy stuck out her lip.

"Aunt Jesse'll pick on us if you're not there," Lou Emma said.

Even Miss Kate looked uncertain. "I've never met these people Jesse's with."

"Kate, I made mud pies with Ardelia Mayfield when she was Ardelia Jones. Jack and I were at Yale together. They're nice people. You must not hold their money against them. I want you to go and take the girls. Understand?"

It was his no-nonsense voice. Lou Emma watched Miss Kate's face.

"All right. We'll go."

"I will check on train times. I think the Colorado Midland makes a stop there. Now we'll go listen to some of Dr. Pettigrew's Red Seal records. He invited us especially.

"Moan-groan," Maddy began, but one look from her father and she hushed.

"If he'd just play records and not talk," Lou Emma said, and got the same look. *Grown-ups stick together like glue 'n' feathers.*

The rocking-chair brigade plus a few husbands sat in the parlor of the Wrenn's Nest. A fire crackled in the grate, and one lone bulb in a colored glass shade gave a dim light. The Millers came in as the last strains of "Un Bel Di Vedremo" from *Madame Butterfly* were being sung by Geraldine Farrar. Dr. Pettigrew held up one finger imperiously; the Millers stood, motionless, until the record came to an end. He nodded, and they found chairs in the back of the parlor while the other listeners applauded politely.

Dr. Pettigrew rewound the Victrola. He took up a record and dusted it with a piece of velvet. Then he cleared his throat and said: "We will now hear the great Nellie Melba in the Mad Scene from the opera *Lucia di Lammermoor* by Donizetti. This opera takes place in . . ."

"Shut-up-up-up-up," Maddy whispered.

Lou Emma nudged her. "Is that Mitch?"

"It sure is. What's he up to?"

Mitch was peering through the glass and grinning. He saw the Miller girls watching and wigwagged for them to turn around. At the same time he put his finger to his mouth in a hush-hush gesture.

Dr. Pettigrew droned on. "In this record Madam Melba reaches great heights in purity of tone and diction. Her rendition—in Italian, of course—is superb. Those of us who know the language—"

"Afraid you're the only one who does, Pettigrew," Dr. Cunningham said.

Dr. Pettigrew went on as if he had not been interrupted. "—will recognize the delicacy of intonation she has achieved."

With great precision he put the record on the turntable, pulled the lever, and placed the tone arm on the wax disk.

"R-r-r-roamin' in the gloamin'
On th' bonny banks o' Clyde. . . ."

The rich homespun voice of Harry Lauder, the favorite Scottish singer and comedian of the whole country, swept into the dim little parlor like a wind from the Peak.

"R-r-r-roamin' in the gloamin'
Wie my Lassie by my side . . ."

With a voice as knobby as a blackthorn stick and *r-r-r-r*'s burring as only a true Scot can sound them, he sang on and on. It was as good as oatcakes, but *Lucia di Lammermoor* it was *not.* The contrast plus the look on

Dr. Pettigrew's face was too much for the boarders at the Wrenn's Nest.

They began to laugh, first hiding politely behind handkerchiefs or coughs or wheezes, then openly. Loud and clear, the laughter filled the parlor. When Sir Harry Lauder began on "A Wee Deoch an' Dorris," they didn't pretend to stop, and even Mrs. Wrenn laughed till tears ran down her face. Dr. Pettigrew seemed unable to do a thing. He stared at the record as if it had betrayed him. When the last Scottish note boomed out, he stopped the turntable. Miss Magruder, who was deaf as a post, spoke up: "Play that one again, Dr. Pettigrew. I didn't get it all."

"I will not play that record, or any other record," the furious little man shouted. "And when I catch that young pup, Mitch . . ."

"Why blame Mitch?" his mother said. "He's not the only person at the Wrenn's Nest. As far as I'm concerned, that record was a big improvement over some we've had to listen to here."

"Really!" Mrs. Pettigrew was on her feet.

"Ladies, ladies," Mrs. Wrenn hurried over. "Only a boyish prank—"

"That Melba record was priceless. One scratch on it, and I'll . . ."

"Come along." Professor Miller shepherded his family from the room to the front porch. "Let's drive to town for some ice cream."

"We'll miss the fight!" Maddy ducked under his arm, but Miss Kate caught her.

Lou Emma searched the shadows of the porch, but Mitch was not to be seen. From the parlor came Miss Magruder's penetrating voice:

"What *is* a wee deoch an' dorris anyway?"

"Whiskey," Dr. Cummingham shouted in her good ear. "And a very good suggestion." He stamped onto the porch. "Anybody seen Mitch around?"

Lou Emma and Maddy squeezed hands.

"I don't think he's here," Miss Kate said.

"If you see him, tell him to hide from me." With that curious remark Dr. Cunningham left the porch.

"Why'd he think Mitch did it?" Maddy asked.

"Who else is smart enough or sneaky enough?" her father asked. "But I must say, he did all of us a good turn."

Lou Emma's heart jumped.

"—though I am sure he didn't intend to."

As they went out to the Great Smith, Lou Emma saw that Mitch was inside, sitting behind the wheel as he had been on the first day. She wanted to warn him, but there was no time. Anyway all her father did was to invite him to join the Millers for ice cream.

"Yes, sir." Mitch helped Miss Kate to the driver's seat and cranked the Great Smith. Then he got into the back with the girls.

"How'd you do it?" Maddy asked sociably.

"Do what?" Mitch said innocently.

"*You know*. Switch records on old Petticoat-grew."

It was the girls' private name for the fussy little man. Maddy clapped her hand over her mouth when she let it slip. Lou Emma waited for a rebuke from her father. To her amazement it came from Mitch.

"You shouldn't speak of Dr. Pettigrew that way. He's a great authority on Shakespeare. Isn't he, Professor Miller?"

"Yes, indeed. Well-known authority in the field." He turned around and Lou Emma could feel his eyes searching Mitch. She hoped he couldn't see that Mitch was holding her hand in the dark. "But I didn't know you were interested in Shakespeare."

"The greatest English writer, sir. I hope to be a writer some day."

"Hmmm. Well, I am sure that whatever you write, Mitch, will be"—he paused so long Lou Emma grew uneasy—"interesting."

"Thank you, sir," Mitch said and squeezed Lou Emma's hand so hard that the birthstone ring hurt her fingers.

Saturday morning breakfast at the Wrenn's Nest was less hurried and more bountiful than any other breakfast. A stream of pancakes came from the kitchen, and home-made brown-sugar syrup was hot and plentiful. At each place was an orange spoon and a half orange topped with powdered sugar.

Word had gone out over the grapevine that Dr. Pettigrew had found his precious Melba record unscratched on his bed and was ready to forgive and forget. But Mrs. Pettigrew and Mrs. Cunningham were still not speaking.

"A good day to take a trip," Miss Kate said after breakfast.

"Did you discourage me from giving an exam yesterday so we would have no papers to grade?" her husband asked.

"I did it for better or for worse," Miss Kate said. "Now, how about going up the Mount Manitou Incline? Mrs. Wrenn says . . ."

The very word "Manitou" was enough to set Lou Emma daydreaming about Mitch's invitation to take her to Soda Springs Park. She still had not told Maddy about it, and she knew she must. If only Maddy wouldn't raise a fuss . . . If only their father would decide to like Mitch . . . If only she could stop feeling guilty about Tommy Biddle . . .

"If Mrs. Wrenn says we should go," Professor Miller teased Miss Kate, "then let's not waste another minute. We might not get veal chops tomorrow."

"Chicken's for tomorrow," Maddy said. "They're in the coop now."

"I won't go near 'em," Lou Emma said. "I hate the way they look at me when I know I'm going to eat 'em."

"They don't know. You know," Maddy pointed out.

"It's the same difference," Lou Emma said.

"We won't be here for dinner," Miss Kate told Mrs. Wrenn. "We're taking a picnic lunch."

The road to Manitou was busy on a fine Saturday morning. Bicycles scorched by. Families packed into buggies and surreys smiled and waved. Trolley cars were loaded to capacity, and people were standing on the platform.

"R-r-r-roamin' in the gloamin'," Maddy began to sing.

"It's not 'the gloamin'," Lou Emma said. "That's almost dark."

"R-r-r-roamin' in the gloamin' with MI-ITCH *by my side!"*

"You'd better stop that." Lou Emma gave her sister a sharp push.

"Why do you like that slick, slimy sap?" Maddy asked. "If you push me again, I'll fall out the Great Smith and be killed. Do you want me dead?"

"I don't want you dead now," Lou Emma said. "But if you keep on . . . I like Mitch, and it's none of your beeswax why. He's different than anybody I ever knew. More grown-up and . . . grown-up."

"Ask me if I like Mitch?" Maddy said. "Dare you."

Lou Emma thought for a moment, then went ahead. "Do you like Mitch?"

"I like him, but I wouldn't trust him far as I could throw Pike's Peak. The way he pussyfoots around grown-ups—Gaaagh."

"He's just polite. Aunt Jesse says good manners are the touchstone of good breeding."

"What's that mean?"

"I don't really know. You can ask her when we get to Greystokes."

As she had hoped it would, the name of the famous hotel set Maddy to repeating what she had heard about its elegance. A coach-and-four to meet the trains, and fingerbowls at every meal. Mrs. Wrenn's cook said it took two hours to eat dinner, from sit down to get up.

"Would you stay at Greystokes, if the Mayfields asked us?"

Maddy shook her head slowly. "Uh-uh. It's too much trouble to be rich."

At a little grocery store on the outskirts of Colorado Springs, Miss Kate bought bologna, cheese, crackers, and apples. She gave out a nickel to each one to buy dessert. Maddy chose lemon drops and began sucking on them at once. Lou Emma took peppermint sticks. Miss Kate got vanilla wafers. Professor Miller settled on a can of sardines.

"For dessert?" Lou Emma squealed.

"We were never allowed to have them at home, so Jesse and I always thought they were a big treat. Once we sneaked a can in and opened it and spilled the oil all over us. Then we wondered how Mama knew what we'd done."

"You and *Aunt Jesse?*" Lou Emma thought of her fastidious spinster aunt. "She must have smelt terrible."

"She did," her father said. "And so will I when I have my dessert today."

They drove on toward Manitou. It was a smaller place than Colorado Springs, although both cities started at about the same time. Manitou was at the foot of Ute Pass. Mineral springs bubbled from the rocks in many places. In the 1870's Dr. Samuel Solly, an Englishman, gave names to many of the springs: the Navajo, the Shoshone, the Iron Ute. And he also wrote about the cures their waters could cause. Drinking the water or taking baths in it, he claimed, was helpful in treating diseases from gout to gallstones. Soon Manitou became popular as a health resort.

Big hotels grew up to take care of those who "came to take the waters." Famous men and women made trips to Manitou. As its fame grew, all kinds of entertainments were needed to keep the summer visitors busy. Bowling alleys, croquet grounds, tennis courts, shooting galleries, were built. Band concerts and dancing were popular. Hiking clubs, card games, and trout fishing took the time of some groups. And there was Soda Springs Park where most of the mineral springs were located. People sauntered from one strange-tasting watering spot to another, drinking from collapsible cups and filling gallon bottles to take back to hotel or boardinghouse or summer cottage to drink some more.

Back of it all rose Mount Manitou. Up this mountain an inclined railway was built to carry materials to the Pike's Peak Highway, which was slowly, but surely, being built to the top of the Peak. Once the highway was completed, it seemed too bad to tear out the inclined railway. So, with a little reworking and a lot of good advertising, it became a mile and a quarter straight-up ride for all comers. At the price of one dollar for adults, fifty cents for children, one could sit in an open cable car with two dozen others, rise to 9,455 feet, stay as long as the cars ran, and come down safe and sound, having had the thrill and chill of real mountain climbing.

Mrs. Wrenn described it to Miss Kate: "It's not the Cog Train to Pike's Peak, of course, but it's a sight you'll never forget. And it's high enough for me!"

Miss Kate drove with great care through Manitou. The streets were narrow and crowded with visitors. She pointed out Soda Springs Park. Lou Emma looked eagerly at the people clustered around the different springs. She could see herself and Mitch—mustn't forget to borrow Maddy's cup—as they strolled among them. A footbridge over Fountain Creek attracted Maddy who wanted to go wading, but Miss Kate was sure the water was icy cold. They drove by the handsome Cliff House hotel, and bumped across the Denver and Rio Grande tracks, and followed a baby burro, lost from its mother, and at last got onto a steep road that went stubbornly up the face of the mountain. The Great Smith labored, choked, and finally stopped. Miss Kate guided it backward off the road and pulled on the brake. Lou Emma and Maddy found rocks to jam under each wheel.

"We can walk from here," Miss Kate told them. "Mrs. Wrenn said—"

"I vote we leave Mrs. Wrenn in her Nest." The Professor gathered the food for the picnic in his good arm. "But did she say how far it is to the Incline?"

"You could ask over there." Miss Kate pointed to a

frame and stone building perched beside a railroad track. On the side was a big sign: MANITOU AND PIKE'S PEAK RAILWAY.

Maddy caught his coat. "That's the Cog Train depot. You can't ask there!"

Sure enough, there was a curious arrangement of metal cogs between the train tracks. A small-size but powerful-looking steam engine waited for a load of passengers to get into the cars in *front* of its tall flared smokestack. People were filing into the cars, coats on their arms, laughing and calling to one another. The engine gave a shrill little TOOT.

"Pike's Peak or Bust!" One man shouted happily to another.

The Millers watched as the tough little engine started pushing the cars in front of it, the forward end tilted, the back end upraised.

"I'm sure they won't mind my asking directions," Professor Miller said taking Maddy's hand from his coat. "And while I'm inside, I'll ask the price of the trip. Mrs. Wrenn *might* be wrong."

He was back in a short minute. "Mount Manitou Incline Railway Depot ahead and to the left. Cars leave every fifteen minutes. Let's hurry."

"Did you ask about you-know-what?" Maddy looked up at her father.

"Mrs. Wrenn was right. Five dollars a trip. Why did I doubt her?"

"Oh Papa, if only we could . . ." She choked, looking after the Cog Train.

"Don't, Maddy. Remember, you're not crying. It's the altitude." He tried to make her smile.

"I know what the Cog Train engine looks like," Lou Emma said suddenly. "Like Swish when he's taking off to butt somebody into Kingdom Come."

They managed to laugh then and walked together up the steep climb to the depot where the Incline waited. In the kinnickinnick a half-dozen chipmunks begged crackers, lemon drops, peppermint chips, and vanilla wafer crumbs from the Millers. Only the Professor's sardines were safe.

The Mount Manitou Incline was an arrangement of two cars that balanced each other. When one was at the station, the other was at the top. As one went up, the other came down. The waiting car was tilted so sharply that getting into it gave Lou Emma the feeling of sitting on a step-ladder step. She and Maddy had the front seat, near the man with the megaphone. Three seats back sat Miss Kate and Professor Miller. At the last minute a freckle-faced boy was hustled up with his family and poked into the seat beside the girls. He sat far over to the side as if to avoid the contagion of being a girl. The man with the megaphone had to make him get his hands, arms, feet, and knees into the car a half-dozen times.

"Looks like Tommy Biddle," Maddy said in a low voice.

"Does *not*. Tommy's better looking."

"Look around Dewey," the boy's mother called. "You too, little girls."

Nobody in the seat moved. The man with the megaphone said it was time to go. "Wait a minute, mister. I want his picture. My boy's picture. And the girls."

"Turn around, you katzenjammers," the man growled. "Or I'll pitch you out at the top and run you down with the car."

They all three turned, but just as the boy's mother snapped the picture, the boy, Dewey, made a horrible face, stretching his mouth with his thumbs.

"Another one," she begged, but the man with the megaphone shook his head.

"Siddown, lady, siddown. This car is now starting up Mount Manitou where it will attain a grade of 68 per cent. . . . a steel cable of one inch thickness protects your lives. . . . everything is done to insure your safety . . . but we can guarantee nothing without your cooperation . . . To your right . . ."

He droned on. The boy grinned. Maddy and Lou Emma moved over.

"Betcha that's the worst pitcher she'll get this trip."

"Why'd you make a face?" Maddy asked.

"Tired of pitchers. I'm gonna bust that Brownie before we get back home."

"Where'd you live?" Lou Emma inquired. "We live in Gloriosa, Kansas."

"We live in St. Louis, Missouri, an' I wisht I was there right now."

"Don't you like Colorado?" Lou Emma was shocked.

"Oh, it'll do. But Ma's been on my neck the whole time. She won't even let me go on the Cog Train because she heard it was bad for kids."

"Is it? Really?"

"Naw. *I* don't see how it could be. But the lady that runs our boarding house says you're not s'posed to take kids under twelve. Heck fire, I'm ten an' three quarters."

"We're twelve and thirteen," Maddy said, carefully not saying which was which. "Your mother prob'ly knows best. It might be bad for little kids."

"Arrrrgh," Dewey growled, and retired to the far side of the seat.

"Why're you so mean?" Lou Emma whispered.

"I'm tired of being polite," Maddy said. "And when I think what we'll have to do at Greystokes, I want to be mean now where it won't count—much."

"We're going up backward," Lou Emma said to make conversation. "Why's that, Dewey?"

"Arrrrgh," Dewey answered.

Clackety-clack, clackety-clack. The car began to rise past the depot. The tilt of the seat changed. Lou Emma broke a peppermint stick into threes and offered the largest section to Dewey. He took it with a suspicious squint.

"Cameron's Cone . . ." the man with the megaphone pointed out.

"Yoo-hoo, Deweeeee," a voice called.

"Arrrrgh." Dewey slid down in the seat.

"There's the Garden of the Gods," Maddy pointed.

Dewey slid up again. "I climbed up to the Kissin' Camels. Almost."

"Me, too!" Maddy said; then she looked at Lou Emma. "I mean I almost did. I mean—I got scared and quit. They had to bring us down with a ladder."

"Hey, that'd be fun," Dewey said. "Next time I'll try that."

Maddy said, "It wouldn't hurt a tough kid like you to go up the Peak. She must have bats in her belfry."

"Maddy! It's his mother." Lou Emma exclaimed.

"Aw, don't get in a tizzy," Dewey said. "I told her that m'self. And she said anybody that had to raise a boy like me had a *right* to bats."

Clackety-clack, clackety-clack, the car rattled its way up. The man with the megaphone pointed out the Antlers Hotel: "Built by General Palmer who died last year, lamented by all . . ."

"Chewing gum?" Dewey whipped out a pack of Blackjack.

The Miller girls looked back, but their parents were watching the scenery. Each girl crammed a stick in her mouth and chewed hard. Professor Miller detested chewing gum.

"We're getting awful high up," Lou Emma said around her cud of Blackjack.

"Don't be scared," Dewey said. "There won't nothin' happen long as I'm here. I was borned on Admiral Dewey's birthday, an' it'll take a silver bullet to kill me. An old woman told my mother that when I was about dead o' the croup."

It was a comforting thought, but as the car continued to rise, Lou Emma wondered if the old woman in St. Louis was reliable.

At the halfway point the car swung to the side, and the second car came sliding down the cable. The people waved and shouted. The man with the megaphone said that if Dewey didn't sit quiet he was going to throw him to the bears.

"Ain't no bears," Dewey said. "Nothin' bigger'n chipmunks."

But Lou Emma noticed he pulled his feet inside.

The view was really glorious now. Far, far out across the world of green, of lakes and trees, was the dim mysterious plain. The clouds touched it and melted into it. They had crossed the plain to come to Colorado, and to see it now was like looking back at a well-remembered past.

Tommy, Tommy. Lou Emma twisted the birthstone ring. *Don't be mad. I just let it pop out.*

"You can see a hundred miles," the man with the megaphone announced.

I can see farther than that.

"We are now approaching the summit of Mount Manitou. An elevation of 9,455 feet, rising from an altitude of 6,000 feet at the depot. Cars leave every fifteen minutes. Stay as long as you like. Picnic tables to the left. Burros to the Halfway House for rent. . . ."

He said more, but Maddy and Lou Emma heard no more. Burros for rent! The car rattled to a stop. Dewey was out in a flash, and the last they saw he was disappearing up the trail as his mother chased him with her camera.

Maddy popped her gum. "I liked him, even if he was little."

"What's the Halfway House?" Lou Emma wanted to know.

"Let's ask Papa."

"Let's swallow our gum first."

Ulp-gulp, and it was down. Only their black tongues showed they had even had it.

"Did you like the trip?" Miss Kate asked as they gathered on the platform.

"Sure," Maddy said. "Papa, can we rent a burro and ride?"

"To the Halfway House. Whatever that is?" Lou Emma said.

"We'll see. Let's walk around here first."

It was chipmunk heaven!

The top of Mount Manitou was scattered with great boulders. Wind-twisted trees made low shelter, and the chipmunks ran like quicksilver. Big black-and-white magpies rasped greetings to each other and quarreled with the chipmunks. Smoke of picnic fires made a good smell in the morning sunshine. People walked about talking to each other in the easy friendliness of vacationers.

"Say you're from Kansas City? Know the McFalls?"

"When we lived in Wichita we knew some McFalls, but they went to Texas."

Professor Miller found a man and his wife from Cleveland. They had a son at Auden College.

Miss Kate "borrowed" a fire from some people who had finished eating and they grilled bologna slices on sticks and ate them hot. Chunks of cheese heated just to melting and popped on crackers burned the tongue with their goodness. Then came dessert, and Professor Miller opened his sardines with his pocket knife. The girls began to beg for bites.

"You're worse than chipmunks," he said, putting bites on the knife blade.

"Next time we'll each have a can. And next time we'll bring steak." Miss Kate tossed her last crumb of vanilla wafer to a magpie. Her hair was ruffled by the wind, and her cheeks were pink.

She's so pretty, Lou Emma thought. Then a strange thing crept into her mind. *I wish she'd do something not perfect. Make a big fat mess of it.* She was so ashamed of herself that she jumped up and began picking up the picnic papers, chasing away the chipmunks and talking about Dewey all at once.

"I saw him," Miss Kate said. "He made me think of Tommy."

"Tommy's better-looking," Maddy teased. *"Lou Emma said so."*

The Halfway House was a mountain hotel built at the fork of Ruxton Creek. It was named from its position on the road to the top of Pike's Peak. From Mount Manitou there was a well-marked trail for hikers to cross over to the hotel. For those who didn't want to walk, a string of burros, saddled and ready to ride, filled a small corral. Gray, brown, mouse-colored, with floppy ears and big mournful eyes, they waited for riders. But when the Miller girls discovered the rental price was a dollar each they knew it was far too high for them.

"Isn't there anything money won't butt into?" Maddy asked sadly.

"Lots of things," her father said, "but this is not the place to talk about them. Did you ever hear of riding and tying?"

"What's that?" Maddy looked suspicious.

Miss Kate said, "I've heard of that. My grandmother—" Then she stopped, her face bright pink. "Go on, Cyrus, tell the girls."

"To ride and tie is very simple. In pioneer times it helped people get where they were going. With one horse and two people, one person sets off on horseback—or burro-back—rides a half mile, gets off, ties up the burro, walks on. The other person sets off afoot, finds the tied burro, rides a half mile—"

"Gets off, ties the burro, walks on—" Lou Emma giggled. "That's fun."

They picked the biggest, stoutest burro named Captain Jack, and Maddy started first. She rode off at a smart pace, Captain Jack's hoofs twinkling in the dusty path. Lou Emma waited until Maddy was out of sight; then she started, jogging on foot. She found Captain Jack tied to a yellow pine tree, and Maddy's green dress just disappearing down the trail. She untied

Captain Jack, got on, and told him to "giddap." He didn't move. "Please, giddap." No motion. She shook the reins; she clucked; she chirruped. Captain Jack stood calmly in the middle of the trail.

"Kick 'im," a man told her.

"Oh, I couldn't do that. He's . . . he's not mine."

"Kick 'im. He's waiting for you to do it."

"Well . . . All right." Lou Emma kicked Captain Jack in the sides, hating herself and feeling terrible. He started off at a smart pace. The man's laughter followed them.

"Hateful," she muttered, but when Captain Jack stopped again, she knew how to start him. And by that time her half mile was up.

Riding and tying, they reached Halfway House, a big log hotel, and ventured inside for a look at the huge fireplace with elk horns mounted over it. When they got outside, Captain Jack was gone. The clerk at the desk comforted them.

"Captain Jack? He's a smart one. Unties any rope he's a mind to. He's prob'ly back on the trail."

And there they found him, blowing at the dust, his tie-rope dragging.

"What'll we do? If he unties ropes, he can go off anytime."

"We can just ride him double," Maddy said. "Ride 'n' tie may be all right for Miss Kate's grandmother, but it's old-fashioned for us."

They found Miss Kate and Professor Miller waiting

at the Mount Manitou Incline. It was late afternoon, and the big clouds that drifted up made a marvelous sight. Just as they started down a rain shower came, and they all got wet and drove back to the Wrenn's Nest as fast as they could go. Mrs. Wrenn had a big fire built in the parlor fireplace. It was beginning to seem like home. Lou Emma looked for Mitch, hoping to tell him about the Incline. He was not in sight. At supper there were several people missing, the Cunninghams among them.

Lou Emma chewed slowly through her mostly-potatoes hash. There must be some way she could think up to see Mitch. As she finished her cup custard, it came to her. She would need to tell him to be sure and bring a cup for drinking at the Soda Springs on Monday. That was certainly reason enough to go up later and knock on the Cunningham door.

She waited until the rest of the Wrenn's Nest boarders were gathered in the parlor, listening to Miss Magruder read poetry. Maddy had complained of a chill and gone to bed. It was simple for Lou Emma to say she must go up and see how Maddy was.

On the second floor she tiptoed to the door of the Cunninghams' rooms. She had been right. There was someone inside. She rapped lightly, and the door was snatched open in her face. The heavy-set maid of all work looked out.

"Is—is—Mrs. Cunningham here?"

She wouldn't ask for Mitch, not if she died for it.

"Moved out today."

"Moved out? But—but—where?"

"Went back to where they come from, an' good riddance. His time was up at the college. Now I've got to get this place ready for new folks comin' tomorrow. Sunday! Movin' in on Sunday! Heathenish, I'd say."

She went back to her work, jerking a folding bed out from the wall. Lou Emma stood, hardly able to understand what she had heard. Then she caught sight of a piece of white cloth, a cloth familiar to her from weeks and weeks of work. It was under the edge of the folding bed. She pulled it out.

"May I . . . have this?"

"Nothin' to me, but don't tell Miz Wrenn." The maid leaned over to sweep under the bed. "Lived here three weeks an' never swep'. Never made up the bed till ten A.M. And that boy . . ."

"Thank you," Lou Emma said, backing out of the room.

She stood in the hall, looking at the handkerchief. It was dirty, and one corner of the hemstitching was torn. Her eyes stung.

He knew he was leaving before Monday. He knew it, and he asked me to go to Manitou anyway. Why? Why? . . . It's so mean . . . so . . . so mean.

Chapter 16

Now the days began to hop, skip, and jump toward the trip to Greystokes. Professor Miller discovered that the Colorado Midland Railroad did make a stop there, but it was at eight thirty in the evening, too late for the dinner for which *everyone dressed*.

After some talk Miss Kate said she and the girls could drive the Great Smith to Greystokes-in-the-Pines. They could leave in the morning, take a picnic lunch, and cover the thirty miles in plenty of time to get *dressed for dinner*.

"Foolish custom," Professor Miller said.

"Papa, when we ate at the Harvey House you said it was right to have a rule to wear a coat. You said a man might decide not to wear pants."

"Well, well, so I did. Why don't you girls ever remember the smart things I say?"

"We're going to wear our white organdies with tatting on the collars."

"And satin sashes—pink for Maddy, blue for me," Lou Emma said.

"Miss Kate's going to wear her white surrah."

"At least the Millers will be properly dressed," he said, smiling. "And anything I have said against the custom of dressing for dinner is *out*."

The boarders at the Wrenn's Nest were all interested in the trip. Mrs. Wrenn offered to pack a picnic lunch. Mrs. Pettigrew gave the girls hair bows to match their sashes. Miss Magruder wrote a poem. Even the new people who took the Cunninghams' room had heard of Greystokes from as far away as Columbia University in New York City.

If Mitch had been around to witness all their glory Lou Emma felt she would have been satisfied. But Mitch was gone—a gone goose—and she had been a goose to pay any attention to him.

For a few days she had asked hopefully at the post-office window, "Anything for Miss Lou Emma Miller?" But there was nothing. Not even a postcard. Mitch didn't care a one-cent stamp's worth what she thought.

Tommy wouldn't have treated a girl that way. And look how she had treated Tommy because of Mitch. She squirmed when she thought of what she had said to the girl from Omaha and to punish herself took off the birthstone ring and vowed not to wear it again until the trip to Greystokes.

Professor Miller was working over the first chapter of his book, and Miss Kate was copying it for him. This left the girls on their own most of the day. Maddy came up with a plan to go to Soda Springs Park in Manitou, and Miss Kate gave them a quarter each. Lou Emma told herself she felt too miserable about Mitch to go to the very place he said he would take her, but it was too hard to explain, so she went along saying nothing.

The trolley got up to high speeds outside the city limits and raced over the hump on Colorado Avenue, right on up to Manitou. Lou Emma had intended to mourn all day, but she got to having such a lot of fun with Maddy she forgot all about it. First of all there was the mineral water!

The nearer they came to the crowd around the first spring the more the water smelled of—rotten eggs. They looked at each other in dismay.

"Maybe it tastes better'n it smells." Lou Emma got her cup full and gulped the sulphur water down, her eyes shut tight.

"How's it taste?"

"Horrible-terrible. Worse'n it smells." Lou Emma refilled her cup.

"Whatcha drinking more for?"

"Mrs. Wrenn says the worse it tastes the better it is for you."

At the Iron Spring Maddy got her courage up and drank first. She gagged. "This must be the best for you. It couldn't taste worse."

They found a mild soda spring and drank some more. People made lemonade from this spring, bringing jars and making it on the spot. It fizzed and had a pleasant taste. A sociable lady gave the girls some from her jar. "Where're you girls from?"

"Gloriosa, Kansas," Maddy said. "Where're you from?"

"Omaha, Nebraska. We've been here a month. Have another cup?"

"No, thank you kindly." Lou Emma stepped away, the good lemonade gone sour in her mouth. She was afraid to look around for fear the girl from Omaha might appear.

They kept on drinking every kind of water that was free. Maddy declared she could hear it sloshing in her stomach when she walked. They watched people having their pictures taken with a blanketed Indian who claimed to be 112 years old and a friend of Sitting Bull. They watched players in a fan-tan parlor and shuddered at a stuffed bear killed in Williams Canyon in 1879. An organ-grinder with a monkey collected pennies, and Lou Emma put one in the tiny dark paw of the monkey and wondered at his sad eyes. They found a man making salt-water taffy in one of the shops. He pulled long ropes of pink-and-white candy, throwing loops around a hook, and then a woman cut them into eating-size pieces and filled sacks and boxes. The Miller girls each bought a nickel sack, but it was so good they came back for more. It was the best and the longest-lasting candy either one had ever had. Maddy put three pieces in her mouth; then she couldn't get her jaws open.

"I 'ot 'ockjaw," she snickered.

"Don't laugh," Lou Emma laughed. "You'll swallow it whole." At that she swallowed a hunk of pink taffy. Maddy had to beat her on the back.

With a nickel each to spend, they bought doughnuts in a bakery and washed them down with mineral water for "dinner." Then they listened to a band concert, peeked at the elegance of the Cliff House lobby, and caught the trolley back to Colorado Springs. It had been an eventful day.

Only when they were almost home did the combination of mineral waters, salt-water taffy, and doughnuts give them violent stomachaches.

"Oooo, I feel awful," Lou Emma moaned.

"Me, too." Maddy clutched her middle. "It must be the altitude."

The girls were up early on August the twelfth, but Miss Kate was earlier still. They found her in the kitchen of the Wrenn's Nest ironing their organdy dresses. Mrs. Wrenn was packing the picnic lunch. She went to the back porch for some peaches set there to ripen.

"I don't like that sky. Rain in the mountains is no joke."

Miss Kate spit on her finger and sizzled the iron. "The sky looks blue to me. Not a cloud when I came down."

"Over around the Peak it's hazy. I've lived here so long, and the weather's so changeable . . . but it may pass as the sun gets higher."

She finished the lunch and gave it to the girls to put in the auto. They promised to tell her every single thing about Greystokes.

Miss Kate took the billowing organdy dresses upstairs and packed them in enough tissue paper to wrap the Great Smith. Professor Miller was there, picking up papers, books, and graded exams. In honor of Dr. Etting, Miss Kate had made him a new sling of Yale-blue silk faille.

"Now Cyrus, don't be nervous," Miss Kate said, dropping a mouthful of pins and knocking her hairbrush from the dresser.

"Nervous? Don't be silly. I'm as calm as Peak's Pike."

The girls giggled, then hushed quickly.

"*Sanguine Saturnini!* Where's my first chapter?"

"In your hand, dear," Miss Kate said. "And whatever Dr. Etting may say it's a wonderful, wonderful book."

"Better'n H-O-G!" Lou Emma shook her fist.

"I dare him not to like it. Double dog dare," Maddy growled.

"We'll see . . . we'll see . . ." Professor Miller said, buttoning his coat wrong. "I'm more worried about you three than anything Etting will say. Kate, don't drive fast. Use the engine to brake, not the brakes. Carry extra water, and watch out for the High Rock Road. If you get in trouble . . ."

He broke off and stood staring at them.

"Why did I ever let you talk me into this fool expedition?"

"We're not going to get into trouble," Miss Kate soothed him. "We're going to have a nice trip, visit with Jesse, dine at Greystokes in our best bibs and tuckers, and be back tomorrow. Hurry, or you'll be late."

"Yes, yes . . . Etting . . . must hurry." Professor Miller let himself be pushed out the bedroom door. As they heard the front door open and close, all three of them collapsed on the bed.

"He had his coat buttoned wrong, but I was afraid to tell him," Lou Emma said.

"He was wearing his old hat, not his good one," Maddy said.

"I used to want Cyrus to write a dozen books, but I don't think I can stand the strain," Miss Kate said.

They gave the back seat over to the dresses packed into three suitboxes. The picnic lunch was on the floor, and Mrs. Wrenn added a thermos of hot tea. The girls cranked the auto, and both got in the front seat with Miss Kate. As they drove away, the windows of the Wrenn's Nest were full of waving hands. Waving in return, Lou Emma admired the birthstone ring, back on her finger.

They drove to the Antlers Hotel, and Maddy pointed out the exact spot where Teddy Roosevelt had stood to make a speech. Miss Kate set the odometer at zero and said, "When it gets to thirty we'll know we're there."

Lou Emma wasn't listening to either one of them. She was looking up at Pike's Peak. The mighty mountain glimmered in the sun like the Promised Land. More than anything she wanted to go to the very, very top. She wanted to stand there and look and look. Fourteen thousand feet, someone had told her.

She whispered the figures over to herself. But other figures—seventeen dollars and fifty cents—came and pushed them away.

"Don't worry about the weather," Miss Kate said.

"I wasn't. I was thinking about . . . the Cog Train. Mitch said . . ."

"I'm glad he's gone," Maddy said. "He was a stuck-up show-off."

"Yes, but—" Lou Emma started and stopped. She couldn't defend Mitch, but she couldn't hear him abused either. She was thankful when Miss Kate began to talk about the Cave of the Winds that Mrs. Wrenn said they must visit.

It was an easy drive west to Colorado City. There they looked at the little log cabin labeled "First Capitol of Colorado Territory." It was too small to get a governor and three mayors into, Miss Kate said. The road took them to Manitou, and Maddy insisted that they stop and Miss Kate taste the water at the Iron Spring. She made a dreadful face and chased the girls back to the Great Smith.

Now the road curved to the right. This was the canyon road to Ute Pass and famous as a testing ground for motor cars. It was graveled, and the Great Smith threw bits of gravel at the kinnickinnick. The road began to climb. The Great Smith went forward slowly but steadily. Miss Kate slipped the gears from one spot to another, seeming as much at home with the big auto as she was with her sewing machine in the millinery shop. The girls stopped talking to watch.

The road turned steeper. The gears ground hard. The Great Smith began to slip backward. Maddy grabbed Lou Emma's knee; Lou Emma grabbed the dashboard. Calmly Miss Kate looked back and let the car slide into a patch of hardened clay that was almost level. Then she hit the gas pedal hard, and the big red auto shot ahead. It began climbing again; the girls began breathing.

Miss Kate patted the steering wheel. "Good boy, good boy."

At the top of the four-mile stretch that was Ute Pass was the town of Cascade. It, too, was filled with summer visitors. While Miss Kate bought a can of extra gas, the girls bought postcards. Lou Emma sent one with a burro on it to Tommy. Maddy insisted on sending one like it to Swish, "care of Hardy Garrett, Esq."

At the edge of Cascade was a sign, UTE PASS 6,800 FEET.

"Good thing I didn't know that," Miss Kate said.

The road leveled off for a short space. A mountain stream came bubbling beside the roadbed. When the Great Smith's engine overheated, they dipped icy water from the stream to fill the radiator. Mountain phlox in pink, white, and lavender colored the banks. By a dripping spring was a clump of bright yellow monkey flowers. The Millers drove through Green Mountain Falls without stopping.

The stream crossed the road to the left. The canyon

widened and the sunlight gleamed on the Great Smith's red hood, polished in honor of the visit to Greystokes. At Woodland Park the odometer read 19.5. They congratulated each other on making such good time.

The words were hardly spoken before a tire sizzled and went flat.

"We'll change it. Tommy taught us," the girls shouted.

Before they even had the jack out, a yellow Thomas touring car pulled up behind, and a man from Fort Worth, Texas, insisted on changing the tire for them. His wife asked Miss Kate to sit in their car and visit. Feeling a little unnecessary, Lou Emma and Maddy wandered down the road and followed a footpath that led them to the right.

Pine and aspen branched over the path; beside it a thread of water trickled down to join the stream below. Ferns grew thick, and deep green moss covered the rocks. A woodpecker drummed on a tree, and an unknown bird sang over and over, *Cher-wee, Cher-wee, Cheo-dee-dee-dee.* The sounds from Woodland Park were as hushed as if they came from another world.

There on a granite ledge they found a cluster of Rocky Mountain red columbine. The flowers rested so lightly on their stems it seemed a breath might carry them away. The bluish-green leaves made a perfect background for the red flowers with their yellow-tipped spurs.

"Should we pick'em for Miss Kate?" Maddy put out her hand.

"N-no. They wouldn't be the same in the Great Smith as they are here."

"We ought to go back, I guess," Maddy said without moving.

It was hard to leave. Stratton Park was theirs because they found it, but it belonged to thousands of other people, too. This place was theirs, alone.

"We ought to go back," Lou Emma said.

This time they walked slowly down the path, looking back now and then at the columbine and the golden sunlight through the aspens.

A patch of red berries was by the path. Lou Emma tasted one.

"Red raspberries!"

They picked and picked, putting the berries by turns into their mouths and into Maddy's big pocket to take to Miss Kate. The berries were plentiful, sweet, and tangy. The pocket bulged. From far-off came the call of the Great Smith. "Oo-*oo*-gah! Oo-*oo*-gah!"

They ran, pelting down the path, Maddy's bulging pocket flopping against her leg. The yellow Thomas auto and the Texas couple were gone. Miss Kate stood by the Great Smith, glancing at her watch.

"Red raspberries for you!" Maddy tumbled them from her pocket onto the Great Smith's wide running board. Not one was perfect; they were a gooey mess. Maddy's pocket looked as if she had been mortally wounded.

"Look!" Lou Emma stamped her foot. "Why didn't you be careful?"

"Why didn't you put 'em in *your* pocket? You priss!"

Miss Kate reached between them and took a few of the mashed berries. "Delicious. We'll come by here on the way back, and you can show me where you got them. Now, it's time to go. Lou Emma's turn to crank."

Laboring over the heavy crank took all the crossness out of Lou Emma. She jumped in beside Maddy and offered her own handkerchief to help take up the seeping stain.

Still climbing, the road turned southwest. They came to Divide.

"EIGHTY-TWO HUNDRED FEET." Maddy read aloud. "Did you know *that?*"

"No," Miss Kate said. "I suppose a girl raised in Kansas naturally thinks all the world is flat. What a funny name for a town—Divide."

"It means the Continental Divide." Maddy had the *Touring Guide.*

"We had that in Geography," Lou Emma shut her eyes to remember better. "All the rain that falls on one side goes to the Atlantic Ocean, and all on the other goes to the Pacific. I never thought it was real."

"The sky's gone sort of gray." Maddy leaned across Lou Emma and looked out, getting raspberry stain on her, too. "Maybe it's the altitude."

"I hope we can find some way to clean up a little

before we see Jesse," Miss Kate said. "Find some water and wash our hands and face."

The road branched. One sign read FLORISSANT, 8 MILES. But the other, a large rustic sign with the words carefully carved, was GREYSTOKES-IN-THE-PINES, 7 MILES.

As if they had been holding their breath all morning, the three Millers heaved a mighty sigh.

"We've made it—almost," Miss Kate said. "Thank goodness."

"And the Great Smith," Maddy said. "Don't forget it."

Lou Emma reached over to the steering wheel and patted it as Miss Kate had done. "Good boy. Good boy."

"When you girls see a spot you'd like to picnic—"

"Right there," Maddy pointed. "Right in the middle."

A dry creek bed was below them, and a big boulder had been left stranded with its upper side flat and white. Maddy said it was the perfect table for a picnic. It took a lot of scrambling from the Great Smith on the high shelf of the road to the creek bed and over the loose stones to the big boulder; but they made it, lunch and all. The sun came out hot and bright.

Mrs. Wrenn had outdone herself. Chicken salad sandwiches, lettuce wedges, sweet pickles, peaches, squares of fudge. The hot tea was heavily sugared, and it tasted wonderful. They ate to the last crumb.

"I feel so lazy." Miss Kate leaned against the boulder. "Back home I'd be at the shop making hats, thinking about supper, or doing the bookkeeping."

Her voice drifted off, and she pulled her cap forward till the visor hid her eyes. "I think I'll take a snooze here in the sun."

"Me, too." Lou Emma leaned against Miss Kate.

"Me, too." Maddy squirmed down till her head was in Lou Emma's lap.

The deep silence of the mountains made sleeping easy. Far above the timberline a hawk rode the wind. A distant cowbell tinkled. A little breeze fluttered Miss Kate's new white scarf.

A bee was buzzing around Lou Emma's face. The sound got into her ears and would not stop. She flapped her hand, but the *buzz-zz* went on. Then it wasn't buzzing any more; the sound was the mutter of thunder in the mountains; the sun was gone.

Lou Emma blinked, and the thunder rolled nearer. Suddenly she jumped to her feet, dumping Miss Kate and Maddy against each other.

"Get up! Hurry!"

A wall of water was rushing down the dry creek bed. Branches of trees were tossing on white foam. Underneath the water was an ugly brown. Jerking at Miss Kate and Maddy, Lou Emma ran, stumbled, fell, scrambled up, and got across the creek bed. They clawed their way up the high shelf of the bank as the wall of water tore past them. Then came the rain, slashing, cold as ice. And with the rain, more thunder and lightning that was like green fire.

"Get in the Great Smith," Miss Kate screamed.

But there was little shelter inside. The wind drove the rain into the auto. Down in the creek bed Lou

Emma saw the water cover the top of the boulder and Mrs. Wrenn's thermos go bobbing away. To the Atlantic? To the Pacific?

"The side curtains," Maddy yelled in Lou Emma's ear.

They dug the side curtains out from underneath the back seat. Black canvas curtains with isinglass peep-holes, and buttons to twist and hold them in place. Now at least there was some shelter, though they were soaked to the skin. Miss Kate sat, almost in a daze, as they crept back inside.

Thunder roared till it jarred the mind. In the green glare of the lightning Lou Emma saw that Miss Kate was crying, her hands clenched.

"Miss Kate? Are you hurt?"

Her stepmother turned a tear-stained face toward her. Never had she seen Miss Kate look like this. Hair plastered by the rain, muddy hands, tears dripping from her chin.

"What's the matter?" Lou Emma and Maddy spoke at the same time.

Miss Kate said, "I'm going to have a baby."

Now she cried harder than ever. Not bothering to hide her face, not wiping away the tears.

"I hate thunder and lightning, and I'm tired and my back hurts, and I never had a baby and I'm . . . scared."

Scared? Tired? Lou Emma had never thought this could happen to Miss Kate. On Maddy's face she saw the same astonishment that she felt.

"I'll have to stop work at the shop," Miss Kate sobbed, "and that means less money. And I never wanted you girls to do housework, but just to have a good time and be free. But now . . ."

"A new baby," Lou Emma said. "It's going to be fun."

"A girl," Maddy said. "We can dress her up and show her off."

"A boy," Lou Emma said. "We can name him Cyrus, only not Junior. I hope he looks just like Papa. And me."

The sobbing stopped. Miss Kate looked at Maddy and then at Lou Emma. "You mean you're not mad?"

"Why'd we be mad?" Lou Emma asked in return. "We'll like it to have you home. And we never had any money anyway, and we like to do housework only you can always do it such a lot better that . . . that . . ."

"Not me," Maddy said. "I hate housework. But I'll do what you tell me, and we like babies. We never had any. There's Joy Wacker, but she's not ours."

"This'll be really ours," Lou Emma said. "Our baby brother."

"Sister," Maddy said. "She can be a suffragette."

CRASH!

Lightning struck a dead tree a mile away. A blaze of fire blinded them, and all three dived for the bottom of the Great Smith. After the thunder had rolled away, they came up as cautiously as T. G., the box turtle. Lou Emma took her handkerchief from Maddy's pocket and handed it to Miss Kate.

"Cyrus told me you'd be glad," she said, getting red stains on her nose. "But I didn't believe him. I was glad, and he was but I thought . . ."

A bellow of thunder shook the Great Smith. Maddy stuck her fingers in her ears. "The baby? When? WHEN?"

"January," Miss Kate yelled back, her fingers in her ears, her eyes tight shut. Lou Emma stroked her arm.

"Don't be scared, Miss Kate. Remember your Grandmother Evangeline that went to California in a covered wagon and had a baby on the way?"

To her absolute horror, this set Miss Kate off on another spell of tears. She cried and shook and hiccupped while the storm raged outside.

"I made her up," she said at last. "She was a lie. I made her up."

"You made up your grandmother?" Lou Emma asked, unbelieving.

Out of the dark sky hail rattled on the Great Smith's red metal chassis. The inside of the auto was like the inside of a drum.

As quickly as it had started, the hail stopped. With one long roll the thunder retreated. A quiet surrounded them. Miss Kate took a deep breath.

"I had a grandmother, but she wasn't like that at all. She never got out of Kansas and she was scared of her own shadow."

"But you told us— You said—"

"I know. Cyrus thought we shouldn't come to Colorado because of the baby. But the doctor said it was all right, and I felt fine. And I thought you girls would never forgive me if I spoiled your trip . . ."

"Course we'd've. Wouldn't we, Lou Emma?" Maddy said.

"Course," Lou Emma answered, but in her heart she wondered. She had been resentful of Miss Kate, of her father's eternal, "Don't overdo." She had even thought things were better BMK. "Please, please don't cry any more."

"It popped out when we were talking," Miss Kate said, "all that wild story. And I heard myself telling my very own girls a . . . a . . . lie."

"But you did it to get Papa to let us have the trip," Maddy said.

"That's no excuse. A lie is wrong. I told Cyrus the truth the next day, but he wouldn't tell you for me. He said it was up to me, and every day . . . every single day . . ." She shook her head. "It popped out as if I'd been planning it for a long time."

The birthstone ring twinkled at Lou Emma. That had been the way she had said to the girl from Omaha: *A boy gave me my ring. Mitch, Mitchell Cunningham gave it to me.* That had popped out, too.

"Now you know," Miss Kate said. "I guess you won't ever be able to believe me again, and I don't blame you a bit. I just wish I could change things."

"I don't," Lou Emma said. "I like you the way you are. I . . . love you, Miss Kate."

"Me, too," Maddy said.

The smallest smile began in Miss Kate's red-rimmed

eyes, spread to her mouth, and lighted her whole face. "I believe you do. I really believe you do."

"We ought to get started," Maddy said. The rain had stopped. The clouds were clearing. Only the creek below, running bankfull, showed what the storm had done.

Miss Kate looked at her watch. "Gracious! It's four o'clock. We ought to be at Greystokes by five to be dressed by six."

"It's only seven miles." Lou Emma remembered the sign.

The rain had left the road slick. At every runoff in the canyon wall a rampant stream of water flooded across in front of them. Miss Kate drove the Great Smith at a snail's pace through the water and the sticky mud. The road was narrow. Sheer rock wall on one side, drop-off of rock and rubble to the roaring water on the other. As they slipped and slid, climbing higher, the road narrowed.

"If we meet somebody—" Maddy shivered.

The road curved around a bulge in the canyon wall. At the outer edge it had crumbled and washed out. Miss Kate brought the Great Smith to a stop. She looked at the girls. "Get out. I want you to walk."

"No!" Maddy said. "No!"

"Yes," Lou Emma said. "Miss Kate wants us to. We'll do it."

Grumbling, Maddy joined her sister in the road. Miss Kate inched the auto forward. At the narrowest point, with the clay crumbling, she accelerated. The clay spun out from the wheels, and she was on the other side in safety. The girls ran to the side of the auto.

"Good for you!" Maddy shouted. "Bet your Grandmother Evangeline couldn't have done that if she was real."

Miss Kate laughed a shaky laugh. "Just be thankful we had the Great Smith and not a covered wagon. It's a good car."

They started to get in, but she stopped them.

"I want you to walk. One by the front wheels, and one by the back. Carry those rocks we use to wedge under the wheels when we change a tire. If the road starts to crumble, jam the rock under the wheel and *get out of the way*—Understand?"

"Yes, ma'am," the girls gulped.

So began the long walk to Greystokes. Maddy by the back wheel, Lou Emma by the front. At times the road was so narrow even a burro would have had trouble passing. But nobody came. The canyon walls dripped from the rain, and the wind was cold.

Lou Emma had time to think as she slogged along, her feet heavy with mud. Things that were like a mixed-up jig-saw puzzle fell into place. She thought of the night before they left Gloriosa and Miss Kate standing by the Great Smith with her head bowed and the sudden flash of understanding, *being a stepmother's not much fun.* But she hadn't gone downstairs and told Miss Kate she understood.

"Are you all right, Lou Emma?" Miss Kate asked.

"I'm fine," she called back, and Maddy echoed,"—fine."

If they got to Greystokes . . . if they got back to Colorado Springs . . . if they ever got back to Gloriosa, Kansas, things would be different.

The road widened. The slope was down now, instead of up. Around a turn in the canyon wall they saw lights twinkling in a huge building. Big glass lamps lighted a wide driveway.

"Yippee . . . yippee . . . yippee . . . Greystokes!" Maddy shouted.

"We made it; we made it," Lou Emma said over and over.

"Shoot-a-mile." Maddy was full of scorn. "The Great Smith coulda done it backward."

Miss Kate said, "Climb in, girls, and ride the rest of the way."

"Can we dress for dinner now?" Lou Emma asked.

"I'm afraid not. It's seven o'clock. We're an hour late."

As they drove through the tall stone columns that marked the entrance to the hotel grounds the Great Smith was stopped by a small crowd of people. Strangely mixed people. Some of the men wore dinner clothes; others had on rough pants and sweaters, and some carried lanterns, pickaxes, ropes, and shovels. With them was a tall woman in a trailing, beige lace gown, trimmed with satin bows. Clinging to her arm was the fragile and ladylike figure of Miss Jesse Miller of Cleveland, Ohio.

At her first glimpse of Aunt Jesse in white embroidered mull with a white crocheted wrap, Lou Emma became conscious of what *she* looked like and of her dirty, muddy, wrinkled dress highlighted with red raspberry stain. Maddy looked as bad, and Miss Kate looked *worse*. As they climbed out of the Great Smith, the best-dressed man with the finest handle-bar moustache came forward. Maddy dropped her tire rock at that instant, and it landed on the toe of his highly polished boot.

"I'll be—confounded!" he said. Then, "Are you the Miller party?"

"I'm Mrs. Cyrus Miller," Miss Kate said, "and this is Lou Emma and Maddy. Are you expecting us?"

"Expecting you?" he shouted. "We never thought we'd see you alive. I'm Jack Mayfield, and there's been a cloudburst in the mountains. We were organizing a search party when you drove up."

Another man said, "That High Rock Road's a killer, lady."

"Is *that* the High Rock Road? I wondered what it was."

"Worst road in the mountains," the man said almost proudly. "All right for a man an' a mule, but nothin' more. Don't recall when an auto made it."

"Miss Kate can drive anyplace," Lou Emma said.

"I believe it." Jack Mayfield put out his hand. "Let me shake the hand of the first woman to drive the High

Rock Road. And I hope the last. Women should never touch a steering wheel, tobacco, or the ballot box."

"Oh, hush, Jack!" the lady in beige lace said. "I'm Ardelia Mayfield, Mrs. Miller. Welcome to Greystokes. Jesse was so looking forward to your visit. But what happened to Cyrus?"

As Miss Kate explained why Professor Miller was not there, Aunt Jesse became more and more agitated. She broke into the story:

"Kate, I am simply aghast that you would try this trip alone."

"But I wasn't alone." Miss Kate put an arm around each of the girls. "Lou Emma and Maddy were with me. I couldn't have made it without them."

"To bring them on such a trip . . ." Aunt Jesse shivered delicately. "To endanger their precious lives . . . to be late to dinner . . . and the Mayfields were to play in the Whist Drive . . . to prostrate me with worry . . ."

Righteous anger boiled up in Lou Emma, the way a kettle of syrup boils up on a hot fire.

"If you had any consideration . . . any feeling for the feelings of others . . ." Aunt Jesse went on, gathering steam.

"Stop picking on Miss Kate," Lou Emma said. "She's going to have a baby."

The silence that descended on the crowd around the Great Smith was so complete that Lou Emma was shocked into realizing what she had done. She had spoken of an unborn child in mixed company. She waited for Aunt Jesse to strike her down with lightning. But as she waited, she felt Miss Kate's steadying arm and heard Maddy's whisper: "Good for you!"

There was a chuckle. Jack Mayfield took a cigar from a silver cigar case. "Tell Skinny Miller congratulations, and I suggest he name the baby Barney Oldfield."

"It's going to be a girl," Maddy said. "She's going to look like Miss Kate. And me."

But Mr. Mayfield and the other men were melting away in the shadows. There was some laughter, but Lou Emma didn't care. She knew who was on her side.

"Kate, is this—true?" Miss Miller dropped her voice.

"Yes, Jesse. I thought Cyrus had written to you, but since he hasn't, I'm glad Lou Emma could tell you."

"Tell me in front of Greystokes-in-the-Pines?" Aunt Jesse's voice went up half an octave. "In mixed company? My poor little motherless—"

"We're not poor, and we're not motherless. Not neither," Maddy said.

At Aunt Jesse's gasp Mrs. Mayfield patted her arm. "Why don't you go up to your room, Jesse? I'll have tea and toast sent up."

"I *am* feeling a little faint, Ardelia." Miss Miller pulled her white crocheted wrap closer. "If you think you can manage—"

"Don't worry, Jesse. The girls and I will look after your sister-in-law."

Lou Emma watched as her Aunt Jesse walked up

the wide stairway to the magnificence of Greystokes, shaking her head at every step. There was something lonesome about her, something that was explained in her father's everlasting remark, "Girls, Jesse means well."

"I'm sorry we upset her," Miss Kate said to Mrs. Mayfield.

"Jesse gets upset very easily. She is a dear friend, and I have known her all my life, but she's always been this way. Thinks Cyrus is her personal property. Couldn't stand his first wife. And the way she carried on when the girls were born . . ."

"Us?" Maddy squealed.

"Couldn't stand *our mother?*" Lou Emma asked, not believing her ears.

"Oh, she came around in time," Mrs. Mayfield said. "And she will again. And she'd never believe she was that way in the past. But why are we standing out here talking? Mrs. Miller, you should lie down."

"I'm perfectly all right," Miss Kate said.

"My dear, I've had five children, and I always say lie down beforehand, for you never have a chance afterward."

"Perhaps you're right," Miss Kate said, meekly. "It was a long drive and the storm and all. Jesse may have been right. I was foolish to bring the girls—or foolish to come to Colorado at all, knowing about the baby."

"Nonsense," Mrs. Mayfield said briskly. "Sensible thing to do. Families should stay together. And as for taking the trip . . . my grandmother went to California in a covered wagon and had a baby on the way. Oh, there's the man I want to send a wire to Cyrus. Can't have him worried." She strode away, her nine satin bows rustling on the beige lace.

The Millers dissolved in helpless laughter on the wide stone stairway. Hand in hand, covered with mud, and not one bit ashamed of their appearance, Miss Kate and her stepdaughters walked into the lobby of Greystokes-in-the-Pines.

Up in the Mayfields' suite, Miss Kate slept under a blue-satin eiderdown *pouf.* Maddy slept on a day bed. But Lou Emma padded around the room. She was supposed to sleep, too, but supposed to isn't the same as doing so. Mrs. Mayfield had put her dress to dry on the steam radiator, and she put it on, stiff and dirty. It was her own, and in the midst of the glamour of Greystokes she needed to remember who she was. At the triple-mirrored dressing table she looked at her face; it was no different than ever. And it ought to be after all that had happened. It was a wonder she wasn't green-faced and purple-haired. In the mirror she saw Miss Kate smile in her sleep. A warm feeling came over her. She nodded to her stepmother's reflection.

Things are going to be better. Wait and see.

Outside a long carpeted corridor led away to the elegance of other suites, other public rooms briefly glimpsed on the way upstairs. Lou Emma tiptoed out and walked, soundless, on the thick carpet. Mirrors hung on the walls, and she nodded at them, and once she made a face like the one Dewey made at his mother's camera.

She heard the tinkle of a piano and polite applause. It was exactly the kind of spot she might run into Aunt Jesse. Lou Emma walked the other way rapidly, found some steps, and went on until she came out on a terrace.

Outside it was dark except for the big lamps on the driveway. There stood the Great Smith, muddy and marked with hailstones. Someone had taken off the side curtains, and it looked dear and familiar in a place that was so different from home. She ran down and got into the front seat, huddling down against the chill. The old lap robe left from horse-and-buggy days back in Auden was there, and she pulled it over her. There was even a little horsey smell left..

She thought about Auden. The house, the barn, the college. All that was BMK. She'd never ever again use those initials out loud, but to herself it was all right. Things were different than they used to be back in Auden. They'd been different since her father married Miss Kate, and now with the baby, they'd be different again.

"Everything changes, Lou Emma. The trick is to change along with it."

"I've changed some," she said to the window in the hotel where Miss Kate was sleeping. "I can change some more."

A train whistled in the night. By craning out of the Great Smith, she could see its lights in the distance.

That must be the Colorado Midland that came up from Colorado Springs. After a while the train huffed along on its way, whistling to the dark mountains, and the coach-and-four came up from the depot in great style. The coachman blew his tally-ho horn, and some people came out to meet the coach. Watching, Lou Emma suddenly came alive and jumped from the Great Smith.

"Papa! Papa!"

A man with his arm in a sling turned abruptly and ran to her. "Lou Emma? Are you all right? Where's Kate? Where's Maddy? Are you all right?"

"We're all all right." Lou Emma hugged him. "Miss Kate's asleep, and so's Maddy. Oh, Papa, I'm so glad to see you."

He was saying "Thank God" over and over, and she knew it wasn't right to interrupt, but he kept it up longer than she could stand. "Why'd you come? What about Dr. Etting? Is he mad?"

"We got word about the cloudburst. They said the High Rock Road would be washed out. I caught the train and came."

"We know about the baby, Papa. Miss Kate told us. It's going to be fun. We've never had a baby. Mr. Mayfield wants to name it Barney Oldfield."

He laughed, "Sounds like Jack."

"And, Papa, Miss Kate told us about her grandmother—the one she made up. She told us in the storm."

"Poor Kate." He stroked her hair. "She suffered over that."

Lou Emma leaned against him, careful of his arm, but so thankful he was there that it was easy to say what was in her mind. "I told a lie, too. It popped out the way Miss Kate's did. And then I wished I hadn't."

"Most of us make mistakes, Lou Emma. Parents and girls and boys. If we love each other and keep trying it works out. Most of the time."

"I won't ever tell a lie again."

"Say 'I'll try not to ever again.' " He kissed the top of her head. "And now I want to see Kate and Maddy. Coming?"

She didn't want to go in right now. Too many things were boiling around in her head, and if she went, they might never get sorted out.

"You go, Papa. I'll be in pretty soon. Did Dr. Etting say it was all right for you to come to Greystokes?"

"I didn't ask him. I just came. But Etting liked my first chapter. In fact he's bought it to use for an article in a history journal he edits." He fumbled in his pocket with his good hand. "Guess what I bought with the money?"

"Something for the baby?"

"The baby can wait." He held up a fan of cardboard tickets. "Four tickets on the Cog Train to the top of Pike's Peak."

"Oh Papa, how wonderful . . . wonderful . . . wonder-full!"

But her father was gone. He was climbing the stone steps two at a time, his coattails flying.

There had to be some way, some special way, to say the thing she was feeling, that surged up like a Roman candle inside her. Not just the Cog Train and Pike's Peak, but everything . . . everything . . .

Lou Emma squeezed the horn bulb of the Great Smith, and at the top of her voice, joined in the sound that rolled from mountain to mountain:

"Oo-oo-GAH! Oo-oo-GAH! Oo-oo-GAH."

They shouted together, she and the big red auto, until the doors of Greystokes-in-the-Pines flew open, and people poured out on the terrace to see what was going on.

ABOUT THE AUTHOR

Alberta Wilson Constant grew up in Tennessee and Oklahoma. She was graduated from Oklahoma City University, and later took classes in professional writing at the University of Oklahoma. The Oklahoma country, with its short exciting span of statehood and its colorful people, has been the inspiration for several of her books. Stories of Kansas told by her stepfather gave her the idea of writing about that state. The many summers spent in Colorado by her husband and his family were the basis for the story of *The Motoring Millers.* Mrs. Constant and her husband live in Independence, Missouri. They have two children.

ABOUT THE ARTISTS

As a successful husband-and-wife team, Beth and Joe Krush have illustrated well over fifty books for children. Both Mr. and Mrs. Krush attended the Philadelphia Museum of Art. Each of them now teaches illustration: Joe Krush at the Museum's school, The Philadelphia College of Art, and Beth Krush at Moore College of Art. Mr. Krush is chairman of the Illustration Committee of the Philadelphia Art Alliance.

The Krushes and their son live in Wayne, Pennsylvania.